THE
HANGING
OF SAMUEL ASH

ALSO BY SHELDON RUSSELL

Dreams to Dust
Empire
Requiem at Dawn
The Savage Trail

Hook Runyon Mysteries
The Yard Dog
The Insane Train
Dead Man's Tunnel

THE
HANGING
OF SAMUEL ASH

SHELDON RUSSELL

MINOTAUR BOOKS ⚎ NEW YORK

THE HANGING OF SAMUEL ASH. Copyright © 2013 by Sheldon Russell. All rights reserved. Printed in the United States of America. For information, address St. Martin's Press, 175 Fifth Avenue, New York, N.Y. 10010.

www.minotaurbooks.com

Library of Congress Cataloging-in-Publication Data

Russell, Sheldon.
    The hanging of Samuel Ash / Sheldon Russell.—First
St. Martin's Minotaur edition.
        pages cm
ISBN 978-1-250-00101-6 (hardcover)
ISBN 978-1-250-03199-0 (e-book)
    1. Runyon, Hook (Fictitious character)—Fiction.   2. Murder—
Investigation—Fiction.   I. Title.
    PS3568.U777H36 2013
    813'.54—dc23

                                        2013009830

Minotaur books may be purchased for educational, business, or promotional use. For information on bulk purchases, please contact Macmillan Corporate and Premium Sales Department at 1-800-221-7945 extension 5442 or write special-markets@macmillan.com.

First Edition: August 2013

10 9 8 7 6 5 4 3 2 1

In memory of my friend
Dr. William Frederickson

ACKNOWLEDGMENTS

It's often said that writing is a lonely business, and it's true that the isolation required to write can lend itself to uncommon doubts and insecurities. That's why I take special comfort in having a team of professionals watching my back. The advice and help I receive is forthright and constructive, its sole purpose always being the making of the best book possible.

Nowhere is this more true than with my editor, Daniela Rapp, and with my agents, Michael and Susan Morgan Farris. It's equally true of Minotaur Books, an organization that runs with the efficiency of a well-oiled machine. Thanks to you all.

THE
HANGING
OF SAMUEL ASH

PROLOGUE

THE KNOT ON the rope, big as a man's fist, scrubbed under his ear. It smelled of hemp and horse sweat. Heat lightning flashed on the horizon, an empty promise of rain, and thunder rumbled over the staked plains. The breeze fell still as death, and from somewhere crickets struck up a dirge.

The rope zinged over the cantilever of the railroad wigwag signal, its tail dancing just within reach. A snap of the rope jerked him onto his toes, and he looked up into the starlit night. Blood rushed beneath his eardrums, and he sucked air through his teeth.

Somewhere beyond the darkness, the whistle of a westbound train rose up. He turned his head against the rudeness of the rope to search out the engine light. His ankles burned, and his legs trembled under him. The rope, cinched tight, cut into his flesh. His thoughts gathered like a moment in eternity.

Hanging done right, he'd heard, proved a sweet way to die, the weight snapping the neck, so powerful its force that a miscalculation could pop the head from its mooring. The headless body, they said, sometimes stood and walked about. But such mercy would not be his, no drop to oblivion, no void, no pity this night.

The thunder rolled once more, and he wondered if it might rain. But then it never rained. The rope jerked tight. He reached for the ground with his toes and found it gone. Grasping the rope, he hung on with all that he had.

The roar of the westbound broke on the horizon. The lights of the wigwag signal, red as blood, flashed back and forth. The bell clanged in alarm, and the train whistle screamed from out of the blackness.

His arms trembled and burned, and when he could do no more, he released the rope. As he rose into the air, his eyes bulged, and his tongue swelled from between his teeth. His back arched, and his engorged genitalia stood erect. A light burned into his eyes, bright as the sun, and then receded to a point in the universe.

The train raced off into the darkness, and the night stilled. Lightning flickered on the horizon, but far away now and silent.

WHEN A FLY whined in his ear, Hook Runyon, Santa Fe railroad bull, sat up and rubbed at his face. The old passenger car waddled down the track like a duck in the shallows, and the air smelled of cigar smoke and stale food. The morning sun blasted through the window, and sweat trickled down his neck.

Now with the war over, both men and equipment had collapsed in exhaustion, and the maintenance shops had surrendered to the excesses of battle. What equipment *could* run *did* run, and to hell with everything else. If rolling stock wore out, the railroad shuttled it off to less-demanding routes, where the dilapidated cars continued to rattle along like tired old men.

Folks despaired with doing the impossible any longer, no matter who asked it, and wildcat strikes, often dangerous and unpredictable, cropped up like grass fires.

In the midst of this, Hook made a run in pursuit of pickpockets, traveling as far south as Pecos. In the end, he'd caught little more than a tequila hangover and a case of indigestion. The train cooler water tasted of chlorine, his back ached from the passenger seat, and both of his legs had gone dead as a side of beef.

To top off this misery, nothing gave him less pleasure than hunting pickpockets. Cowardly by nature, and opportunists of the lowest order, they preyed on the weak and defenseless. Relying on stealth, deception, and the goodwill of others, they stole whatever they could without regard for the consequences of their actions. Like coyotes, they hunted in packs for the easy kill, tugging the carcasses about among them before slinking off into the night. To make matters worse, Hook found the bastards almost impossible to catch.

He lit a cigarette and stared out the window at the passing landscape. In this country one direction looked as another, and the miles stretched out as monotonous as a cotton string. He checked his watch. The train should be arriving in Carlsbad, New Mexico, soon now. He'd be glad to get back to his caboose in Clovis, a modest abode to be sure, but home nonetheless and where he wanted to be.

The Santa Fe had towed his caboose from Albuquerque to Clovis shortly before he left for Pecos, parking it on a siding close to the depot baggage deck. Though not the most private place in the world, it beat the hell out of the Arizona salvage yard in which he'd been living the past few months.

The cook at the Clovis Harvey House promised he'd keep an eye on Hook's dog, Mixer, providing a sawbuck showed up come payday. Hook hadn't much confidence in the cook's commitment to Mixer's well-being but had agreed to the arrangement, figuring Mixer could take care of himself under most circumstances anyway.

Hook leaned back and scanned the car for any new passengers who might have boarded the train while he slept, spotting an old black lady sitting in the Jim Crow seat at the back. Across the aisle from her, a young soldier dozed with his hat pulled over his eyes.

A Mexican couple, with two kids in tow, sat near the bathroom. The little girl, thumb in her mouth and forefinger over her nose, slept in her mother's lap, while the boy drew pictures in his Big Chief tablet. The mother, looking minutes away from her next delivery, propped her feet up on a cardboard box to ease the swelling in her ankles.

In the aisle seat next to the exit, a woman—young and fresh and dressed in a pink summer outfit—worked at her makeup. When the train slowed for the approaching depot, she hooked her black leather purse over her shoulder.

The engineer blew his whistle, and Hook checked his watch again. He'd have time to call Eddie Preston, the divisional supervisor, from the Carlsbad operator's phone, though he didn't look forward to reporting his failure to catch the pickpockets.

Having grown more belligerent over the years, Eddie now bordered on the intolerable, while at the same time Hook had become less inclined to suffer fools—the end result being war without resolution.

Hook figured to deal with Eddie first and then to find a lavatory where he could wash the Chihuahuan Desert from his body. After that, he'd catch the next milk run into Clovis. By tonight, he'd be sipping Beam and water and sleeping in his own bunk.

The passenger car lurched to a stop as they pulled into the station. Hook took a single suitcase down from the rack. He traveled light, often with no luggage at all. In this case, he knew the trip to Pecos to be a long haul and with little chance of a layover, so he'd thrown in a change of clothes and a couple of titles to read along the way.

He waited at the door of the car for the girl in pink to work her way down the steps. He paused at the bottom for a last look back. Failing to see that the girl in pink had stopped in front of him, he bumped into her, nearly spilling her onto the platform.

"Oh, Christ," he said, catching her by the arm. "I'm sorry. Are you okay?"

Recovering, she brushed the hair back from her face. "No harm," she said, smiling. "My fault."

Hook watched her walk away. At the corner she turned and looked back at him.

He found the operator working up tickets. Hook didn't recognize him, but then the company bumped operators around from depot to depot like traveling salesmen.

Pushing the tickets aside, the operator said, "Yeah?"

"Need to use your phone," Hook said.

The operator pushed his glasses onto his forehead and looked at Hook's arm prosthesis.

"This phone ain't for public use, fella. Gotta keep the line open. Never know when a train might arrive on time and stampede the whole goddang place."

"I'm railroad security," Hook said. "What's your name?"

"John Beauford," he said.

"Been chasing pickpockets down in Pecos. I need to get hold of Division."

The operator took his glasses off, fogged them up with his breath, rubbed them clean with his shirttail, and slipped them back on. His eyes grew big behind the lens.

"That so," he said, peeking around Hook's shoulder. "Guess you got them pickpockets cuffed up outside so's they don't crowd up the waiting room?"

"Pickpockets is like trying to catch mice," Hook said. "Grab one and three more run up your pant leg."

The operator nodded. "I seen one steal a candy bar right out of an old lady's mouth," he said. "Took her false teeth right along with it. Wasn't nothing left but a dab of chocolate on the end of her nose."

"About that phone?" Hook said.

"Anything to help out the law, but I'll need to see your badge. You know how persnickety the railroad can be about its equipment."

"Right," Hook said, searching for his badge.

The operator drummed the counter with his fingers while Hook went through his pockets.

"My badge and wallet seem to be missing," Hook said.

"That a fact?"

Hook clenched his jaw. "Sons of bitches must have lifted it."

"Now ain't that irregular?" he said. "A man might think a rail dick would know better than to get his own pockets picked while tracking down pickpockets."

"Let me use the phone," Hook said. "Division can clear this up."

"You better move on downline, mister," he said.

"And how the hell am I supposed to get a pass to Clovis?"

"Buy a ticket like everyone else. I never knew a bum yet what didn't think he had the right to get something for nothing. I get up every day, put my britches on, and go to work, so I figure you can do the same. If not, there's the Salvation Army down on Fifth."

Hook leaned into the window of the cage. "Listen, brass pounder, I'm the yard dog out of Clovis. Maybe I'll just come around there and kick your ass to prove it."

The operator stepped back. "You better move on, mister, or I'll call the cops."

Hook took a deep breath. A yard dog's authority didn't hold much water with local cops, and he had enough trouble going already. He walked to the door and turned.

"When's the next milk run to Clovis?" he asked.

"Three o'clock," he said. "But I wouldn't be thinking of hopping her if I was you. Bums don't get far on this line. Anyway, that engineer's a ballast scorcher, and he don't slow for boes or no one else."

Outside, Hook checked his watch. He hated to admit it, but the son of a bitch had a point. A rail dick ought know better than to get his pockets picked. He figured that dame in pink had set him up, and he fell for it. While he mumbled apologies, she could have lifted his boxer shorts, and he'd never have known it.

He peeked through the depot window and could see the operator talking on the phone. Hook didn't believe in revenge, being above it morally, but he figured to get even with that bastard someday.

Having bummed the rails in another life, he knew how to hop a freighter with the best of them. If that's what it took to get home, then that's what he'd do. In the meantime, he'd find some shade and wait it out.

As he turned to leave, a patrol car with two uniform cops in it pulled up next to him.

The driver stuck his head out the window. "Hey you," he said.

Hook paused. "Me?"

"That's right. You."

"What do you want?" Hook asked.

The cop on the passenger's side got out and walked around the car.

"Want you to put your hands on the hood," he said.

Hook held up his prosthesis. "I only have one."

"Hey, chief," he said, kicking Hook's feet apart. "We got us a smart-ass here."

The other cop got out.

Going through Hook's pockets, he said, "Threatening a railroad operator can get you into serious trouble around here. But being a smart-ass can get you hurt."

"I'm the Santa Fe railroad bull," Hook said.

"A one-armed cinder dick? Now there's a rarity. Let's see your badge."

"Hey, chief," the other cop said, holding Hook's weapon up by the barrel. "He's packing, too."

"I lost the badge," Hook said.

"Say what?" the chief said.

"I lost it."

He pulled at his chin. "You lost your badge, did you?"

"That's right."

"Well, let's see your driver's license then."

Hook shrugged. "It's in the billfold with my badge."

The chief twisted his mouth to the side. "You've had a run of bad luck, haven't you? Cuff him up, Joe. We'll run him in for vagrancy and carrying."

Officer Joe slipped cuffs from his belt and paused. "But he's only got one arm, chief."

"Then cuff him to your own damned self, Joe."

"He could kill a man with that hook, chief."

"Put your gun on him then."

"But what if he tries to run?"

"Jesus, Joe, then shoot him," he said.

2

HOOK SAT IN the cell studying the beetle that climbed up the wall. Just as it reached its destination, it tumbled to the floor, flipped itself over, and started up again.

He reached for a cigarette, remembering that Officer Joe had taken them before putting him in the cell. At least they hadn't brought the drunks in yet. That usually didn't happen until the bars had been open for a while.

Just as he stretched out on the bunk, with its layered odors, Officer Joe opened the cell door.

"Chief says you can make a call. One," he said, holding up his finger.

"That's all I've been trying to do since I landed in this dump," Hook said.

"Make it a good one," he said. "A smart-ass can get thirty days in this hotel with no trouble at all."

He led Hook to the office, where the chief sat behind his desk reading the funny papers. Hook's cigarettes lay on his desk.

"Mind if I have one of my smokes?"

The chief tossed them over to him. "Phone's there," he said. "You got two minutes."

"I'd like a little privacy," Hook said.

"And I'd like a stripteaser cooking my breakfast," the chief said.

Hook lit a cigarette and picked up the phone. He turned his back to the chief and dialed Eddie Preston.

"Security," Eddie said.

"Eddie, Hook here."

"Runyon," he said. "Don't you ever check in?"

"Jesus, Eddie. That's what I'm doing."

"I get this call from Clovis," he said. "From the operator at the depot. He says there's a dog spraying up the baggage every time a train comes in. So I says, 'What kind of dog is it?' And he says, 'What the hell difference does that make?' And I says, 'It don't make a goddang bit of difference, so just handle it your own damn self.' And he says, 'I ain't altogether sure it's even a dog. It might be an African hyena, though I don't know what an African hyena would be doing in New Mexico.' So I says, 'What the hell does an African hyena have to do with me?' And he says, ''Cause it's living under Hook Runyon's caboose, and he's one of your crack detectives, if I ain't mistaken.'"

"Look, Eddie, maybe we could talk about African hyenas some other time. I'm in a bit of a jam-up here, and I only have a couple minutes."

"What kind of jam-up would you be in now, Runyon?"

"I lost my wallet and badge."

"You lost them?"

"Not exactly lost. They were stolen."

"Stolen? How the hell does someone steal a yard dog's badge and wallet?"

"Pickpockets."

He could hear Eddie breathing on the other end. "For Christ's sake, Runyon, you're telling me pickpockets stole your wallet and badge while you were hunting pickpockets?"

"These bastards are good, Eddie. The best I've ever seen."

"Where are you now?"

"Carlsbad jail."

"They ain't likely to be in jail what with you on their trail, Runyon."

"I'm the one who's in jail, Eddie. I need you to verify who I am."

"You're the biggest idiot in New Mexico," he said.

"Come on, Eddie. My time's about up here. Tell the chief who I am, and then call the operator at the depot so I can get the hell out of this place."

"I'd let you sit until you grassed over, Runyon, if I didn't have urgent business that needed attending. Let me talk to him."

"Thanks, Eddie."

"And phone me the minute you get back to the depot."

"Right," Hook said, handing the phone to the chief. "It's Eddie Preston, division supervisor. He wants to talk to you."

The chief took the phone. "Yeah," he said, leaning back in his chair. "Pickpockets, you say? You're shitting me, right?

"Yeah, okay. You might want to pin a note to your boy's shirt," he said, looking up at Hook. "I'll send him on his way. Wouldn't want to hold up a crime fighter like him, would I?"

The chief hung up the phone and rolled his shoulders. "Looks like you're free to go, Runyon."

"I'll take my sidearm, if you don't mind," Hook said.

The chief pulled open a drawer and handed it to him. "Don't let someone take it away from you and shoot you in the ass," he said.

"And how about a ride back to the depot, chief?"

"Joe, give Clark Kent here a ride back to the depot, will you? He's in a rush to flush out some more pickpockets."

Hook rode in the backseat of the patrol car in silence. Every once in a while, Officer Joe would look at him through the rearview mirror and shake his head.

When they'd pulled up to the depot, Officer Joe said, "Just give us a call if anyone takes your lunch money. It's a dangerous world out there."

Hook got out and paused at Joe's window. "You might consider taking up a second job, Officer Joe, maybe security out to the drive-in theater or guarding the ticket gate for the high school football games."

"What the hell you talking about?"

"Just something I overheard the chief say. I wouldn't worry about it if I was you."

The operator looked up at Hook, folded his arms over his chest, and said, "How was I supposed to know?"

"'Cause I told you," Hook said.

"You got to admit you don't look like no yard dog."

"And you don't look like a moron. Now, do you think I could use that phone?"

"Sure," he said, pushing it over to Hook.

Hook paused. "You mind?"

"I'll be out front. Jesus," he said.

Hook dialed Eddie, who picked up on the second ring.

"Security," he said.

"Eddie, this is Hook. I'm at the depot."

"You know that siding north of Carlsbad, the one that goes to the potash mine?"

"More or less," Hook said.

"The engineer on the short haul, while coming back from the mine about three this morning, said the wigwag signal had something hanging over it."

"What was it?"

"How the hell do I know? That's why I'm telling you. Probably some Halloween prank."

"This is June, Eddie."

"The union's been stirring things up and down the line. Maybe they sabotaged the signal to get attention."

Hook clenched his jaw. Union problems were even more disagreeable than hunting pickpockets, and he didn't like being caught between strikers and the company.

"How am I supposed to get out there, Eddie? It's in the middle of nowhere, you know."

"Hang on, let me see if I can locate something."

Hook rolled the operator's chair over and sat down. From there he could see the operator out front. Every once in a while, he would peek through the window to see if Hook had hung up yet.

"Runyon," Eddie said.

"Yeah."

"There's a road-rail over at the Artesia depot. The track crew won't be using it for a few weeks. Catch the next train over there and pick it up. Make damn sure you get clearance before pulling onto the line with that thing."

Hook dropped his head. A road-rail, being a vehicle with hydraulic equipment for running both road and track, was neither fish nor fowl. Its claim to fame lay in the number of railroad employees it killed every year.

"Jesus, Eddie, can't you just get me a car?"

"I can get you a long vacation."

"Alright, Eddie. How about sending me another badge?"

"It's coming out of your pay, Runyon. They don't give those things away." He paused. "At least most people don't."

"Alright, Eddie. I'll catch the next run."

"By the way, Runyon, the department has taken on a new man, a crackerjack, a smart son of a bitch, dictator of his graduating class."

"Valedictorian, Eddie."

"Whatever. He's shy on experience, so I'm sending him to Clovis."

"That's great, Eddie. Clovis could use a dictator. But what does it have to do with me?"

"I want you to show him the ropes."

"I don't have time to deal with some kid, Eddie."

"Did I ask? I don't remember asking, and don't be teaching him bad habits. Stay off the hooch. This kid is the goddamn future, and his old man is important. Oh, and call me soon as you get that wig-wag thing cleared. The railroad don't stand for no one tampering with its signals."

Hook hung up. He could hear the milk run in the distance. The operator stuck his head in the door.

"I got work to do, you know."

"Radio a slow to that milk run," Hook said. "Official business."

Hook waited on the platform for the caboose to come downline. He set a pace, latched on to the grab iron, and swung up. So far, it had been one hell of a day. The way he figured it, things could only get better.

3

WHEN THEY CAME into Artesia, Hook swung down from the caboose and waited for the train to pull out. He made his way into the depot. The operator sat with his feet up on the desk and his hands behind his head.

"I'm the bull out of Clovis," Hook said. "Division says there's a road-rail here that I can use for a couple weeks."

"Gotta badge?" he asked, grinning.

"Operators got anything to do besides gossip?" Hook said.

"It's parked around back. I'd about as soon ride a mule myself."

"I'm heading back to the potash switch. Is the line clear?"

Checking the board, he said, "There's a mail run out of Pecos coming through about three, and a westbound short haul on the potash spur due about midnight. After that, she's clear 'til morning."

"I should have been an operator myself," Hook said. "Sit around with my feet up while everybody else is working."

"Someone's got to do the headwork around here," he said.

"Division says there's signal trouble on that spur," Hook said. "I figure kids covered up the wigwag lights. I'm going to check it out."

"If I was you, I'd *road* that road-rail to the crossing just this side of the potash switch and get on the tracks there. Stay off that god-dang line long as you can. A road-rail don't set off the signals, you know, and the odds of some drunk running you over is about fifty-fifty. On top of that, it's Friday the thirteenth. Then there's wildcat strikes brewing, too. Uncle John's been hiring up scabs, and tempers can run pretty high, you know."

Hook nodded. "I could see it coming. The War Labor Board and the union bosses been sleeping in the same bed ever since the war started. The union guarantees no strikes, and the government guarantees no one can quit the union. Everybody else sleeps on the floor."

Hook paused. "You wouldn't spot me five 'til payday, would you? I'm a little short."

"Someone pick your pocket or something?"

"That Carlsbad operator's on my list," Hook said.

The operator grinned. "Here's a fiver. It's worth it for the laugh."

"Thanks. I'll get even with you come payday. You have the key to the road-rail?"

"Key's in her, far as I know."

"Pretty slack security, isn't it?"

"No one in his right mind would steal that thing," he said.

"I could use a flashlight, too. It can be pretty dark at those crossings."

"They keep one in the glove compartment and extra batteries under the seat," he said. "Never know when you might need to flag off an oncoming freighter."

"But you'd know if there *was* an oncoming, you being the operator. Right?"

"Oh, sure," he said. "Most of the time."

Hook walked around the old road-rail, and then he walked around it again. Pilot wheels hung underneath like a cat crouched on a sandbox. A cable wench had been mounted on the front and the cable end looped around the bumper to keep it from dragging on the ground. The front fender had been crushed like an accordion, and a grease rag plugged the gas tank.

Hook got in and searched for the ignition. The cab smelled of oil and sweat, and empty cigarette packages covered the dash. A hole the size of a coffee can had been poked through the door by something, and a wad of electrical tape served to hold on the gear-shift knob.

Hook pumped the accelerator a half-dozen times and cranked her over. To his surprise, she fired up, and a cloud of blue smoke drifted away.

He took off down the road, rumbling like a thrashing machine. When he hit forty, the front wheels started wobbling, and a high-pitched squeal emanated from the differential.

By the time he got to the crossing, his arm ached from hanging on to the steering wheel, and his eyes burned from the smoke boiling into the cab.

He checked his watch. The mail run should have passed Artesia and be headed for Clovis by now, so he pulled onto the crossing, lined up his tires on the rails, and lowered the pilot wheels. Dropping her into gear, he eased off down the tracks.

The old road-rail, transformed into a track vehicle, clipped along as light and easy as a summer breeze. As he sped into the desert, he released the steering wheel and leaned back. With luck, he'd make the wigwag and be on his way home before the short haul left from the potash mine.

Vandalism had taken its share of his time over the years, and odds were that's what awaited him at the wigwag. Boys, cranked up on beer and testosterone, had probably covered the signal lights as a prank. Kids often didn't know the difference between fun and funerals. Tampering with a crossing signal came as close to mur-der as a person could get without pulling a trigger. He'd picked up enough body parts at crossing accidents to know.

After switching onto the potash spur, he brought her up to speed. The moon climbed into the sky, and the stars slid overhead like sequins. Out here in the desert, the clatter of the world fell away, and a man's thoughts lined up one behind the other like soldiers.

When the wigwag signal rose up in the darkness ahead, he coasted in. At first, he figured the engineer to have been right, that someone had covered the lights. But as he drew near, he could see a body hanging from the cantilever, and it had blocked the signal arm. Heat rose into his ears. He'd seen his share of death over the years, but it never came easy.

At the crossing, he lifted the pilot wheels, pulled off the tracks, and backed down the slope of the road until the headlights lit up the body.

"Bastards," he said.

For a man with only one arm, getting a body down from that high up would be impossible. Maybe he could drive back for help, but that would take hours. In the meantime, the crossing would be unprotected, and the railroad hated nothing more than paying compensation for crossing fatalities.

He climbed out, kicked his foot up on the bumper of the road-rail, and that's when he spotted the cable wench again. Getting back in, he pulled up to the wigwag, tied off the rope, and hit the switch. The body turned in the moonlight as the wench lowered it inch by inch to the ground.

When it had come to rest at Hook's feet, he knelt for a closer look. He guessed it to be the body of a young man, no more than a boy, though in the darkness he couldn't be certain.

The rope had been knotted and then looped over the victim's head. Whoever did it hadn't bothered to secure the boy's hands. A ligature mark cut deep into his neck, and the veins in his eyes had ruptured and bled. Without a fall to break his neck, he'd strangled in the slowest and most cruel way.

"Bastards," Hook said again.

He sat back on his heels. Sometimes his work pressed in like a weight, and then there would be the images flashing in his head for months to come.

He searched the victim's pockets, finding nothing, no identification, no indication of who he might be or what brought him to die in this place.

The moonlight reflected from the signal's red eye. The victim could be a hobo, he supposed, though he doubted it. Most boes hit the rails to escape their pasts, moving from place to place, broke and hungry most of the time, and of little consequence to anyone. On occasion there would be a knifing or a beating, some random act of violence over a stolen meal or a bottle of whiskey. But rarely did boes suffer anything as deliberate and time-consuming as a hanging.

He looked for prints in the hard-packed road. He walked the tracks with the flashlight and found nothing that might reveal who had been there.

The Artesia operator had been right about the anger generated in a strike. Given the absence of individual responsibility in a group, men's capacity for violence increased. If strikers had been involved here, there would have been a number of them trampling about, a gang of fired-up and angry men, which would increase the chances of leaving behind some sort of clue. But he'd found nothing, not a cigarette butt, not a shoe print, not a hint as to anyone having been there.

Suicide, while always a possibility, struck him as unlikely as well, given the proximity of the body to the cantilever, which was easily within arm's length for the victim. What man, given this option, could have resisted reaching up and liberating himself from suffocation? This fellow was either dead or unconscious by the time he got up there.

Hook looked at the time. The search had taken longer than he realized, and he needed to contact the New Mexico State Police, who complained if they didn't get their hand in from the outset.

They'd probably run prints on the chance that something would turn up in their files. If that failed, they'd write the whole thing off as just another dead tramp, and he'd be right back where he started.

When the short haul's whistle lifted in the distance, he turned up track to wave it down. Two-way radios had been installed in most of the equipment by the end of the war, and with luck, the engineer might be able to call in and save him a trip back to Carls-bad.

When the engine's glimmer broke, the wigwag, freed of its en-cumbrance, fired up behind him, its lights swinging and its bell clanging.

Hook swung his flashlight in a stop signal, and the short haul set her air. The ground trembled under Hook's feet, and the heat from the engine warmed him as the engineer eased her up next to him. He leaned out of the cab window and pushed his hat back.

"What the hell is going on?" he asked.

"I'm rail security out of Clovis," Hook said. "A man's been hung off the wigwag. Could you radio the Carlsbad operator and have him send out the state police?"

"Hold on." When he poked his head back out he said, "The fire-man's putting in a call."

"Appreciate it," Hook said.

"Know how it happened?" he asked.

Hook shook his head. "Not yet."

"Some folks need hanging," he said. "Like this fireman I got in here."

"Hanging a fireman isn't illegal," Hook said. "Long as he doesn't obstruct the wigwag signal."

"I'll keep that in mind," he said. "There are wildcats popping up here and there, you know. Maybe they hung a scab?"

"Think you could tell them to send out a meat wagon, too?" Hook asked.

"Hang on," he said.

Hook listened to the thump of the diesel engine as he waited.

The engineer leaned out over his elbow. "They're sending a trooper out and an ambulance. Anything else?"

"No. Thanks," Hook said.

The engineer nodded and brought up the engine. The rumble filled the night as he bumped out the slack and eased off down track. Hook waited until the end light disappeared before going back to the crossing.

He sat down on the bumper of the road-rail. Moonlight cast onto the body lying crumpled and silent in the road. Hook rubbed the tension from his neck and wondered what plans and hopes had also died on this night. He pulled his collar up against the evening cool.

"They're on their way, my friend," he said. "They'll be here soon."

4

THE PATROL CAR, with the ambulance close behind, rolled down the road with its emergency light on.

Hook stepped into the road and signaled with his flashlight. The adrenaline could run high in these situations, and he had no intention of being mistaken for a criminal.

The officer opened the door and stood behind it. "Identify yourself," he said, his voice tight.

"Hook Runyon. I'm the Santa Fe bull out of Clovis, the one who called in."

Closing his door, the trooper came forward, his hand resting on the grip of his weapon. His hat was squared, and gray stripes ran the length of both pant legs. The gold badge on the front of his uniform shined.

"Officer Payne," he said. "Step into the headlights, please."

Hook moved forward and waited as Officer Payne looked him over.

"You only got one arm," he said.

Hook looked at his prosthesis. "Been wondering why it took so long to button my shirt."

"I'll have some identification. You don't look like no bull I ever saw."

Hook rolled his eyes. It had been two years since anyone asked to see his badge. Now that he didn't have one, every son of a bitch between here and Pecos wanted a look.

"Must have left it on my bedside table. You can call my supervisor if you got a problem."

"Well," he said. "I guess you wouldn't be driving no railroad vehicle otherwise. You might want to consider carrying it in the future. Someone might mistake you for a bo."

"Yeah, I'll keep it in mind," Hook said. "The body's over there."

Officer Payne walked around the body, knelt, and then looked up at Hook.

"How many goddamn ways can a man figure out how to die?"

Hook said, "A call came in that the wigwag had malfunctioned. Turned out to be this fellow hanging from the cantilever up there."

Officer Payne shined his light onto the wigwag and then back onto the body.

"You ought know better than to move a corpse. This here is a crime scene."

"A short haul was scheduled in from the mine," Hook said, shrugging. "Had to get that signal up. Safety, you know."

"Who is he?"

"No identification."

Officer Payne stood and clicked off his light. "Maybe he left it on his bedside table," he said.

"Or maybe the sons of bitches who hung him took it," Hook said.

Officer Payne searched for a cigarette. Hook offered him one. He popped it between his teeth and lit up.

"Bums, be my guess," he said, blowing smoke out the corner of his mouth. "The country's crawling with them, what with the war over. Found one in a grain elevator the other day after he'd eaten a bellyful of treated seed corn." He shook his head. "Blew up like a goddamn toad."

"Times can get hard on the rails," Hook said.

Officer Payne flipped his cigarette ash onto the ground. "I figure this one here bailed off the wigwag his own damn self."

"Possible," Hook said.

"You could search from here to hell and not find out who he was, 'cause he didn't want no one to know. He maybe didn't know hisself.

"In the end, it don't matter a damn, if you ask me. All of 'em got the same story one way or the other. Their wives left 'em; they couldn't find work; they've been jilted or otherwise screwed by society. Or maybe they're just plain too lazy and stupid to get along."

He dropped his cigarette next to the body and squashed it out with his foot.

"Every man's story should be worth a hearing," Hook said.

"Right," Payne said, motioning for the ambulance to pull up. "I'll have the coroner in Carlsbad take a look-see. We'll run prints, but I wouldn't count on it coming to much."

"I can be reached through the Clovis operator if you come up with anything," Hook said.

The ambulance driver and his assistant dropped the gurney and lifted the body onto it.

Hook turned to the patrolman. "Who's the coroner over there?" he asked.

Officer Payne rubbed the toes of his shoes against his pant legs.

"Broomfield, the local dentist. I know as much about ballet as he knows about being coroner."

Hook arrived at the Artesia depot about dawn. The operator, busy digging an apple out of his lunch box, looked up.

"Get them little bastards rounded up?" he asked. "I tell you, kids nowadays."

"Turned out to be a dead body jamming up the wigwag," Hook said.

"I'll be," he said. "Never know what's running the tracks these days. I took to keeping a pistol in the desk drawer over there just in case."

"Mind if I use your phone?" Hook asked.

The operator slid the phone over to Hook.

"Don't tie it up too long," he said. "The yard office raises hell if they can't get through."

Hook pulled up a chair and dialed Eddie.

"Security," Eddie said.

"Eddie, this is Hook."

"You know what time it is, Runyon?"

"Later than you think, Eddie. Look, I just got back from that wigwag out on the potash spur."

"You called to tell me that?"

"A body had jimmied the thing up."

"A body? What the hell's a body doing on the wigwag?"

"Just hanging there."

"Dead?"

"When you're hanging from the wigwag, you're pretty much dead, Eddie."

"Who was it?"

Hook leaned back and studied his fingernails. "He had nothing on him, Eddie, no identification, not even pocket change."

"It's against the law to hang on railroad property, Runyon."

"I don't think he gave a shit, Eddie."

"Where is he now?"

"Who?"

"Jesus, Runyon, the body. What the hell we been talking about?"

"The state police took it to the coroner in Carlsbad."

"Is that signal back up?"

"It's up."

"Then get on over to Clovis soon as possible. We got strikers kicking up dust over there. The sons of bitches break the law, you nail them. The union's got a no-strike agreement with the company. These bastards don't follow their own rules."

"Right, Eddie."

"It's your job to see that no one breaks the goddamn law, strike or no strike."

Hook rubbed at his temple. An ache had settled in behind his eyes.

"About this wigwag thing, Eddie?"

"What about it?"

"Don't you think there should be an investigation?"

"Let the state police handle it. Give those boys something to do besides write traffic tickets."

"I got this feeling, Eddie."

"Keep it in your pants, Runyon. Feelings can turn a man's brains to shit. Stick with the facts for once."

"Yeah, I know, Eddie. It's the first thing you learn in detective school."

"And that new man should be arriving in Clovis anytime."

"Come on, Eddie. I've got a lot going on here."

"His name is Junior Monroe. He's highly educated, and he's got manners. Maybe you can learn something from him. I want him trained right, see. We need men who respect their superiors."

"I respect you, Eddie. You're like a father to me."

"Well, that's a possibility," he said, hanging up.

Hook turned to the Artesia operator, who had just come back from the can.

"Is the line clear to Clovis?" he asked. "I want to take the road-rail in on the track. It drives like a Sherman tank on the road."

"You can't run that road-rail to Clovis," he said.

"Want to see my note from home?"

"The line's been closed to through trains 'til further notice."

"I'm running a road-rail, not a train."

"You can run it to hell for all it matters to me. I'm just telling you what they're telling me."

Hook turned in his chair. "So, why is the line closed?"

"Crossing is down. Probably an accident or something. I just follow orders around here and wish the hell others did the same."

"I'll be needing fuel for that road-rail," Hook said. "She drinks gas like a road grader."

"You'll have to go to the yard for fuel. While I have to kiss every fool's ass who comes through that door, I don't have to fill up their gas tanks."

Hook pulled onto the crossing outside town, dropped the pilot wheels onto the rails, and sped off downline for Clovis. With luck, he could be home in a few hours.

He was anxious to get back. Rummage sales had been blooming all over town. While not the best for book hunting, the prices couldn't be beat. He'd catch a little shut-eye, get himself a burrito down at Pepe's Pepper Shack, and head out for the nearest sale. It had been a hard week, and he deserved a break. Even if he didn't come up with a rare first, the hunt just might save his sanity.

He closed his eyes against the sun. By noon it would be a hundred, by five, a hundred and ten. Already heat waves rose up in ribbons down the right-of-way, and the dry air crackled.

He thought about that boy hanging from the wigwag, how men like him died in obscurity, men forgotten by family and country alike. He'd seen his share of them, been on the run himself, for all that. If nothing else, maybe they would locate the poor bastard's family and rescue him from the indignity of a pauper's grave.

The road-rail hummed down the tracks like a Cadillac. Given a choice between road or rail, the old hermaphrodite clearly preferred the rail.

At the Roswell signal, he brought her down to check the traffic.

Pulling through the crossing, he goosed her up and clacked off into the desert. The miles clicked away, and as he approached the Clovis signal, he could see that the crossing had been blocked by a truck. A dozen men sat about, some with signs across their laps. When they spotted his road-rail, they stood. Hook slowed down and eased to a stop just short of the truck.

One of the men, an ax handle cradled across his arm, stepped up.

"Where you think you're going?" he asked.

Hook got out. "I'm headed for Clovis," he said.

The men gathered in a line across the right-of-way behind the man, who then lowered the ax handle to his side.

"Not this way, you ain't," he said. "This line is closed until further notice."

5

Hook RECOGNIZED THE man with the ax handle as Moose Barrick from the signal gang out of Clovis. He'd been nicknamed Moose for obvious reasons. His nose flattened out on the end, and his eyes bulged from his forehead in perpetual astonishment.

Hook knew him first in Amarillo, where Hook had investigated him once for stealing railroad supplies. He'd not pinned Moose, but he had little doubt that the suspicions were justified. Moose, having taken offense at the investigation, never forgave him.

"Hello, Moose," Hook said. "What you doing with that stick?"

"Killing rats," Moose said.

The men laughed and gathered in close.

"Looks to me like you got the line shut down. Your union know this is going on?"

"We *are* the brotherhood," one of men said from the back. "We ain't had a raise in five years. All the company cares about is profit, and all the union cares about is keeping its membership guaranteed by the company. And that's just the way Truman likes it. We ain't looked up since this war began, and it's time we changed things."

The men rumbled their agreement and moved in closer.

Moose said, "Get your road-rail off the track, Runyon. There ain't nobody running this line without our say-so."

Hook moved to the front of the road-rail, and Moose stepped back.

"I just took a dead man off the potash wigwag," Hook said. "It's left a sour taste, and my temper's running short. Whether you strike or don't strike is between you and your union. But you don't have a right to break the law. Shutting down the line is breaking the law. Move the truck off the crossing."

When Moose started to lift his ax handle, Hook spun about and shoved his elbow into his nose. Moose staggered back, his eyes wide, blood oozing into the corners of his mouth.

Moose tried to bring the ax handle up again, but Hook stuck him with three short ones to the belly. Air rushed from Moose's lungs, and his eyes glazed. Hook caught him again with a solid whack across the head with his prosthesis. Moose staggered and then wilted to his knees. His ax handle clattered into the cinder bed.

Hook glanced around to make certain the others hadn't taken up the fight before delivering a shattering uppercut that sent Moose sprawling across the tracks.

Stepping back, Hook lowered his hand onto his sidearm. The men looked at each other and then backed up.

"Now, move the truck, boys," Hook said. "And take this lard bucket here with you."

"Whose side you on, union buster?" the man in the back said.

"This is not about sides," Hook said. "This is about keeping it clean. Stay off the property, and we won't have a problem. Is that understood?"

The men nodded, and Hook said, "You might want to pick a new leader while you are at it. This one's not feeling so well."

Hook waited until they'd carried Moose off and backed the truck down the road before he cranked up the road-rail and headed for Clovis. He blew on his knuckles, which were bruised and swelling. Moose Barrick had a head like an anvil and a brain the size of a rabbit's.

Hook did understand the men's frustrations. Those same fellows had worked twelve-hour shifts seven days a week for the duration of the war. Prices had increased, but their wages hadn't. They were feeling the squeeze.

In this business, he had no choice but to walk the line between the company and the union, so it had to be about the law and nothing else. If either side perceived him as partial, his effectiveness was shot to hell.

He pulled off at the Clovis crossing and parked the road-rail behind his caboose. When Hook got out, Mixer came bounding from beneath the caboose.

Hook knelt and pulled his ears. "What's this I hear about you claiming the baggage?" he asked. Mixer dropped down on his front legs and stuck his butt in the air, his tail swinging. "You're treading on dangerous territory, buster, 'cause I been thinking I might like to have a cat instead. They eat half as much and cover up their mistakes."

Mixer, knowing he'd been chastised for something, slinked away, looking back over his shoulder now and again as he went.

Hook made his way to the depot to check in with Popeye, the Clovis operator. Everyone called him Popeye because, when young, he had biceps the size of Christmas hams, and he wore a cocked hat everywhere he went.

He found Popeye bent over in his chair tying his shoe.

"Where'd the operator go?" Hook said from behind him.

Popeye jumped and bumped his head on the drawer he'd left pulled out on his desk.

"Goddang it, Hook. Do you have to sneak around like that?"

"You'd think an operator would be a little more alert, given he's charged with keeping trains from crashing into each other," Hook said.

Popeye took off his hat, rubbed his head, and then poked his hat back on. "Where the hell you been, Hook? That dog of yours has been tormenting humans and animals alike around here."

"Mixer's just good-natured, unlike a sour old operator I know," Hook said.

"Humph," he said. "That mongrel waits for hours out there for a passenger train to pull in. Then he runs out and sprays up the luggage when it's set off. Course he don't spray up just any old luggage. Oh, no. He favors the alligator and pigskin luggage, the expensive stuff."

"I never knew an operator who could keep from blowing up a story," Hook said.

"That mutt's turned over trash cans, stole T-bone steaks out of the Harvey House kitchen, and chased the line inspector's speeder car halfway to the Belen Cutoff."

Hook sat down. "You about through bitching, Popeye? 'Cause I feel a migraine coming on."

"Why should I complain? It's just been dandy all around, hasn't it. Finished up the week with a truck blocking the Pecos run, tying up the whole line and setting off every official from here to Chicago. There's a million square miles of desert, and some son of bitch stalls out on the main-line crossing. You have to figure it's a shit cloud just hanging over my head. There's just no other way to explain it."

"The line's cleared," Hook said.

"You checked on it? Was it a farmer or a drunk?" he asked.

"There are more possibilities than farmers and drunks in New Mexico, Popeye."

"Not far as I can tell. Course, could have been a drunk farmer, or a yard dog, I suppose. But then here he sits sober as a Baptist deacon."

"Farmers," Hook said.

"Well, I thought so, and the Artesia brass pounder said you found a bo dancing off the potash wigwag?"

"Is there anything else you'd like to know for your newspaper column, Popeye?"

He took off his hat and pushed back a wisp of hair that lay across his bald head. He put his hat back on and checked the clock.

"There's a package came in on the mail train for you," he said.

"Oh?"

"Looks like a security badge to me," he said.

"Jesus, Popeye, that's my private mail."

"I hear there's pickpockets working the line. Course, *you*, being a lawman and carrying a sidearm, wouldn't have to worry about pickpockets like the rest of us."

Picking up his new badge, Hook dropped it in his pocket.

"Tampering with the mail is a federal offense, Popeye. I'll thank you to mind your own business in the future."

"Well, I'd tell you about that fellow whose been looking for you, but then it ain't none of my affair, I guess, so I'll just sit here and mind my own business like I was doing before you came in."

"It's been a while since I shot up an operator, Popeye, but I'm seriously considering it at the moment."

"He's a stiff-necked little guy what looks like he just ate a lemon. You can't miss him. He's all dressed up for a wedding, or a funeral, which comes mostly to the same thing."

Hook drove to the dime store downtown, bought a wallet for a buck, and slipped in the new badge. Back at the depot, he parked the road-rail in the shade and made his way toward the caboose.

A young man, just coming out of the bathroom, waved him over. He wore a starched white shirt, black suspenders, black bow tie, and his black shoes shined like axle grease in the sun. He'd slicked his hair back without a part, and he flashed a set of teeth straight as a picket fence.

"Excuse me, sir," he said, setting down his luggage. "I'm looking for a Mr. Walter Runyon. You wouldn't happen to know him?"

Hook studied him against the sun.

"He have one arm with a hook on the end of it?"

"Yes, a prosthesis, I believe."

"Like this?" Hook said, holding up his arm.

"Why, yes. I believe so."

"Never heard of him," Hook said, turning away.

"Oh wait. Sir? Sir?"

"Me?" Hook said.

"If I could have a moment."

"You can have a couple of 'em, providing you aren't selling snake oil or saving souls."

"You wouldn't be Walter Runyon yourself, would you?"

"I would be if I had a choice," he said. "But I don't, so I'm Hook Runyon, not Walter Runyon." He held up his prosthesis. "You might figure why?"

"I see," he said. "Are you the security agent?"

"I would be if I had a choice," he said. "But I don't. There's not enough security around here for me to be a security agent, so I'm a yard dog instead."

"My name is Junior Monroe," he said. "I've been assigned to you."

"Look, Junior Monroe, Eddie can assign you wherever he chooses, but what you need to know can't be taught by me. It's got to be experienced, and you got to do that on your own."

"Look, Mr. Runyon, Hook, I know you have your hands full."

"*Hand*," Hook said. "I've got my *hand* full, and I have enough trouble keeping out of the deep end without worrying about a greenhorn."

"I won't be of any trouble," he said.

Hook looked through his brows. "I don't own this railroad,

Junior, and I can't keep you from hanging around. Just don't expect me to teach you anything. I'm not your instructor, so don't get in my road, and don't interfere with my way of doing things. I'm too goddang tired to change."

"Yes, sir," he said.

"Keep your eyes open and carry your own water."

Junior stuck his hands in his pockets and rolled up on his toes. "I will," he said.

"Come to that caboose over there in the morning, after ten."

"Right," he said.

"In the meantime, you might want to meet my dog, Mixer."

"Your dog?"

"The one whizzing on your luggage there," he said, walking away.

6

Hook AWOKE TO someone knocking. Sunlight shot through the cupola window and into his eyes. He rolled out of bed and opened the door to find Junior Monroe standing on the platform. He sported a bow tie, vest, and a Panama cocked down over one eye.

"I thought I told you after ten," Hook said.

Junior checked his watch. "I guess I'm a little early."

"Look, I haven't slept for two days and then what with trains coming and going all damn night."

"Sorry," he said again, looking down at his feet.

"Nice outfit," Hook said.

Junior looked at his arms. "A man's clothes are the key to . . ."

"Right," Hook said, scratching his face, which had grown dark with a beard. "You just as well come in, Junior. I'm damn sure awake now."

"Thank you, sir," he said, taking off his hat.

"Coffee?" Hook asked, searching for his prosthesis.

"Tea, please," Junior said.

Hook pulled his prosthesis out from under a stack of clothes.

"I didn't ask you if you wanted tea. I asked you if you wanted coffee."

"Coffee's fine. With cream, please."

Hook slipped his britches on and looked over at Junior. "I didn't ask you if you wanted cream, 'cause I don't have cream."

"Black's fine," Junior said, holding his hat in front of him.

"Sit down," Hook said, working on his shirt.

Junior looked around for a place to sit, deciding to move a stack of books off the bench by the stove.

"You live here?" he asked.

"No, I just visit, 'cause it's so goddang peaceful and quiet," Hook said.

Hook lit the fire and set the water on to boil. He looked out the window. Mixer sat on the dock waiting for the eastbound.

"You read all these books?" Junior asked.

"I collect them," Hook said.

"Collect them?" Junior said, fanning through one of the books. "Why would you want old books around if you don't read them?"

"I didn't say I didn't read them. I said I collect them. Sometimes I read them. Sometimes I don't. It's no different than someone collecting measuring cups. Just 'cause they have a hundred measuring cups doesn't mean they go around measuring a hundred things with a hundred cups."

"But I don't see why anyone would need more than one cup in the first place."

"Something tells me you never will."

"I could understand dry measurements versus liquid measurements."

"It's not about *using* the damn things. It's about *having* them. Don't you have things that you don't use?"

"I've a couple shirts that are way too garish," he said.

"Jesus. They're my books because I want them. If you don't like that, just keep it to yourself."

Hook found his cigarettes. The knuckles on his hand had swollen even more from banging Moose Barrick's hard head.

"Cigarette?" he asked.

"Smoke irritates my skin," Junior said.

Hook lit up and blew smoke out the corner of his mouth. He looked at Junior through the blue haze. Junior dropped an eyelid.

"Irritates your skin?" Hook said.

"Makes me prickly," he said.

"That so?"

"I've very sensitive skin. I was in the hospital once with second-degree burns in my crotch."

"Someone set your crotch on fire?"

Junior flushed and straightened his bow tie. "No, of course not; my mother washed my boxers in bleach. Any kind of bleach product, I get these enormous blisters."

Hook drew on his cigarette. "Well, you're safe enough from any bleach products around here.

"So, Junior, what kind of experience you had working law enforcement?"

"I have an undergraduate degree in political science and a minor in criminology," he said. "I plan on going to law school eventually and then into public service."

Hook poured the coffee. "Public service?"

"Prosecutor."

"So what does that have to do with being a railroad dick?"

"My father feels I should have some real-life experiences with the darker side before I make my decision. He's an acquaintance with Eddie Preston, so here I am."

"An acquaintance?"

"Mr. Preston owes him money."

"Well, it can get fairly dark around here at times."

"That's what Mr. Preston said."

Hook swirled his coffee and examined the grounds in the bottom of his cup.

"I remember one time when a new prosecutor showed up down in Pecos. He swore to clean up the whores working Main on Saturday nights. Folks advised him against it, whores being a long-held tradition in that particular part of town. But the prosecutor, being highly educated like yourself, and knowing the ins and outs of criminal behavior, couldn't be discouraged."

"Being informed of the law can be critical in these situations. What happened?"

Hook rubbed at his whiskers. "Within a month's time there wasn't a whore within two hundred miles of Pecos. The crime rate dropped, and church attendance soared to an all-time high."

Junior nodded. "The theory is to stamp out the small crimes and the big ones will take care of themselves. It's a tried and true concept of criminology."

"So, the deacons got together and voted to make the prosecutor citizen of the year," Hook said. "Only one problem."

"Oh?"

"They couldn't find him. The cops looked everywhere, even called his aging mother back east, who swore she hadn't seen nor heard from him since he left for Pecos."

"What happened?"

"A year later, his body, shriveled up like an old shoe, turned up in the Chihuahuan Desert."

"Oh," he said.

"Just remember, Junior, that doing the right thing is good but never as good as staying alive. There's always some bastard willing to kill you, eat you, and spit your bones in the desert dirt."

Junior, his brow wrinkled, looked at Hook. "That's a rather cynical view of life, isn't it, sir?"

Hook looked out the window. "Yesterday I cut a boy down from the wigwag signal out on the potash spur. He'd been hoisted to the top of the cantilever with a rope around his neck. They left him there to strangle. It's the sort of thing that can make a man cynical."

When a knock came at the door, Junior jumped, sloshing his coffee onto his hand.

Hook opened it to find Popeye waiting on the platform. He took off his hat and dabbed the sweat from his bald pate with his bandanna.

"Hook," he said. "Eddie Preston called and said to tell you them pickpockets are working the Clovis to Amarillo run. Said they stole the conductor's watch right out of his pocket. Said if you were sober and able, he wanted them rounded up before they closed down the entire line."

"Right," Hook said.

"So I told him you were most likely able, but I couldn't be certain about the sober part."

"Thanks, Popeye."

"He said there'd be hell to pay if them pickpockets ain't caught soon and that you were to take the boy with you, 'cause he needs the experience if he's ever going to become an executor."

"Prosecutor," Hook said. "Jesus. What time is the Amarillo run?"

Popeye checked his pocket watch and snapped the cover shut. "She's due in a couple hours, providing the wildcatters don't shut down the system somewhere."

"Alright. Radio them that we'll be hitching a ride, will you, Popeye?"

Hook met Junior on the platform thirty minutes before the Amarillo passenger train was due to come in. He secured Junior's wallet to a piece of string, tied a pencil on the other end, and poked a hole through Junior's hip pocket

After threading the pencil through the hole, he said, "Let them try to steal that."

Junior examined his pocket. "This is a brand-new suit, sir."

"Stop calling me that, Junior. I don't know who the hell you're talking to half the time.

"Just keep in mind that yard dogs are called upon to make sacrifices now and again in the fight against crime. A hole in your pocket is little enough to pay to catch these bastards."

"How will we recognize them?" Junior asked.

Hook lifted the wallet between his index and middle fingers. "Feel that?"

"Yes."

"Good. They look just like everybody else, Junior, except more so. That's the problem, and they can lift a thought right out of your skull.

"Now, when we get in there, I want you to sit up front, and I'll sit in the back. At some point you parade up and down the aisle a few times to make sure you're seen. What with you dressed up like a penguin and with that fat wallet in your pocket, they'll be certain to cut you out from the herd."

Junior turned to look back at his wallet. "Shouldn't I have a weapon?"

"If worse comes to worst, I'll shoot them myself. Most likely, they'll make their move when things crowd up on arrival at a depot. Soon as you feel a tug on that wallet, let out a yell, and I'll move in."

In the distance the whistle of the train rose and fell. Hook hollered at Mixer to get off the tracks. He slinked away to the caboose, crawled under, and peeked out from the shadows.

"Now," Hook said. "Remember, you're to look around as if you don't know where to go. You let me take care of everything else. Do you understand?"

Junior nodded his head. "You want me to board first?"

"I'll board first, and don't look at me when you get on."

"Okay, Hook, but I'd feel better if I had a weapon to carry."

"Well, I wouldn't. Anyway, prosecutors don't carry weapons, so you just as well get used to it."

When the train arrived, Hook boarded and worked his way to the back of the car. From there, he had a good view of the passengers.

Junior found a seat near the front and put his hat on the overhead rack. An old lady with knitting in her lap sat in the seat next to the window. She looked at Junior over the tops of her glasses before returning to her knitting.

Hook considered the back of Junior's head, which struck him as particularly large for his neck. He had the look of a boy headed to summer camp. If there was ever a mark in the making, it had to be Junior Monroe, public servant.

The passenger train slid away from the platform and climbed up to speed. A young couple sat near the back. The girl's hair, raven black, fell about her face as she leaned into the boy. She popped a stick of gum into her mouth and reached up to fondle his face.

Across from Hook, a soldier slept on his duffle, his hat drawn over his eyes. His jacket, having fallen onto the floor, displayed a variety of multicolored ribbons that had been pinned over the pocket.

Hook looked the passengers over once again. They struck him as unlikely candidates for being pickpockets. Maybe Eddie Preston had it wrong. Maybe they'd already moved to a different run.

When the train pulled into the Hereford depot, Junior stood, ran his hand through his hair, and then walked slowly to the end of the car and back, the top of his wallet visible in his back pocket.

Several more passengers got on and fanned out across the car. The old lady with white socks and varicose veins walked to the back. Two women, each with a blond kid in tow, took up seats near the middle of the car. A businessman with a calfskin briefcase moved as far from the others as possible and proceeded to go through his notes.

As they pulled off, Hook yawned and scrunched down in his

seat. Pickpockets rarely struck on a moving train, too much chance of getting caught and with nowhere to run.

When the conductor walked the aisle announcing their arrival time in Amarillo, Hook checked to make certain Junior had been alerted. Some of the passengers stood to retrieve luggage from the overhead racks.

The engineer blew the whistle. The train decelerated and pulled to a stop at the station. The passengers stood and moved into the aisle. Hook could see Junior as he worked his way to the door.

Hook scanned the car but spotted no signs of a problem. He ducked down for a peek out the window. People on the platform had moved forward as they waited for the passengers to get off.

When Hook stepped out onto the platform, he moved into the crowd. He could just see Junior's hat above the others. Pushing his way closer, he scanned the passengers.

Suddenly, Junior's hat disappeared, and someone screamed. Hook shoved his way forward. Junior sat on the ground, and the old lady with the knitting bag lay sprawled out in front of him. Her skirt had hiked up, exposing her garter belt and the hairy backs of her legs.

Hook pulled his sidearm. "You're under arrest," he said.

The old lady whimpered and buried her face in her hands. A collective gasp rose up from the passengers, who had crowded in about them.

"But Hook, what are you doing?" Junior said. "I didn't call for help."

"It's a ruse," Hook said. "She falls. You get distracted, and someone lifts your wallet."

"She just tripped, and I fell over her. Anyway, I still have my wallet. See."

"Let her up," a woman said from the crowd. "She's an old lady, for heaven's sake."

"Yeah, let her up, you creep," a man said from the back.

The soldier who had been on the train stepped forward. "What kind of asshole pulls a gun on an old lady?"

"I'm the railroad dick," Hook said. "She's a pickpocket."

"Someone check her knitting bag," the lady in the back said.

The soldier knelt and dumped the bag onto the walk. A ball of yarn, a small magnifying glass, and two knitting needles fell out.

"Nothing," the soldier said, helping her to her feet. "Since when is knitting against the law?"

The old lady swooned and leaned into him.

"Someone should call the law," the lady in the back said.

Hook turned. "I *am* the law, lady."

"Really," she said. "You should be ashamed."

The whistle blew, and Hook turned. The old lady had disappeared into the crowd, which now drifted toward the train.

Hook walked to the luggage wagon. Junior, the brim of his Panama bent from his fall, followed behind.

"I didn't feel anything, Hook, or I would have called out as you suggested."

"Forget it," Hook said.

"First thing I know, she fell, and I went right over the top of her."

"You have any money?"

Junior looked at him from under the Panama. "Money?"

"To buy tickets home."

"But can't you just show them your badge?"

Hook turned and headed for the depot. "Which is just what I'd do, Junior, if they hadn't lifted the damn thing."

7

POPEYE PUSHED THE phone across the desk. "Eddie isn't going to be happy about them pickpockets getting away, Hook."

"How is it operators can predict the future without ever leaving their chairs?" Hook asked.

"It's a matter of uncommon intelligence," he said.

"It's for sure uncommon," Hook said.

He could see Junior waiting for him on the bench outside, his Panama drooped down in front like a broken bird wing. Hook dialed Eddie.

"Security," Eddie said.

"Eddie, Hook."

"What the hell you doing, Runyon?"

"Chasing crooks, Eddie."

"You get them pickpockets?"

"The bastards teamed up on me."

Eddie fell silent. "Have you considered early retirement, Runyon? I'm sure the company would be willing to make an exception."

"What I *have* considered could put me on death row, Eddie."

"So, I get this call from Amarillo," Eddie said. "This guy says a one-armed man pulled a gun on an old lady in the middle of a crowd at the depot. 'What the hell kind of railroad you running?' he says. So I asked myself, who would be crazy enough to draw down on an old lady and in a crowd? Guess who came to mind?"

"She wasn't that old, Eddie. Anyway, it's not always easy to tell who the criminal is."

"You got that right. So what's next, a pistol-whipping down at the old-age home?"

"Those pickpockets are probably working the competition by now, anyway, Eddie."

"They have no reason to leave *us*, Runyon. It couldn't be safer right where they are."

"I've got their number. It's just a matter of time."

"Put that boy on it, Runyon. He's college, you know."

"He drinks tea."

"What the hell does that mean?"

"And cigarette smoke irritates his skin. Jesus, Eddie, why don't you just pay your bills so I don't have to babysit?"

"That coroner called from Carlsbad," he said. "He has something he wants you to look at before he releases that wigwag body for burial."

"Like what?"

"Check it out, Runyon, and there's an old bus parked in the right-of-way west of Gallup. See it's removed."

"Right," he said. "Listen, I thought you were going to send me a new badge."

"What the hell you talking about? I sent it a week ago."

"Well, it didn't arrive."

"What do you mean, it didn't arrive?"

"You'd think the railroad could deliver the goddang mail without losing it."

"This is coming out of your pay, Runyon. And if that other

badge shows up, send it back. I don't want them floating all over the country. Pretty soon the only one without a badge will be you."

"Send it by stagecoach, Eddie. Maybe it will get here that way."

"And there are wildcat strikes breaking out up and down the line. Remember it's your job to protect company property."

"Got it, Eddie."

"Truman's threatening to nationalize the railroad if these strikes don't stop. How would you like working for Truman?"

"Maybe he could get my badge here without losing it, Eddie. And you might consider sending some decent transportation out here. That road-rail is like sitting a camel.

"I got to go, Eddie. The operator's making ugly noises about his phone."

Hook waited for Popeye to come back from the john. "I've got to make a run to Carlsbad," he said. "I'd like to put that road-rail on the line. You got a slot open?"

"Why don't you just road it, Hook? That way I don't have to do the board over."

"My kidneys won't take another road trip in that thing."

Popeye looked at the schedule. "There's a blacksnake with a load of coal coming through in about an hour. After that, the line's open until three. You want an order?"

"Write it up, Popeye."

Hook joined Junior on the bench. Mixer hopped up to greet him. Junior stood and brushed the hair off his lap. Hook lit a cigarette and looked downline.

"Eddie has an assignment for you," he said. "There's a bus on the right-of-way west of Gallup. He wants you to have it towed off company property."

Junior fanned away the smoke that drifted over his head. "But how would I get there?"

"There's a tanker train through here in an hour. Hop her and run on out there. The company will pick up the tow bill for the bus."

"Hop a freighter? You mean jump on it without a ticket?"

"That's right," Hook said. "And don't fall under the wheels. It makes a hell of a mess."

"And where will you be, Hook?"

"First, I'm taking a nap, and then I'm herding the road-rail over to Carlsbad to see the coroner's gold-teeth collection.

"Come on, Mixer," Hook said, pausing. "And when you get back, find yourself a place to stay. I didn't sign on to share my caboose with a prosecutor."

Hook stretched out on his bunk and perused his copy of Hemingway's *For Whom the Bell Tolls*. He'd owned a reading copy, too, but this one was in fine condition. Someday it would bring a nice return, and he never tired of Hemingway's clean style. His dialogue shot from the page like a rifle bullet.

If things ever slowed down, he intended to find some of Hemingway's other work. When a book, long after it had been set aside, still lingered in his head, he took it as a sure sign of collectability.

When he awoke, his copy had slid to the floor, and Mixer, with both paws up on the bunk, stared into his face. Hook pushed him away and sat up. He dug out his watch. The blacksnake should have come and gone by now, and, with it, Junior Monroe.

Hook himself had abandoned riding coal cars some years ago. Eating coal dust in a fifty-mile-an-hour gale had taken some of the fun out of it. Still, it would be a good learning experience for Junior.

After setting out some extra food for Mixer, who had apparently worn out his welcome at the Harvey House, Hook checked on the road-rail. One of the tires had lost air, and a bird had deposited a calling card on the windshield.

By the time he cleaned the window and pumped up the tire, the sun had lifted high in the east. He pulled onto the crossing, dropped the pilot wheels, and headed off for Carlsbad.

The countryside slid by like a silent film, and the blue sky, laced in white, swirled about in the exact pattern of an agate shooter marble he'd had as a kid. The smell of heat and thistle rode in on the wind.

Days like this brought back the freedom he'd experienced when he bummed the rails. Being a bo took little from a man's spirit. Some of his happiest times had been tracking through the night atop a boxcar with no plans, no destination, and no expectations. But more often than not, fear and hunger trumped freedom, until at last the fare had become too high to pay.

At dusk he passed by the Clovis signal, and he slowed. He could smell smoke and figured it to be the strikers' campfires somewhere beyond the hill. He brought the road-rail back up to speed. As long as they stayed off company property, he had no quarrel with them.

He hoped the strikers had taken his advice about dropping Moose Barrick as their leader. Moose had worked for the railroad for a long time. Hook never understood how a company would fire a man for sitting down on the job but keep a lowlife like Barrick on the payroll for years.

Night fell, and the stars popped into the sky. The zing of locusts rose up above the hum of the tires. And when the Artesia depot came into view, Hook thought to pull off for a break. But then he remembered the fiver he owed the operator and decided to press on to Carlsbad.

The moon had set, and the night had darkened to ink by the time he hit the crossing in Carlsbad. He found the operator paring his nails into the trash can.

When the operator looked up, he said, "Oh, it's you."

Hook squinted his eyes into slits. "You ask for my badge, Beauford, and it'll take three surgeons to find where those clippers went."

The operator shoved the trash can back and dropped his clippers into his pocket.

"What you want, Runyon?"

"You know where the coroner lives around here?"

"Broomfield? Sure. His office is just off Third downtown."

"Where does he do his coroner work?" Hook asked.

The operator opened his mouth and showed Hook a missing tooth. "In his chair."

Hook looked up at the clock. "There some place I could catch a nap?"

"I heard the jail's right comfy," he said, grinning.

"That's real funny. You thought about applying for Eddie Preston's job?" Hook said.

"There's a spot behind the water heater in the baggage room. You get caught, I don't know you," he said.

"Thanks," Hook said. "I figured you might have located yourself a roost."

When Hook awoke, a spider ran across his chest and disappeared under his arm.

"Damn it," he said, sitting up.

Sunlight struck through the window and lit the wall. He could smell the diesel fumes from the freighter idling outside and hear the men as they went about their maintenance check.

When he came out of the baggage room, a different operator sat behind the desk. He looked like a kid taking up his first job.

The operator looked up at Hook. "Who are you?" he asked.

"I'm Hook Runyon, the bull out of Clovis," he said. "Where's John?"

"John who?"

"Beauford, the operator who was here."

"Last shift," he said. "They bumped him to Needles."

"What's your name?" Hook asked.

"Clyde."

"Clyde who? Never mind," he said. "You goddang operators aren't around long enough for it to matter, anyway."

"Say, what you doing in the baggage room?" he asked.

"Security," Hook said. "Why the hell wasn't the door locked?"

"I thought it was."

"Well, it wasn't. You might want to check on these things when your trick starts."

"Yes, sir," he said.

"I'll let it go this time," Hook said. "But don't let it happen again. I'd hate to have to write you up."

Hook's road-rail took up two spaces in front of Dr. Broomfield's dentist office. Hook waited in the waiting room for thirty minutes while Broomfield completed an extraction.

"Dr. Broomfield will see you now," the receptionist said. "If you will follow me."

Hook followed her into a small area off the waiting room. It smelled of burnt coffee. Boxes of dental supplies were stacked along one wall.

When he came in, Hook stood. "Dr. Broomfield?"

"Yes," he said.

"I'm Hook Runyon, security agent for the Santa Fe."

Dr. Broomfield looked at Hook's prosthesis. "I've been expecting you, Mr. Runyon. Please, have a seat. I've no patients scheduled for a bit."

Hook sat down and adjusted a droopy sock. Dr. Broomfield sat on the edge of the table, locked his knee in his hands, and bobbed his foot. He was tall, six two, maybe taller, and he had the hands of a woman. His hair, the color of straw, hung over an eye. He sported a blond mustache that curled into the corners of his mouth.

"You asked to see me," Hook said. "What's the deal?"

"Yes," he said. "It's about the body that the highway patrol brought in from the potash spur."

"Right," Hook said. "I found no identification on him. Have you found something?"

Dr. Broomfield's pant leg pulled up, revealing the hair on his leg, which was the exact color of his mustache.

"I found no identification, if that's what you mean. Perhaps it had been removed by someone else."

"That's how I figured it," Hook said.

Dr. Broomfield reached for the cabinet drawer and opened it. "I did, however, find something of interest while preparing the body for examination."

"Oh?"

"This," he said, dropping a medal into Hook's hand. "It was tied about his neck with a piece of string."

"A star?" Hook said.

"Yes," he said. "A Bronze Star for valor."

8

A WAR HERO?" HOOK said, cradling the medal in the palm of his hand.

Dr. Broomfield rolled his shoulders. "Or a thief. Who knows? Look at the back."

Hook turned the medal over. The name Samuel Ash had been engraved on it.

"His name?" he asked.

"Possible," Broomfield said. "But folks steal the damndest things, given a chance."

"Have you checked it out?"

"Mr. Runyon," he said, running his long fingers through his hair. "How many Samuel Ashes do you figure occupy this country?"

Hook shrugged. "Thousands, I suppose."

"Exactly. Look, I'm a county coroner appointed by the judge to determine if there's been foul play in a person's death. And the judge, being the frugal sort, is dead-set against me pissing away money on hopeless causes. On top of that, I have my practice.

"There are four possible causes for a person's death as I see it: accidental, natural, suicide, and homicide. Now it's clear this fellow didn't die of natural causes, being young and healthy by all appearances, and I doubt he had an accident while climbing a wigwag signal with a rope around his neck.

"According to my calculations, that leaves suicide or homicide. My examination revealed no evidence of wounds, no signs of struggle, not a scratch or a bruise anywhere. No fingerprints were left behind, no footprints, no tire tracks, and no weapons. No hangman's noose had been used, and his neck wasn't broken.

"If I'm not mistaken that probably leaves suicide. In my judgment, he tied off that rope, climbed up that cantilever, and let himself over the side. Who knows why? Maybe he had a love affair gone wrong. Maybe he suffered a disappointment so devastating that he couldn't pull out of a nosedive. Maybe he killed someone himself for all I know. I figure he set out to do what he had to do, and that's where my responsibility as coroner ends. If the railroad wants more information than that, then I say, have at it."

"The cantilever was an arm's length above his head. How does a man strangling at the end of a rope not reach up and save himself?"

"A person's will can be strong. I once investigated the death of a widow who shoved a pencil up her nose and into her brainpan.

"Look, Mr. Runyon, to investigate this further, I'd have to convene a coroner's jury and pay them stipends. I'd have to transport the body to Albuquerque for an autopsy, and I'd have to bear the wrath of Judge Bellow for squandering funds.

"I'm not prepared to do that because, in the end, it's unlikely that we'll ever know exactly what happened anyway. Even if we did find out, it wouldn't make a damn bit of difference to that fellow. He's as dead as he's ever going to be and knowing the reasons why won't change a damn thing for him."

The bell on the front door signaled, and Dr. Broomfield looked at his watch.

Hook rubbed at the back of his neck. Riding that road-rail had taken its toll on his spine.

"What happens to the body?" he asked.

"It's been released to the funeral home. He'll be given a Christian burial in the pauper's cemetery at county expense."

"Can I keep this star for the time being?"

"I don't see why not. I'll put it in the record."

"You may be right about all this, Dr. Broomfield, but there is that name, Samuel Ash? I don't see how it can be ignored. I'd like a chance to track it down before you put this man into a pauper's grave. If he's got family, they deserve to know."

Dr. Broomfield rose and checked his hair in the mirror on the back of the door.

"As long as it doesn't cost the county. I'll ask the funeral home to delay internment."

"I'd appreciate that," Hook said. "And I'll let you know what I find out one way or the other."

Broomfield reached for the doorknob. "I've a patient waiting." He paused. "You understand that there's a limit as to how long this can be postponed? A matter of a few days at most."

"I understand," Hook said.

Hook herded the road-rail back to the depot. Unable to find a parking space large enough to accommodate it, he parked under a tree nearly a block away and walked in.

Clyde, the new operator, stood up. "I locked that door to baggage like you said."

"That's good," Hook said. "Passengers got a right to have their belongings secured. All and all it's a deceitful world, Clyde; besides, some slacker might slip in on company time and take a nap behind the water heater."

"Oh, no sir," he said. "There's none of that going on around here."

"I figure you as a stickler for the rules," Hook said.

"Yes, sir."

"Well, that's good. Now, I need to use your phone to call Division."

"Right over there."

Hook pulled up a chair. "In the meantime, maybe you could write up a clearance order for my road-rail to Clovis."

"Well, I don't know," he said. "The company don't like putting road-rails on the line unless it's necessary. They don't hold up so well against an oncoming."

Hook took the receiver off the phone and hung it over his shoulder. "I understand that, Clyde, but this here is a security matter. I'm sure you wouldn't want to stand in the way of the law."

"No, sir. I'll work it up right away."

Hook dialed Eddie and waited.

"Security," Eddie said.

"Eddie, this is Hook."

"Where the hell are you now, Runyon?"

"Carlsbad, checking in with the coroner on that wigwag deal like you asked."

"So, what did he say?"

"He said that fellow died by hanging. Course, I had an idea that might be the case when I cut him down from the wigwag."

"Get it off the books, Runyon. I smell a lawsuit here, and you know how the railroad hates a lawsuit. On top of that, we got strike problems cropping up everywhere."

"He had a Bronze Star around his neck, Eddie."

"A Bronze Star?"

"You know, like for heroism in combat."

"I know what it's for, Runyon."

"There was a name on the back of it."

"On the back of what?"

"The Bronze Star. Jesus, Eddie, am I going too fast?"

"What name?"

"Samuel Ash."

"Who's Samuel Ash?"

"I don't know, Eddie. That's the point."

"Everyone has a name. I have a name."

"Yeah, I know what they call you, Eddie."

"Don't stir the pot, Runyon. I'm telling you."

"I want to check the company employment records. You know how those bastards are about the records. Maybe you could clear it."

"It's against my better judgment."

"Something like this could come back on the company, Eddie."

"Okay, but I don't want this thing strung out, you hear?"

"Right. I'll check with Topeka when I get back to Clovis."

Hook hung up and leaned back in the chair. He could use a shot of Runt Wallace's shine about now. Talking to Eddie Preston could make a man dive headfirst off the wagon.

The operator came in and handed Hook his clearance. "You'll have to wait until the eastbound comes through. After that, you should have plenty of time to make it to Clovis."

Hook tucked the order into his pocket. "Thanks, Clyde," he said. "I think you're going to go far in this company."

Hook killed a few hours scouting books down at the Salvation Army thrift while he waited for the eastbound to clear. When he heard the whistle go through, he made his way back to the road-rail. He hoped the damn thing didn't fail him in the middle of the Chihuahuan, and him with only a half-pack of cigarettes left.

He checked his rearview mirror. At least it would be dark soon and a hell of a lot cooler. As he drove through town, he thought about what the coroner had said. Maybe he'd been right. Maybe tracking down some indigent served no purpose in the end. In fact, the uncovering of his past may have been the thing he least desired in the hour of his death. And, like the coroner said, finding out whether Samuel Ash or someone else bailed off that wigwag would not change his circumstances one iota.

Still, a man had died on railroad property, and Hook had never been one to walk away from a case. He'd tracked down many a man in his time and lived with the consequences of doing so, good or bad. The day he lost the drive to find the truth would be the day he turned in his badge, if he could manage to keep one that long.

He took a left on Main and headed for the nearest crossing. If the man hanging from that wigwag turned out to be Samuel Ash, Hook figured him to be a war hero, and he had no intentions of letting them bury him in a pauper's grave.

He stopped on the first crossing at the edge of town and pulled onto the rails. Driving onto railroad tracks with a vehicle struck him as against the laws of nature, and his heart picked up a beat as he lowered the pilot wheels into place.

But, once moving, he relaxed. Leaning back, he listened to the hum of the wheels as he sped off into the fading light. He figured, with luck, to be back at the caboose in time for a whiskey and water before bedtime.

The old road-rail gathered up speed, the smell of oil and gas fumes drifting up about him. He turned over the steering to the pilot wheels and let the wind blow in his face through the window. Such moments as these were singular, dreamed of by boys and men alike.

Much of his life he'd burned away in passions of one kind or another, be it women, hooch, or the lust for a rare book. But more and more he'd found sweetness in solitude, in moments like these when thoughts washed up like an ocean tide.

He dozed, or so it seemed, and when he opened his eyes, red lights glowed about him in the darkness. He'd often imagined death this way, not violent and noisy, but an oozing away from one realm into another.

But when the siren blasted from out of the blackness, he sat erect, his heart pounding in his chest. From the corner of his eye, he spotted the throb of emergency lights beating in the blackness like a bloody heart. The oncoming vehicle, unaware of his presence in the absence of a signal, raced headlong down the side road toward the crossing in front of him.

Hook grabbed the steering wheel and slammed on the brakes with both feet. But the pedal sank to the floorboard, and the road-rail raced down the grade like a runaway steam engine.

As he entered the crossing, Hook glanced up to see the car looming on the tracks in front of him. His stomach waded into a knot, and his mouth turned to cotton. He closed his eyes and clenched his jaw against the inevitable.

The road-rail caught the back fender of the vehicle, and the impact drove Hook forward into the steering wheel. His lungs emptied of air and refilled with fire. Sparks sprayed up into the blackness, and the sound of breaking glass filled the night. The lights of the other vehicle spun about and shot skyward as the car skidded up the bank of the opposite bar ditch.

How long it took him to stop the road-rail, he couldn't be sure. But by the time he climbed the embankment and pried open the car door, his heart pounded in his ears like a steam jenny. Inside, he found a man lying on the floor of the car, his hat crushed over his eyes and his legs jammed under the dash.

"Jesus," Hook said, pulling him out. "You okay?"

The bill of Officer Joe's hat stuck out over his ear like the porch on a shack, and his badge hung loose from his pocket. A smear of dirt ran from one eye to the other like an eyebrow gone feral. Weaving, Officer Joe looked at his car and then at Hook. He screwed his hat back on his head and clenched his jaw.

"No, I ain't," he said. "But I'm a hell of a lot better off than you're going to be, Runyon."

9

HOOK POURED A cup of coffee from the thermos and took up a chair. He scratched at his beard, the consequence of two days in the Carlsbad jail, and watched Clyde, the Carlsbad operator, finish off the last of his bologna sandwich and an overripe banana.

The judge had fined Hook the cost of repairs on Officer Joe's patrol car, the total of which had yet to be determined. He released Hook on his own recognizance with the understanding that full payment would be made to the court when the appraisal arrived. Officer Joe, being less than civil about the situation, had made Hook's two-day stay in the clinker as miserable as possible.

In the end, Hook figured he'd escaped with only minor damage to his otherwise spotless reputation. All had worked out except for one small detail: Officer Joe had towed the road-rail, and they wouldn't release it until someone paid the ten-dollar tow fee.

Hook considered calling Eddie but hadn't yet informed him of the accident. Anyway, Eddie had enough responsibilities without having to deal with every small detail of an investigation.

"Thanks for the coffee," Hook said to Clyde.

Clyde shut his lunch box and kicked his feet up on the desk.

"Why is it you had to come back so soon, Mr. Runyon?" he asked.

"It's Hook to you, Clyde. That goddang road-rail broke down on me and had to be towed."

Clyde lit a cigarette, blew a smoke ring, and watched it wobble across the room.

"Damn good job it didn't break down on line," he said. "I heard a Flagstaff track foreman tried to beat a highwheeler to the Hackberry spur with his road-rail over to Shattuck."

"He didn't make it?" Hook asked.

"Oh, he made it, just not in one piece. They did find his silver-plated belt buckle and a set of false teeth."

Hook sucked at the hot coffee. "I don't remember hearing that. Guess I must have been on vacation."

"So, what's wrong with your road-rail, Hook?"

"It's not altogether clear. But the wrecker service wants ten bucks to release her. Seeing as how my cash is in Clovis, I'm stuck in Carlsbad talking to you."

"That's a real shame, but ain't that a company expense?"

"Which is why it would be a secured transaction if a man got an interim loan. Thing is, there's paperwork to be done and then a wait. You know how long it takes these bastards to do anything. Maybe you'd spot me the ten so I could get on with my business?"

"Aw, hell," he said. "I'd sure do one of those interim things for you, but then I couldn't buy milk for the babies."

Hook poured a shot of sugar into his coffee to tame it down and stirred it with his little finger.

"I didn't realize you were married, Clyde."

"Who's married?" he said, grinning.

"I wouldn't ask but for the circumstances I find myself in," Hook said.

"Ten bucks is a pretty good bite out of a man's check," he said. "And I've been figuring to buy a new pair of boots come payday."

"It takes a generous man to give up a new pair of boots for a friend, and it's not my way to mention the fact that I didn't report that breach of security with the baggage room, even though it could put my job at risk for not doing so. But then I've always said that friendship shouldn't come with a price. I'd do the same thing again this very minute, even though it could well cost me my job. You can't see your way clear, don't you worry about it. I'll figure something out."

"Well, hell," he said, reaching for his billfold. "I guess I can get by for another two weeks without them boots, seeing as how there's company money behind the loan."

Hook took the money and slipped it in his pocket. "Clyde, my boy, I predict a bright future for you in the railroad business."

Hook handed the tow truck operator the ten bucks and pointed out the road-rail, which had been parked near the fence.

"What the hell kind of vehicle is that, anyway?" he asked. "I seen August grasshoppers looked prettier than that thing."

"It's a road-rail," Hook said. "She goes either way, so to speak."

The truck driver said, "I heard of them."

"Well, she comes in handy in a pinch," Hook said.

"If I was you, I wouldn't be driving her until them brakes are fixed."

"Low on fluid?" Hook asked.

"Oh, she's low alright and likely to stay that way."

"What do you mean?"

"The brake line squirts like a humpback whale."

"Cut?"

"Worn through, I'd say. Why, you got enemies around here?"

"Officer Joe's been out of sorts lately."

"Yeah," he said, searching for his Beech-Nut. "Officer Joe pouts up every time someone runs over his patrol car." He opened the package, smelled the contents, and loaded his jaw. "I got an extra brake line back there. Can put her on for three bucks. Won't take that long."

"Thanks, anyway," Hook said. "But I don't have that far to go."

"Here's the keys," he said, reaching into his pocket. "You might want to scratch Officer Joe off your hit list, though. He's got a reputation for getting even."

Hook pulled off and eased his way through town. At the rail crossing on the outskirts, he coasted to a stop and studied the tire tracks where Officer Joe had launched up the embankment.

The drive back on the road promised to be a long haul, but he had little choice. Stirring up more attention getting a clearance order didn't strike him as the prudent thing to do at the moment.

Popeye leaned against the door and watched Hook come up the Clovis depot steps.

"What the hell you parking that thing on the sidewalk for, Hook?"

"'Cause I like it on the sidewalk," Hook said, rubbing his back. "You got a problem with that?"

"No, no," Popeye said. "I guess the sidewalk's as good a place as any for parking a road-rail.

"Where the hell you been, Hook? That dang dog's got the whole place in a stir. He chased a woman's poodle right through the Harvey House dining room the other day. The damn thing ran into the ladies' room and wouldn't come out. They had to cover its head with a blanket and carry it out the back door."

Hook took off his shoe and worked out a rock that had embedded itself in a hole.

"He probably figured it to be a rabbit," Hook said. "Mixer's a born hunter."

"A *white* rabbit?"

"There're white rabbits known to exist," Hook said.

"Yeah, in Alaska," Popeye said. "And I don't think they wear pink ribbons in their hair, either."

"Anyway, that dog don't belong to me," Hook said. "So I'm not responsible for what he does or doesn't do."

"He don't belong to you?"

"No, he doesn't, strictly speaking. He just showed up one day, and I haven't been able to run him off. Kind of like an operator I know."

"Then maybe I'll just shoot him next time he sprays up the baggage."

"Go ahead," he said. "But make damn sure he's dead because Mixer doesn't make a distinction between white rabbits and old depot operators."

"It's sure good to have security back in town looking out for my well-being," Popeye said. "I can't tell you how much safer I feel."

"It's all in the job," Hook said. "By the way, you haven't seen that Junior Monroe around, have you?"

Popeye pushed his cap to the side. "No, I ain't. He probably took off, and if he's smart, he won't look back."

Hook tossed the piece of rock away.

"How about spotting me a sawbuck until payday, Popeye?"

"Hell, Hook, I loaned you money last month."

"I'm running a little short," he said. "Just to get me over the hump."

"Last time I had to wait two weeks to get my money."

"I had a lot on my mind, Popeye."

"Right after that, Ted Burnham saw you buying old books at the rummage sale."

"That's a black lie, Popeye. I was just looking 'em over."

"Well, I don't have ten, but here's a five if you promise to spare me the details."

"Thanks, Popeye. Now, if you're finished disparaging me and my dog, I need to use the company phone."

Hook dialed Topeka. A man answered.

"Personnel."

"This is Hook Runyon, railroad security. I need to check on a Samuel Ash. He might have been one of our employees."

"Company employment records are not available to just everyone," the man said.

"Eddie Preston, the divisional supervisor, has cleared it," Hook said.

"Please hold," he said.

While Hook waited, he watched Popeye work the office. No better operator in the country existed, though he'd never admit it to Popeye.

"Sir?"

"Yes."

"Samuel Ash was recently hired as a temporary by the Clovis signal department."

"A temporary?"

"That's correct."

"You mean a scab?"

"I mean a temporary," he said. "Is there anything else?"

"No," Hook said. "Nothing else."

Determined to wash away two days' worth of jailhouse grime, Hook showered in the sleeping-room quarters before returning to the caboose. Too weary to put his prosthesis back on, he carried it under his other arm. When he stepped out the door, the callboy, just coming in to wake the next crew, stepped back and looked at the prosthesis dangling from under Hook's arm.

"Jesus," he said. "What happened to your arm?"

Hook looked down at the prosthesis. "Be careful what you play with in the shower, boy. You never know what might fall off."

Mixer greeted Hook from the steps of the caboose, his rear swinging to and fro.

Hook knelt and pulled his ears. "No more chasing white rabbits with pink ribbons, you understand?"

Hook fixed himself a whiskey and water and took to his bunk to read a little from the Hemingway. Mixer crawled underneath the bunk and fell fast asleep.

Twenty pages in, Hook doubled his pillow and rolled onto his side. He'd seen in the paper where the local library had scheduled a book sale for 9:00 Saturday morning, an annual event designed to move old editions off the shelves to make way for new ones.

Given the fact that security rarely gave a man a break and given that he'd worked more than his share of overtime hunting pickpockets, Hook figured the company owed him some time off.

Though he had two pretty good copies of *The Hound of the Baskervilles*, they were both 1927 London reprints. What he needed to fill out his collection was a 1902 American first edition.

Most librarians, possessing small interest in the collectibility of books, had been known to put some valuable stuff on the bargain table. Though ex-library books were not the most collectible, having often been abused by the public, sometimes the rarity of the book offset the disappointment of coffee stains and folded corners.

The next morning Hook took breakfast in the Harvey House. Not only could he put the bill on his tab, but he could partake in a meal of the highest caliber. Harvey Houses adorned nearly every depot on the line and held fast to a reputation for cleanliness and fine dining. Some said Fred Harvey had an eye so keen that he could pick gnat shit out of black pepper and would fire an employee for a single smudge on the water glass. But one thing sure, even in the remotest corners of the desert, a man could experience a Harvey meal that came in second to none in the country.

Hook pulled up to a table set with Irish linen, silver utensils, and Mimbreño china. A Harvey girl, dressed in a fitted uniform, took his order. She smelled of soap, and when she leaned in to fill his glass, he could feel the heat of her arm against him.

He ordered from memory, and his breakfast arrived in minutes: dippy eggs poached in milk, sourdough pancakes served with warm Vermont maple, a slab of hickory-smoked Kentucky ham, buttered biscuits, and a crystal saucer burgeoning with Oregon raspberry preserves.

"Coffee?" she asked, flashing a smile. Hook nodded and waited as she filled his cup with a steaming rich brew. She held up a crystal creamer. Hook nodded again, and she poured a dollop of fresh cream into his cup. He sipped at his coffee and listened to the rustle of her skirt as she made her way back to the kitchen.

When he'd finished breakfast, he retrieved an old briefcase from under his bunk. After admonishing Mixer to stay on his best behavior, he headed on foot for the Clovis library.

By the time he arrived, a passel of women and a few old graybeards had already lined up for the bargains. Some of the women carried large purses or shopping bags to fill with books. One of the men had a cardboard box on the floor, which he advanced now and again with the toe of his shoe.

A large oak table, groaning with discarded books, had been placed in the middle of the room. All books, good or bad, carried the same ten-cent price.

Hook questioned whether he should be spending his money on books, given that he now owed his next paycheck to the judge and half the railroad operators in the country.

But after careful thought, he concluded that giving up his money for rare books constituted a selfless act, a sacrifice that might well save some of America's finest literature from the trash heap.

When the sale opened, everyone crowded in. Books disappeared in quantities, dragged to the counter by satisfied patrons who would read away the summer at bargain prices.

Hook picked up a first-edition Sherwood Anderson, and *Exiles, A Play,* by James Joyce. He spotted a first edition of *Cabbages and Kings,* by O. Henry, under a stack of magazines. But the *Baskervilles,* the one book he wanted most, could not be found.

He filled out the remainder of his purchases with reading copies of whatever struck his fancy, and by then the stack had dwindled to a few ragged pulps and a random assortment of encyclopedias.

Hook placed his purchases on the floor next to the overstuffed chair by the newspaper rack and sat down for a rest.

At what point the thought came to him, he couldn't be sure. In fact, it might not have been a thought at all, at least not a conscious thought, but a feeling, a drawing by some force from outside of himself.

He rose and worked his way into the stacks, and there it sat on the shelf with its crimson cover. He pulled it down and took it back to his chair to peruse.

He thumbed its pages, and the smell of time and promise rose up from them. This copy, were it his, would bring closure to a collection he had worked on for a good long while.

Looking around, he slipped it into his stack of bargain books, gathered them up, and made his way to the counter.

BACK AT THE caboose, Hook filled Mixer's water dish before laying out the day's acquisitions. When he came to the *Hound of the Baskervilles* he'd taken from the library, a small knot twisted in the back of his throat. He'd never considered himself a thief, except for the usual childhood transgressions: a pack of cigarettes from his father's nightstand and a comic book from the drugstore, which he'd hidden for days in a coffee can buried under the front porch.

So maybe it hadn't been right, him taking the book like that, but then he could trade it out, couldn't he? His London edition would be considered in very good condition by even the most meticulous collector. Anyway, the library and its patrons would never know the difference. They could not care less about editions and points and impressions. Such things mattered only in the minds of collectors with their obsessions for rarity.

Taking his knife out, he removed the library-card pocket from the American first and attached it to the London edition, after which he slipped the book under his belt and pulled his shirt down over it.

He waited until nearly closing time before returning to the library, where he placed the London edition on the shelf.

The librarian, who stood behind the checkout counting the day's receipts, only nodded as Hook made his way out the door.

Mixer awakened him at eight with a slurp across his ear.

Hook sat up and rubbed his cheek dry with his shoulder. "Damn it, Mixer," he said. "Can't you hold it?" Mixer went to the door and whined. "Okay, okay," Hook said, looking for his shoes.

Determined to make up for the money he'd spent on books the day before, Hook skipped breakfast and walked to the signal department in the yards. The smell of oil and grease filled the morning, and the drum of idling diesels pooled in his core as he picked his way over the tracks. Pigeons pranced on the roof of the roundhouse like sentries and chortled their disapproval.

He found the day shift just arriving, men in overalls and denim shirts with their lunch boxes in tow. Slope Hurley, the signal foreman, sat on the tailgate of the crew truck.

They called him Slope because, according to Slope himself, his skull had been squeezed through a birth canal no bigger than a banana. So narrow had been the passageway that he shot out like a champagne cork and with his skull cast into a permanent ski slope. Slope claimed that he remembered the exact moment still after fifty-odd years, though he was just a newborn at the time.

Hook figured maybe more than his skull had been damaged, because Slope enjoyed the reputation as the meanest son of a bitch to work for in the southwest division. Moose Barrick had become his right-hand man. Between them, the turnover rate in the Clovis signal department rivaled that of the battle of Okinawa. Both Slope and Moose knew how to make men miserable and never passed up the chance to do just that.

The crew stowed their gear and watched Hook walk across the yard toward them. They mumbled among themselves and turned their backs. Slope stood and pulled at his chin, which had accommodated his profile by banking skyward on the end.

"Slope," Hook said. "Nice morning."

"Would be if I didn't have a stack of calls coming in," he said.

"Backed up, are you?"

"There hasn't been nothing fixed on this line since the war started, and now that it's over the brass wants it done overnight."

Hook looked around. "Your boys look a little unhappy this morning."

"Maybe they heard the news about Moose Barrick," he said.

"And what would that be?"

"That some bastard shut him down for exercising his American right to strike."

"Moose can strike all he wants long as he doesn't block the line. It's my job to see the law's not broken, Slope. Simple as that."

"Most these lazy bastards should back up to their paychecks, anyway," Slope said. "Up to me, I'd send them all to the county farm and start over with a new crop."

"I guess it's your optimism what brightens the day for everyone, Slope."

"There's damn little reason for grinning around here," he said.

"I'd like to ask you a few questions, if you don't mind."

He pulled his pocket watch out and looked at it. "I've got men waiting, Runyon. Maybe another day."

"I can take your boys into the shop one at a time to talk to them, if you want it that way."

Slope's nose reached for his chin. "I don't know nothing about Moose Barrick, except he shows up to work and keeps these bastards away from the water bucket."

"It's not about Moose," he said.

"Well, make it quick. Some folks work for a living around here."

"You ever heard of a man named Samuel Ash?"

Slope took out his watch again, wound the stem, and then dropped it back into its pocket.

"I heard of him."

"Did he ever work for you?"

"I didn't hire him, if that's what you mean. Topeka sent him down. I figure the company smelled a strike and decided to beef up the workforce with scabs while they could."

Hook took out his knife and worked at another stone that had lodged in the bottom of his shoe.

"How'd he get along with the crew?" he asked.

"Scabs ain't welcomed with open arms around here or those what take their side. You might remember that, Runyon."

"Anyone in particular find him disagreeable?"

"Everyone in general, I'd say. Thing is, I couldn't have that kind of problem brewing in the crew, so I pulled him."

"And did what with him?"

"Put him on the road painting wigwag bases. I didn't hear nothing back for a week, and then I get this call that the company truck had been abandoned at a crossing. I figure the son of a bitch cut and run. Wouldn't surprise me if he picked up what he could before he left."

"He didn't get off with much, Slope, given I found him hanging from the wigwag cantilever out on the potash spur."

"Dead? Too bad."

"I'm thinking one of your boys maybe gave him a ride to the top of the cantilever and forgot to bring him down."

"It's all I can do to put in a shift around here, Runyon. I make it a point not to know what these men do or don't do after hours. I don't much give a damn if they're killing scabs or not, though I got my doubts there's one among them with the grit for hanging a man."

Hook searched for a cigarette. "Did Samuel Ash say anything about being in the army?"

"He didn't say nothing about nothing, and that's more than I wanted to know."

Hook turned to leave. He paused.

"It's hard to understand why a man decides to kill someone, Slope. Maybe he just wants to know what it feels like. Or maybe he reaches his limit. Maybe he's just pushed too far on the wrong day. It's something to think about, though."

Hook cut by the Harvey House on his way back to the depot. He stopped to light a cigarette just as the chef stepped out the back door.

"Hook," he said. "You come to pay that ten dollars. It never showed up in my tip jar."

Hook hiked his foot on the bench and lit his cigarette. "I meant that money to be for taking care of my dog while I solved crimes," he said. "Far as I can tell, Mixer didn't get any attention whatsoever. Poor devil could barely stand on his feet. Another day and he'd have starved to death."

"He ate better than I did, Hook, not to mention what he stole out the back. On top of that, he terrorized an old lady's poodle so bad it went into shock and had to be revived."

"I didn't pay ten dollars for my dog to be set loose on stray animals. Intelligent dogs, being high-strung as they are, shouldn't be coaxed into fighting without cause."

"If Fred Harvey ever hears what happened in his dining room, I'll lose my job and maybe my life."

"Look," Hook said. "I'll pay you the ten, even though you failed to earn it, strictly speaking, but I've had a run of bad luck with my health." Hook rubbed at his shoulder. "I'll just cut back on the medicine and make payments along, if that will be alright?"

"I don't remember you saying nothing about making late payments when you left that dog here in the first place, Hook."

"A few days' wait is the least a man can do for a sick friend," Hook said.

"If I have to wait for my money, I should be getting fifteen dollars instead of ten, interest for the inconvenience, so to speak."

"I could do twelve, though a man's health is not under his control, you know. Anyway, if Fred Harvey gets word of Mixer's indiscretions, I'll take full responsibility for it myself."

"Twelve, then," he said. "But no more delays."

"Your patience and understanding of my situation is noted, Chef, and I don't forget a favor. I'll be doing business with you again."

The chef opened the kitchen door. "You and your business can go to hell, Hook, and that crazy mutt right along with you."

Popeye pointed to the desk drawer. "Another security badge came," he said. "They must have a factory working overtime."

"Maybe you could just point it out minus the commentary, Popeye."

"It's in that drawer," he said.

"Thanks," Hook said, opening the drawer.

He dropped the badge in his pocket and helped himself to the peanuts Popeye kept hidden in the back.

Popeye lifted his brows. "You'd think a yard dog could keep track of his own badge, wouldn't you?"

"Need to use your phone, Popeye, if you're through questioning my ability."

"Just go ahead but try not to lose it somewhere before you're done," he said.

Hook kicked his feet up and dialed Eddie Preston.

"Security," Eddie said.

"Eddie, Hook here."

"Runyon, I've been trying to reach you all morning."

"I've been working that wigwag case. Turns out the company hired Samuel Ash for scabbing on the signal gang. I'm thinking one of Slope Hurley's crew may have taken matters into his own hands."

"I get this call from the Carlsbad police department, see," Eddie said. "He claims some idiot ran over their patrol car with a road-rail."

"That bastard ran the signal, Eddie, and I couldn't get stopped. Brake line's broke. I don't think it will cost the company much."

"You got *something* right," Eddie said. "It won't cost the company nothing. Operating company equipment safely is your responsibility, broke line or no broke line. I expect you to get this straight with Carlsbad. Are we clear?"

Hook popped a peanut into his mouth. "We're clear, Eddie."

"What about that bus thing over to Gallup?"

"It's under control."

"And Junior Monroe?"

"Junior's fine, Eddie. I got him a sugar tit to keep him from crying."

"I don't want nothing to happen to that boy."

"We're like goddang brothers, Eddie."

"Every time you call, it's trouble, Runyon. You're supposed to solve problems, not make them."

"Believe me, Eddie. If I had my way, you'd never hear from me again."

Hook hung up the phone and tossed another peanut into his mouth.

Popeye pushed Hook's feet down from the desk, took the peanuts, and put them back in the drawer. Just as he started to say something, the phone rang.

Popeye picked it up. "Clovis depot. Yeah, he's the yard dog here," he said, looking over at Hook. "You want to talk to him? Okay, sure. I'll tell him."

Hook stood. "Tell me what, Popeye?"

"You might want to get on over to Gallup, Hook. They got Junior Monroe locked up in the city jail for stealing the B&B company bus."

11

Damn IT," HOOK said. "Junior Monroe has been on the job ten minutes, and he's already in jail?"

"A finely held tradition of yard dogs, as I remember it," Popeye said.

Hook walked to the window and looked out. From there, the tracks shot off into the yards like the rays of a desert sunset.

"You got a passenger train scheduled that way?" he asked.

Popeye checked the board and shook his head. "There's an old teakettle getting serviced out in the yards. She's pulling a couple steamers to the graveyard. You might catch her if you hurry."

"Right," Hook said, heading for the door. "Keep an eye on Mixer for me, will you, Popeye?"

"Don't worry. I'll watch that son of a bitch every second," he said, waving Hook off.

Hook found the steamer just as she backed off the siding and onto the main line. Deadheading two old engines at her back, she reached down hard to break them loose from a cold start. Black steam thundered out her stack, her drivers slipping and spinning under the enormous weight of her load. Her bell clanged again and again, filling up the morning.

Hook waved her down from across the yards, and steam shot out her sides as she idled back to wait for him. Holding his hand over his eyes against the sun, Hook waited at the bottom of the ladder.

Frenchy stuck his head out the cab window. "I'll be shot," he said, looking over at the fireman. "It's that one-armed yard dog, Hook Runyon. Hide the hooch and lock up your daughters."

"Frenchy, is that you?" Hook asked.

"No," he said. "It's Franklin D. up from the grave. Who the hell you think it is?"

Hook had known Frenchy for a good many years. Though short on diplomacy, no man on the line knew the makings of a steamer better than Frenchy.

"How about a hitch to Gallup?" Hook said.

"Well, now, I don't recall you ever *asking* to ride before. Mostly you just hop like any other bo."

"You think this ole calliope will get that far?" Hook asked.

"Climb aboard, and don't worry about her getting there. She'll be making steam long after you're smoldering in your grave."

Hook worked his way up by slipping his prosthesis under each rung while pulling up with his good hand. For a one-armed man, climbing a ladder and tying shoes could be tough as brain surgery.

When Hook stepped in, he nodded at the fireman and then searched out a place to sit. Frenchy lit his cigar and checked the gauges. Turning to the fireman, he said, "Dust her out. She choked down while waiting on this cinder dick to make up his mind."

The fireman opened the boiler door and pitched in some sand to blow out the clinkers. Fire from the boiler lit his face and filled the cab with heat.

Frenchy bumped her ahead and then leaned into the throttle. The old engine groaned and stepped up to a walk. With each stroke, she picked up speed, and they were soon clipping down the track.

Relighting his cigar, Frenchy turned to study Hook. "You still collecting those goddang books?" he asked.

"It's a gentleman's pastime," Hook said. "And as such is outside your realm of appreciation."

"You got that right," he said. "Now, I'd understand something useful, like collecting baseball cards or girls' underwear."

"I rest my case," Hook said.

"Say, I heard someone run down the Carlsbad police with a road-rail. Some kind of maniac. Course, you being a gentleman and all, I guess you wouldn't know nothing about that."

"I avoid hearsay and gossip whenever possible," Hook said.

"Heard he had but one arm and had a snootful when he done it," Frenchy said, grinning.

Hook rolled his eyes. "Well, you're half right."

"Listen, Frenchy, you coming back through anytime soon?"

"Tomorrow late. You need a free ride home, do you?"

"Might."

"I'll keep an eye out for you, long as I don't have to listen to no book collecting."

"I thought you were going to retire, Frenchy."

"Well, someone's got to lead these teakettles to the cemetery, you know. There are lines of these old bullgines three miles long waiting for the scrap furnace. I figure when I put the last one to rest, then maybe I'll take mine. I don't think I could be a railroader no more, anyway."

"You featherbedders have it easy, Frenchy. Me, I've got wildcatters tying up the high rail, scabs hanging from wigwags, and a college-educated yard dog cooling his heels in the Gallup jail."

"So, you're bringing up a new yard dog, are you? Guess jail is as good a place as any to start him out."

"Experience on line isn't important anymore, Frenchy. These kids think they can talk their way out of trouble."

Frenchy lit his cigar, puffing it to life. "Well, all of America is sinking to hell if you ask me. We're feeding half of Europe and running up the cost of living in our own country. Truman's locked in price controls and threatening to draft the strikers into the goddang army. It takes five years to get a Pullman on line, and wages been frozen since forty-two."

"But you got the union, Frenchy. All I have is Eddie Preston."

"Any fool knows the union is in management's pocket, and there's a hole in it the size of a half-dollar. We employees work our asses off, pay our dues, and for what? Eight hours and ice water, that's what."

The fireman shoved his hat back. "You bastards don't quit, I'm going to jump," he said.

"Save us from having to push," Frenchy said, winking at Hook.

Hook waited in the office of the Gallup jail for Junior Monroe to come out. When he stepped through the door, Hook hardly recognized him. He looked like he'd been hung out to dry on a windy day. The brim of his hat had been torn loose, and a grease smear ran the length of his cheek. Dark rings encircled his eyes, and his ears glowed red as a signal lamp.

The deputy behind him pushed his hat back and said, "Is this here your boy, Runyon?"

"Appears so, though I can't be certain," he said.

"He don't resemble no real yard dog to me," the deputy said.

"No, he doesn't, I admit," Hook said.

"Maybe you better take him home to his mother before he gets himself in real trouble."

"Good idea," Hook said. "You called that B&B foreman yet?"

"Couldn't reach him. He's staying in a crew car out on the line somewhere."

"Well, no need to bother him. I'll see that bus gets back soon as I get the boy here on his way."

Junior followed behind as Hook walked down the street. At the Around the Bend Café on the edge of town, Hook turned.

"You hungry?"

Junior ran his finger under his nose and sniffed. "Famished. I lost my wallet, and I haven't eaten anything but jail food since."

"They have pancakes in here big as boiler plates. Don't be ordering meat, though. What with the expenses of chasing you down, I'm nearly broke myself."

The waitress came to the table with menus. She looked at Junior, whose bow tie sat at three o'clock under his chin, and whose hair hung over one eye like Clark Gable.

She turned to Hook. "Fathers ought not let their sons out drinking half the night in my way of thinking. It ain't right."

Hook started to protest but changed his mind. "You know how boys are," he said.

"Oh, do I," she said. "Okay, what will you have to drink?"

"Coffee for me," Hook said. "Hot tea for the boy here."

"Hot tea?"

"With cream."

She slipped her pencil behind her ear. "Maybe he'd like a crumpet with that, too?"

"Just tea," Hook said.

After she'd gone, Hook said, "I'd be interested in how you wound up in jail, Junior."

Junior coughed and rubbed at his eyes. "I jumped on that train like you said. It nearly tore my arm off. No offense, sir. Those cars were so slick, I couldn't go up or down, so I just clung to the ladder in hopes that I could make it to the next stop."

"Getting on a blacksnake is only half the job, Junior. You have to figure how to stay on once aboard and then get off without killing yourself."

"The train just kept gaining momentum," he said. "The faster it went, the worse the wind became until it took the breath right out of me. The dirt nearly blasted the skin from my face. When I thought I couldn't hang on another second, the train slowed and came to a stop."

"Did you jump?"

"I considered it but then I didn't."

"Why the hell not?"

"Because we were sitting on top of a trestle so high I couldn't see the bottom. And then a swarm of mosquitoes arrived, humming and whirling around my head in a black cloud. I thought they would surely drive me mad. For a moment, I reconsidered jumping, trestle or no trestle."

The waitress arrived with their drinks. "Two coffees," she said. "Boss says we don't do tea and crumpets for no one, 'cept the queen, and this ain't her week to be here."

"We'll manage," Hook said.

They both watched her top off cups as she worked her way back to the kitchen.

"Go on," Hook said.

Junior pushed his coffee to the side. "Somehow I made it to Gallup. But by then my fingers had turned blue from hanging on, and my eyes had clogged with dirt. Frankly, my resolve had begun to weaken. I decided then to jump the moment the train slowed for Gallup."

"Good thinking, Junior."

"But it never did," he said, staring into his plate. "It only accelerated."

"Lay asides can be unpredictable," Hook said. "One time I rode a coal car clean to Winnipeg, Canada, before she stopped."

Junior nodded. "And then we went by these stock cars filled with cattle." He ran his fingers through his hair. "The thing is, they urinated just as we passed."

"Urinated, you say?"

He nodded. "Collectively, as if premeditated."

"Well, you can never be certain what cows are thinking," Hook said.

The pancakes arrived, and both fell silent as they slathered on butter.

Hook held up his knife. "You mind if we get to the jail part now, Junior?"

Junior shoved large portions of pancake into his mouth as he gathered up his story.

"So I'm thinking perhaps I made a serious mistake not jumping when I had the opportunity. But then again, perhaps the train would slow enough when we came to the bus. I calculated that the road couldn't be that far off."

Hook poured syrup over his cakes. "The jail, Junior? I got pressing matters."

Junior laid down his fork and stared off into space. "We shot past that bus so fast I could barely see it. We must have been going seventy miles an hour.

"In the end, I didn't get off until the train stopped in Fort Defiance. I walked all the way back to the bus and discovered the keys under the seat. Though the bus was in a state of disrepair, I thought it only logical that I attempt to drive it back."

"The jail, Junior."

"Apparently the bus belongs to the bridge and building foreman, who had parked it there while attending a job in Amarillo. He'd requested the police to keep an eye on it.

"When I arrived in town, I was promptly arrested for stealing railroad equipment. I explained to the deputy that I was in fact a real railroad detective, that I had been directed to remove the bus by railroad officials."

"He didn't believe you?" Hook asked.

"He said he was a real cop, too, and would be directing me straight to jail."

Hook leveled his prosthesis at Junior. "It's the job of yard dogs to put *other* people in jail. They're not supposed to be put in jail themselves."

"Yes, sir."

"A yard dog has to set an example, be an ideal citizen, so to speak. He can't go around getting picked up by the authorities. His life has to be whistle-clean and his integrity beyond question."

"I'm sorry, sir. Had I known . . ."

"Being put in jail cast the company in a bad light. You don't want that."

"I can do better. I promise."

Hook pushed his plate aside.

Junior cupped his elbows in his hands. "Are you going to release me, Hook? I'm afraid my father will not understand."

Hook twisted his mouth to the side. "I'm prepared to give this a second chance, Junior, though I do so with considerable doubt."

"I won't disappoint you a second time. I promise."

"Thing is, I found a boy hanging off the potash wigwag. He might have been a murder victim."

Junior's eyes widened. "Murder?"

"Possible. Turns out he'd been scabbing, and hard feelings had developed among the signal crew. The coroner found a Bronze Star around his neck with the name Samuel Ash engraved on it. So far, it's the only lead I have."

"A war hero?"

"I want you to go back to Clovis and see if you can find out anything about this Samuel Ash."

"Where should I begin the investigation?"

"Where the answers are, Junior. In the meantime, I'll see if I can clear the air around here."

"Yes, sir, but . . ."

"But what?"

"Do I have to jump on another train? Perhaps you could arrange a permanent pass?"

"There's a mail car comes through this afternoon. I'll see if they'll take you on." Hook stood. "And check on my dog when you get back. He pines something terrible when I'm away."

"Yes, sir."

"And, Junior, let's keep this between us for the time being. Eddie Preston doesn't always understand the ins and outs of criminal investigation."

12

AFTER GETTING JUNIOR on his way, Hook located the old bus parked behind the police station. The front grill had been replaced with chicken wire, and a board had been bolted over the back window. He found the keys under the seat and cranked her over while pumping the foot feed a half-dozen times to bring up the fuel. Bridge bracings and bolts of every ilk had been stacked on the passenger seats, and the smell of grease permeated the air.

The bus fired up, and a cloud of blue smoke sailed over the police station. Hook worked the gearshift into reverse. The bus jerked back as the clutch caught and slipped like an old washing machine.

He brought her up to forty and checked his watch. There should be plenty of time to get her parked back in the right-of-way before Frenchy came through.

Eddie deserved an ass chewing for ordering a tow on a company vehicle in the first place. But at the moment, given his own standing, Hook figured to let it pass.

Dusk fell as he rattled along the country road toward the crossing where the bus had been parked. Dust boiled in from around the windows, and a trickle of sweat raced down Hook's neck.

He considered having a one on one with that B&B foreman about leaving his equipment on the right-of-way. Such carelessness encouraged others to do the same thing, and security, being overworked and shorthanded, had all it could manage now.

As he approached the crossing, he slowed to check for trains before turning down the right-of-way. A couple hundred yards in, he backed the bus around and shut off the engine. The first stars of the evening clicked on, and a mourning dove cooed somewhere in the distance. Hook checked for Frenchy's light in the rearview mirror.

The death of that boy on the wigwag lay on his mind as heavy as a sad iron, not so much because of the business of dying, death in itself being unremarkable, but because he couldn't shake the manner in which it had been dealt—the injustice of a man hauled up by the neck and left to strangle at the end of a rope. It struck him as reprehensible to discard a war hero in a pauper's grave and without a soul in the world to give a damn.

When he looked up again, Frenchy's glimmer lit the horizon, and the wail of his whistle lifted into the night. Hook turned the ignition key and flipped on the stoplights. The clicker ticked and tocked, and the red glow of the lights pulsated in the mirror. The chug of the steamer deepened as she slowed, and Frenchy lay in with short blasts of his whistle to announce his stop.

Hook tossed the keys under the seat and made his way to the track to wait. Frenchy brought her in as easy as a rocking chair and slid up beside him. The steamer huffed and sighed, and the smell of heat filled the night. Frenchy stuck an elbow out the cab window and leaned over it.

"You boarding or taking hostages?" he asked.

"I haven't thought it out," Hook said, working his way up the ladder.

The fireman ducked his chin at Hook before turning back to his gauges. Hook located a perch. Frenchy bumped her ahead, and they were soon making time.

"Running light, aren't you, Frenchy?" Hook asked.

"Just this here bullgine and a couple of hopper cars I'm deadheading back to Belen. Picking up an old louse box there and hauling her into Clovis."

"Sometimes they don't even bother to run a caboose anymore," Hook said. "Don't know what the world's coming to."

Frenchy dug out a new cigar and rolled it between thumb and index finger next to his ear. He bit off the end and struck a match on his overalls' button.

"Did you get that greenhorn out of jail?" he asked between puffs of smoke.

Hook said, "Didn't know the B&B work bus from his ass and took her for a spin."

"Too dang much education," Frenchy said. "Causes a man not to think his own thoughts."

Hook nodded. "Junior Monroe wears a bow tie, drinks hot tea, and fans his face every time someone stokes up a butt."

Frenchy turned and pushed the bill of his hat up. "The hell? He should have got twenty years hard labor, if you ask me."

Hook smiled and leaned back for a nap. "Bat the stack off her, Frenchy, and wake me when we get to Belen."

Frenchy kicked the bottom of Hook's shoe and pointed at the door.

"Belen," he said. "I'm taking her into the yards for a drink, and I'll be picking up that old louse box after that. Be about an hour."

Hook rubbed the sleep from his face. "I'm headed for the Harvey House to eat. You want anything?"

"I brought a nosebag," he said. "The Harvey's too ritzy for the likes of me."

Hook searched out a table near the back of the restaurant and had just pulled up his chair when the waitress arrived. He ordered the blue plate special and a glass of milk.

The dining area, nearly empty, smelled of baked pies and fresh-brewed coffee.

A woman sat at a table near the front and dabbed her linen napkin against her mouth. For a moment, Hook thought he recognized her but decided that it must be the familiar remnants of old age that he recognized.

He considered the possibility of hot apple pie topped with a slab of cheddar and had nearly caught the attention of the waitress, when the old lady stood, took up her purse, and made for the restroom.

When she passed by Hook's table, she glanced at him. Only then did he notice the white socks and realized that the purse looked exactly like the knitting bag the old lady had that day in the Amarillo depot.

He started to get up but hesitated, not anxious for yet another public confrontation with an old lady. By then she had disappeared into the ladies' room at the back.

Minutes passed, and she didn't come out. They brought his dinner, and he ate it. He ordered apple pie, and she still hadn't come out. After finishing his pie, he drank another cup of coffee. Perhaps she'd recognized him, found a different exit, or perhaps she had simply decided to wait him out.

He checked his watch. Frenchy would be coming soon. He paid his tab and then made his way to the restroom hallway. Pausing at the ladies' door, he listened. After a second look down the hallway, he pushed the door open and went in.

The lights were off, save for a single bulb over the sink, and he could see no one inside. He moved into the nearby stall and bent over for a look-see under them. From there, he spotted the old lady standing in the back stall, her white socks clearly visible.

Hook flushed the toilet, waited a few seconds, and then opened the bathroom door as if to leave. Slipping back into the stall he waited, quieting his breath.

First came the squeak of her stall door and then the shuffle of her feet as she made her way to the exit. When she opened it, Hook stepped out and grabbed her by the arm.

She yelped and struggled to get loose. Hook clamped his hand over her mouth.

"Railroad security," he said. "Keep your voice down or we're off to jail."

He slowly removed his hand.

"Rapist," she said. "Murderer. I'll scream."

He laid his hook against her cheek. "I twisted a man's tongue right out of his head with this thing one time. I suggest you not scream."

"What do you want from me?" she asked.

He pulled her in close, and his fingers disappeared into the soft flesh of her arm. She smelled of stale perfume and menthol.

"You been working diversion for those pickpockets," he said. "I never forget a thief's face."

"I don't know what you're talking about," she said. "I'm just an old lady traveling alone."

"This could mean prison," he said. "Maybe years, and, believe me, that's not the way you want to spend your old age."

"You're going to arrest me?"

"An accomplice is just as guilty as a perpetrator. We'll go out the back way and have a talk with the cops."

"I'm just an old lady. They said all I had to do was pretend to fall. I needed the money. I'm alone and have to make my way. The world doesn't care about old ladies."

"The world doesn't care about anyone, and neither do I."

He started for the door with her in tow. "No, wait," she said, pulling back. "Isn't there something I can do?"

Hook hesitated. "Maybe you know where those pickpockets are working?" he said. "Maybe you could provide a little information?"

"They paid me to kick up a disturbance. I did and then I left. That's all I know, I swear."

"Too little too late," he said. "Let's go downtown."

"No, wait. Maybe I did overhear something. I mean, maybe I did hear them talking."

"Hear what?"

"If I tell you, will you let me go?"

"No," he said. "But then it's hard to watch someone every second."

"I heard them say that the Amarillo to Wellington run had heavy passenger traffic and light security. That's all I heard, I swear."

Hook relaxed his grip. "I dropped my cigarettes in that stall. You stay here. I'll be right back."

When Hook stepped out of the ladies' room, a woman coming down the hall stopped and put her hand over her mouth. "Oh, my," she said.

Hook shouldered past her. "That toilet's fixed now," he said. "But be damn careful what you put in it."

13

HOOK SWUNG DOWN from the steam engine at the Clovis depot. With nothing but the louse box in tow, they'd made good time out of Belen.

"Thanks for the lift, Frenchy," he said.

Frenchy lit his cigar and waved as he pulled off down the high rail.

Back at his caboose, Hook kicked off his shoes and fixed himself a Beam and water. He favored Runt Wallace shine, but he only had the one bottle of twenty-year-old that Runt had presented him a few years back. Someday, given a celebration, he'd open it up and see what the years had wrought.

He pulled back the covers of the bunk and collapsed into bed. For now, sleep would do. Tomorrow, he'd pick up his check and see if he couldn't get the road-rail repaired.

The westbound blew her whistle and sat Hook straight up in his bed. Swinging his legs over the side of the bunk, he rubbed at the stubble on his face.

He located his prosthesis and looked out the window. He'd slept half the day away.

"Damn," he said, slipping on his pants.

After making certain the chef wasn't smoking at the back door of the Harvey House, he cut through the alley to the road-rail. Cranking her up, he nursed her out to the yards and pulled around to the back of the machine shop, where he found the machinist helper working on the steam jenny.

The helper propped his foot up on the jenny and tied his work boot. "I don't know nothing about fixing brake lines, Hook; besides, I got three bushings to turn, and some son of a bitch ran a switch engine through a buffer stop."

Hook opened the door to the road-rail. "I heard you could fix anything, but then I understand you're a busy man. Far be it from me to bring up that little incident, anyway."

The machinist helper dropped his foot down. "What little incident would that be, Hook?"

"Those welding rods I found in the back of your truck that day. Hell, I knew you wouldn't carry off railroad property on purpose, even though that's the way it appeared at the time."

The machinist helper walked around the jenny and paused. "I got some fittings might work, if you ain't in a hurry?"

"No hurry," Hook said. "Drop her off at my caboose when you get finished, will you?"

Hook stopped at the paymaster's and then walked the line back to the depot, where he found Popeye sitting behind his desk, his glasses pushed to the end of his nose.

"Well," Popeye said. "If it isn't the crime fighter hisself."

"Hello, Popeye."

"You get that road-rail off the sidewalk yet? If an official comes through here, there will be hell to pay."

"Yes, I did," Hook said. "Though, I'd thought a good friend might have taken care of that himself, seeing as how I put my life on the line for this company every day."

"I loan you money and sit your dog, Hook. I figure that's about as far as I can stretch a friendship. And if I'm not mistaken, it *is* payday."

"And that's why I'm here, to pay you those two dollars I owe you and with my thanks, I might add."

Popeye pushed his chair back and looked at Hook over the tops of his glasses. "It isn't two dollars. It's five, and it ought to be seven, given the time I've had to wait for my money."

"Five was it? Are you sure?"

"Sure as sure."

"Well, damn," Hook said. "Here I've been thinking two. Take these two, and I'll get the other three to you next payday."

Popeye stuck the money in his pocket and shook his head. "Don't forget it, either, Hook, 'cause I damn sure won't."

Hook opened the desk drawer and took a handful of peanuts. "That Junior Monroe get back?"

"Yes, he did, smelling like he'd been riding in a cow cage. Why don't you get that boy a pass?"

"I been meaning to," Hook said. "Where is he now?"

"Hotel Clovis."

Hook rolled his eyes and popped some peanuts into his mouth.

"Hotel Clovis, is it? Drinking tea and eating crumpets, I suppose?"

"Not everyone lives in a caboose, Hook. Some folks sleep in real beds, take their baths on a regular basis, and pay their bills on time."

"Where's my dog, Popeye, or is he staying at Hotel Clovis, too?"

"Headed east last I saw, chasing an old highwheeler steam engine. Guess he figured it to be a giant rabbit with wheels."

"He'd as soon fight a giant as a midget."

Popeye closed the drawer to the peanuts. "They have a derailment over to Lubbock. Half-dozen reefer cars jumped track just north of the signal. Said the rail buckled up like a ribbon, so the line's tied up for who knows how long."

"We've had an unusual number of accidents the last few weeks," Hook said.

"Acts of God, you might say," Popeye said.

"You might, though I have my doubts God had anything to do with it," Hook said.

"And another thing: that digger called from Carlsbad. Said he couldn't delay burying that wigwag body no longer. Said he only had the one cooler, and folks were waiting."

Hook dusted the peanut salt off the front of his shirt. "You have any more bad news, Popeye? If not, I'm going home and get some rest before my head explodes."

When Hook awoke from his nap, he dug his books from under the bunk and laid them in a row across the table. He drew his finger over the covers. There were few enough things in life that could be finished, zipped up from beginning to end with nothing left undone. Perhaps that's why he liked collecting books so much, the passion, the pursuit, but most of all the completion.

He slid out the American first *Baskerville* from the row, a fine copy to be sure. Without it, the collection remained incomplete. He slid it back. That's where it belonged, not hidden away on some dark shelf in a library; besides, libraries cared only about the latest romance novel, or political rant, or high suspense. They didn't give a damn about some obscure first edition.

When a knock came at the door, Hook said, "Who is it?"

"Junior Monroe? Are you home?"

"No, I'm still in Gallup," he said.

"May I come in?"

"Door's open."

Junior stepped in with his hat in his hand. He shined like a newborn, and he smelled of soap.

"Where's my dog?" Hook asked.

"At first I couldn't catch him, and then I was afraid I would," Junior said.

"Well, he's not my dog, strictly speaking, so I can't be held responsible for any transgressions, real or imagined.

"I'm about to work up a drink here, Junior. Care for one?"

"No, thank you," he said. "I don't drink. My father doesn't approve."

Hook fixed two Beam and waters and slid one over to Junior. "Did you find out anything on that Samuel Ash deal?"

Junior smelled his drink. "I called the National Archives. They weren't too forthcoming, but I got a little information."

"You're supposed to drink that, not smell it."

Junior sipped his drink and wrinkled up his nose. "Samuel Ash enlisted in Oklahoma City," he said. "He received the Bronze Star with valor and was discharged from the army a few months ago."

"Samuel Ash is from Oklahoma City?"

Junior took another sip of his drink and shuddered. "That's where he enlisted, but he put his hometown as Carmen, Oklahoma."

"Parents?"

"Deceased."

"Carmen?" Hook said. "I've been through there, a jerkwater and mail stop of a few hundred people or so."

"Anything else?"

"He earned a Purple Heart somewhere along the line, in addition to the Bronze Star, and was promoted to sergeant first class just prior to mustering out. That's about it, I guess."

"Well, it's more than we had. Wonder what brought him to New Mexico in the first place?"

Junior finished his drink and pushed the glass to the side.

"It's my understanding that vets have trouble settling in after war, after living on the edge for so long, and then jobs are hard to come by. They do a lot of wandering about, I hear."

Hook poured Junior another drink and topped off his own.

"How is it you didn't join up, Junior, or maybe you had too much education to die for your country?"

Junior held up his foot. "Flat feet. What about you, Hook?"

"Flat head," Hook said. "Finish that drink before the Beam goes bad."

Junior polished off his drink and slid the empty over to Hook, who poured him a thumbful. Hook lit a cigarette.

Junior turned his glass in the puddle of condensation on the table and said, "Sunbeam reminds me for the world of caviar."

"I was just thinking that myself," Hook said.

"At first it tastes a little off, but after a while, you just want more and more."

Hook drained his glass and looked through the bottom of it. "I can't remember the last time I had caviar."

Junior propped his elbows onto the table. "It's like these books," he said. "If everybody had them, you probably wouldn't want them."

"I wouldn't even have them on this table," Hook said.

"Because it's the wanting that counts, isn't it? I mean, there are some things a man just has to have because no one else has them."

Hook refilled their glasses. "I've seen men fight to the death over a bottle of Sunbeam. I guess there's just not enough Sunbeam and caviar in this world to go around."

Junior rubbed at his face. "Hook, I think I may have had a stroke."

"A stroke, you say?"

"My face just slid down, and I can't get it up again."

"Well, I wouldn't worry about it, Junior. Trouble getting it up comes along to most men sooner or later."

Junior studied the tabletop. "Maybe I'll have another Sunbeam," he said. "And maybe I'll have a cigarette, too, if you don't mind."

Hook lit him up, and Junior blew smoke out his nose. He coughed and rubbed at his eyes.

"A smoke does a man good," he said.

Hook paused. "Junior," he said. "Have you ever stolen anything?"

Junior straightened his bow tie. "I don't understand the question, Hook."

"It's a philosophical inquiry, Junior. Do you think there is ever a justifiable reason to steal?"

"Stealing is against the law and morally unacceptable," he said. "Philosophically speaking."

"Say a man stole something for posterity, to keep it from being destroyed or neglected, and by doing so, he saves something important that would otherwise be lost to the human race."

"The law's the law, Hook, no matter the cost to mankind."

"Are you telling me you never stole anything, Junior?"

Junior puffed on his cigarette, and smoke boiled about his head.

"You think the strikers will shut down the line, Hook?"

"What is it you stole, Junior?"

Junior hung his head. "An angel."

"A what?"

"A Christmas angel. I stole it from the dime store when I was a kid."

Hook took another drink. "An angel? That's just terrible, Junior."

"My mother hung it on the Christmas tree every Christmas for twenty years. I had to look at that angel hanging on the tree my whole life."

Junior took a swig of his drink. "Did you ever?"

"Ever what?" Hook said.

"Steal anything?"

Hook held the bottle up to the window to check the level of its contents and then poured them each another round.

"Real lawmen don't steal, Junior, and if they did, they sure wouldn't steal no damn Christmas angel."

When the knock came on the caboose door, Hook opened it to find the machinist helper wiping his hands on a grease rag. The orange rays of sunset shot into the clouds behind him.

"It's fixed, Hook, though it took all damned day."

"Thanks," Hook said.

"And about that other thing?"

"What other thing?" Hook said.

The machinist helper nodded and worked his way down the steps. He stopped and looked up at Hook.

"You might want to take it to a real mechanic first chance. Get a new line put on. Them fittings could give way, you know."

Back inside, Hook said, "Drink up, Junior, and I'll give you a ride back to Hotel Clovis."

Junior walked around the road-rail and scratched at his head.

"Exactly what is this vehicle, Hook?"

"It's a road-rail. She runs on road or rail, either one. She might even run on water, though I've never tried it. Climb in."

Hook fired her up, and they headed down the street.

"It really runs on the track?" Junior asked.

"Sure it does. There's a crossing just ahead. I'll give you a demonstration."

"Aren't we supposed to get clearance, Hook?"

"Just a run to the yards and back," he said. "No clearance necessary."

Hook pulled onto the crossing and lowered the pilot wheels. Junior leaned out for a better look as they clipped off down the track. His hair blew in the breeze, and he grinned. Hook released the steering wheel.

"You better not let go, Hook. We're moving pretty fast."

"It tracks on its own," Hook said. "Why, a man could take a nap or read a book if he wanted."

"Maybe you could acquire one for me as well," he said.

"Road-rails are for officials and trusted employees, Junior. Privileges like that have to be earned."

"Say, is that a light behind us?"

"That's the sunset, Junior. Don't they have sunsets at Hotel Clovis?"

Junior turned for another look. "It looks more like a train to me, Hook."

"A train?"

"Maybe we should get off the track now."

"Why the hell didn't you say something, Junior?"

"But you said it was the sunset."

"Any fool can see it's not the sunset, and a road-rail can't just hop on and off the track like a rabbit. It's got to have a crossing or a spur switch."

The train whistle blew behind them, and the roar of the engines pooled hot in Hook's belly.

"Look, there," Hook said, pumping the brakes, which had improved but little in their stopping ability. "A spur. Get out and throw that switch, Junior, and you might want to step on it."

Junior bailed out and leaned into the switch. The train's glimmer brightened behind them, and its engines rumbled down the line. Hook shoved the road-rail into gear and drove onto the spur.

"Switch it back!" he yelled over his shoulder. "Now!"

Junior shoved the switch back just as the train thundered by, her brakes screeching as she slowed for the upcoming yards.

Hook dabbed the sweat from his forehead as Junior made his way back to the road-rail. Junior leaned into the window.

"Maybe we should get off the track now, Hook."

"We're sitting on a spur, Junior, and it doesn't go anywhere except to the roundhouse, and we can't switch back onto the high rail with that train laying by, can we?"

Junior rubbed at his face. "How long will it lay by there, Hook?"

"How the hell should I know?"

"So, what are our plans?" Junior asked.

Hook drummed the steering wheel. "If we could get on that other spur over there, I'm pretty sure it dumps out at the crossing."

"But how is that possible, Hook? I don't see a switch to that one."

Hook studied the line of cars and then fired up the road-rail.

"Get in, Junior. I've got that plan you mentioned."

———

Hook pulled into the yards and eased up to the turntable. The yard lights lit the tracks into streaks of silver, and the smell of steam and smoke settled in about them like fog. The chug and wheeze of a half-dozen engines grumbled from out of the yards.

"Go over to the control house, Junior, and wheel us around to that other spur. There's nothing to it, a motor and a brake. If she slips, throw a little sand under the friction wheel."

"But Hook . . ."

"Jesus, just do it, Junior," Hook said.

When Junior reached the control house, Hook gave him the high sign. The turntable growled and moved toward the crossing spur. Once aligned with the track, Hook signaled again, and Junior brought her to a stop, after which he dashed to the road-rail and jumped in.

Just as Hook pulled onto the spur, the yardmaster charged out of the yard office, his head down and his arms swinging. Stepping in front of the road-rail, he stuck his arm in the air.

"Stay in here, Junior," Hook said, opening the door. "Let me do the talking."

"What the hell is going on?" the yardmaster yelled, spittle flying from his mouth.

Hook turned and then looked back at the yardmaster. "You're the yardmaster around here, aren't you?"

"You goddamn right. What the hell you think you're doing?"

Hook pulled his badge. "Security," he said. "We got a call that someone had parked this road-rail on the turntable. You know anything about that?"

"Hell no," he said, tugging at his collar. "First thing I know I see you driving this thing off it."

"It's your job to know what goes on in these yards, isn't it? You're the yardmaster, aren't you?"

"Well, yes, but . . ."

"The company can't have people driving road-rails onto the merry-go-round for the hell of it, you know."

"Yes, sir. I know."

"Well, it could have been strikers, I suppose. I'll see if I can't get this business headed off. This sort of thing can't happen again, or I'll have to report it."

"No, sir. It won't happen again, not if I have to post a man out here all night."

"Now, this spur will get me to the crossing, won't it?"

"Yes, sir, straight to the crossing."

"Good," he said. "I'll talk to my associate back there. I believe in giving a man a second chance."

"Don't worry," he said. "These bastards won't do it again, you can bet on that."

Hook pulled the road-rail in front of Hotel Clovis and waited for Junior to climb out.

"Thanks for the ride, Hook. It's one I'm not likely to forget."

"Don't mention it. And, Junior, tomorrow, I need you to go over to Lubbock and check on a hoptoad."

"Hoptoad?"

"Derailment. See if the line's been tampered with."

"Alright, Hook," he said, steadying himself against the road-rail.

"And you need to keep check on your drinking habits, Junior. The railroad is fussy about that."

"Yes, sir."

"And when you get back to Clovis, stop in and pay the Harvey House chef twelve dollars. I'll reimburse you soon as I get back."

"Where you going?"

"Carlsbad. I've a date with the undertaker."

"Hook, about my face?"

Hook cranked up the road-rail. "Don't worry about it, Junior. Come morning, you won't even know you have a face."

14

AFTER STOPPING AT the Artesia depot to pay off the operator, Hook rumbled on to Carlsbad. When he pulled up in front of the undertaker's house, he shut down the road-rail. She continued to bump and grind from the motor heat until Hook put her in gear and popped the clutch.

He found the undertaker in the backyard digging up the ground with a spade.

"Yeah, I'm the undertaker," he said, leaning the shovel against the house. "Name's Bruce Jenson."

The undertaker's front teeth crossed over one another like a row of fallen dominoes, and he had the hands of a violin player: delicate, long fingers.

"Hook Runyon," Hook said. "I'm the railroad bull out of Clovis. You burying folks in the backyard now?"

"I admit to considering it on occasion when the north wind's blowing," he said. "But I'm digging worms. I like to fish. No," he said, wiping the sweat from his brow. "That's not right. I *love* to fish. I'd rather fish than sleep in a bed full of women. You like to fish?"

"Not that much," Hook said. "I'm here about that wigwag fellow."

"Well, he's in the cooler, but the coroner's released him for burial in the pauper's cemetery. The county keeps a little money back for indigents. It's hardly worth my doing, you know, but running that cooler day and night isn't cheap neither."

Hook pointed to a worm that had crawled under a clod. "The thing is, this boy had a Bronze Star hanging around his neck with his name on it. Strikes me that he should be buried with honors and among his own people."

The undertaker squatted down, retrieved the worm, and dropped it into his coffee can.

"Those goddang catfish go for them big ones," he said. "I caught a twenty pounder on one just the other day."

"I've done a little checking on this boy. According to the military records, he's from Carmen, Oklahoma."

"I got a cemetery full of folks, and all of them are from somewhere," he said.

"Why couldn't he be shipped back to his home and buried there?"

"Everything's possible with enough money. Maybe you have enough?"

"The quest for justice is a noble one, but it doesn't pay worth a damn," Hook said.

"That's sort of what I figured. Look, Mr. Runyon, shipping bodies isn't quite as simple as it sounds. First, you have to get a burial transit permit, and then two first-class tickets, one for the escort and one for the corpse.

"The body has to be shipped within a specified number of days. Those days have already lapsed, so the body will have to be cavity-disinfected and embalmed, orifices plugged, wrapped in two layers of cotton and hermetically sealed. The coffin itself has to be shipped in a structurally sound outer container in the event of wrecks and other potential mishaps. Do you hear the cash register ringing yet?"

Hook squashed out his cigarette. "You couldn't trim that back a little, given this boy went into combat for his country?"

"I'd be happy to, except once the body arrives at its destination, a report is sent back to the licensing agency about its condition. While I love fishing, I love eating even more. Do you get the picture?"

Hook bent down and picked up another worm with his hook. "How much?"

"A couple hundred, give or take."

"And if I come up with the money and agree to be the escort?"

"Then I'll do what is necessary, and he's all yours."

Hook dropped the worm into the can. "Thanks," he said. "I've some calls I need to make."

Hook sat in the Carlsbad operator's chair and dialed Eddie Preston.

"Eddie," he said. "Hook here."

"Where are you, Runyon?"

"I'm in Carlsbad trying to clean up this mess with the road-rail accident."

"Why are you calling me? I told you that road-rail was your responsibility."

"The thing is, Eddie, the city is threatening to sue if the company doesn't pay damages on their patrol car."

"Why does everyone think they can sue the goddamn railroad, Runyon?"

"They want two hundred, Eddie. It's a hell of a lot cheaper than a lawsuit."

"This doesn't smell right."

"I didn't want to bring this up, Eddie, but that bus you ordered towed turned out to be the B&B work bus. I had to bail your boy out of jail for stealing company property."

"Company bus?"

"That's right, the B&B bus. Not to worry, Eddie. I worked it out. No one knows you ordered it towed. I mean, hell, everyone makes stupid mistakes sometimes."

Hook could hear Eddie thinking. "What did you say the bill was on that patrol car?" he asked.

"A couple hundred. If you could wire it here to the Carlsbad operator, I'll see it's paid."

"Alright, Runyon, but I don't like it. I'm telling you, I don't like it."

"Thanks, Eddie. I can't put into words my feelings about you."

Hook hung up and watched Clyde finish counting out his ticket drawer.

Clyde turned. "About that money I loaned you, Hook?" he said.

"You mean that boot money?"

"That's right."

"The railroad will work you into the ground and bunk you in a cattle car, but it always meets its debts, Clyde."

"Not that I was worried about it or anything," he said.

"That's good, Clyde. Now I'll be back later and see if we can't work something out, but a man's duty always comes before money. You need to remember that."

Hook spent the afternoon obtaining a burial transit permit from the Department of Health, after which he stopped by the undertaker's and advised him that the money was on the way. The undertaker agreed to have things in order for transit by morning.

That night Hook parked the road-rail in the alley behind the depot and slept in the seat. He dreamed that a corpse was riding next to him on the *Super Chief.* They ate steak dinners together in the dining car and drank Beam and branch water. But when Hook failed to pay for the meals, the conductor twisted his arm up behind his back and threw him and the corpse off in the middle of the Chihuahuan Desert.

When Hook awoke, his prosthesis had caught in the door latch, and he had to remove his harness in order to extricate himself.

The next morning, Hook found Clyde pouring coffee from his thermos.

"Coffee?" Clyde asked. "You look like you need it."

"Thanks," Hook said. "That money come in?"

"Two hundred," Clyde said, pulling an envelope from the drawer. "I could sure use my share now, Hook."

Hook sipped on the coffee, which had cooled in the thermos.

"I'd be happy to pay you this minute, Clyde, were it my money to spend. But this money is to be used for the proper burial of a war hero. You wouldn't want to stand in the way of that, would you?"

"No, sir, but I understood I'd be paid with company money."

"Well, in most cases that's true, Clyde, but this money is intended for something altogether different."

"I'm short no matter how it's intended, Hook. Maybe I should just turn the whole thing over to Division to figure out."

"No, no. I'll just take the money out of my own pocket. Far be it from me to spend money meant for a war hero and put it on a new pair of boots. You couldn't get by on a little less for now, I suppose?"

"Well, I might get by with five."

"You're a man of honor, and it warms my heart to do business with you, Clyde. Here's five and the other five's coming soon enough. You can bet on that."

After pulling into the drive of the undertaker's place, he waited for the road-rail to stutter to a stop. The undertaker answered the door with his fishing hat on, which had been decorated with all manner of fishing lures.

Hook presented the transit permit. "I'm here to pick up Samuel Ash," he said.

"Finished up this morning," the undertaker said. "You understand that the container is not to be breached?"

"My intent is to ship him off to relatives to bury, soon as I get some located," Hook said.

"I'll make arrangements with the funeral home there to receive the body. There's a loading dock around back. Pull around, and we'll load him up."

The shipping container, a reinforced metal box with grips, caused Hook to groan when they lifted it into the road-rail. The lid had been sealed, and a plastic envelope had been attached to one of the handles.

"What the hell kind of vehicle is this, anyway?" the undertaker asked.

"It's a long story," Hook said, dropping down from the road-rail. "I hope the tires don't blow."

"That shipping container is lead-lined and guaranteed leak-free," he said. "None better for the money."

Hook dabbed the sweat from his brow with the back of his hand. "So how much do I owe you?"

"One eighty, counting the prep and the equipment," he said. "No charge for the lifting."

Hook counted out the bills. "That's a pretty hefty price if I do say so."

"Traveling isn't cheap," he said. "Say, you interested in doing a little fishing this afternoon?"

"Thanks the same, but I've a train to meet," Hook said.

Hook pulled off, the casket looming dark and quiet in the back. He took the side streets to the depot and parked under the tree down the way. He found Clyde with his feet kicked up on the desk. He laid down his newspaper and waited for Hook to pull up a chair.

"Clyde," Hook said. "I need you to work up a first-class ticket to Carmen, Oklahoma."

"Hell, Hook, you don't need a ticket. You have a pass."

"It isn't for me," he said.

"Who's it for?"

"That feller waiting out there in my road-rail."

"Why don't he buy his own ticket, Hook?"

"Because he's dead, Clyde. It's a corpse ticket to Carmen, Oklahoma, if you don't mind."

"Alright, Hook. You want the observation car?"

Hook lit a cigarette and squinted up an eye. "I don't think that will be necessary, Clyde."

"One way or round-trip?"

"Let's make it a one way."

"That's nineteen dollars and fifty cents," he said.

"Charge it to the company."

Clyde scratched at his head. "I can't do that on my own, Hook. I'll have to have clearance from Division."

"Damn," Hook said. "Sometimes I think I'll just go back on the bum. Life's a hell of a lot less complicated."

"You want the ticket, I got to have the money."

"I only have fifteen," he said.

"I don't set the prices, Hook."

Hook walked to the window and looked up the tracks. "How much would a ticket be from *Clovis* to Carmen?"

Clyde dug through his notebook once again. "Fifteen even," he said. "That's one way. But you have to get him to Clovis first. How you going to do that?"

Hook held up the road-rail key. "The same way I got him here," he said.

15

THE OLD ROAD-RAIL kicked and bucked down the street, and the coffin rattled in the back as Hook made his way through Carlsbad. If he could make it back to Clovis intact, his fifteen bucks would buy a first-class corpse ticket. That, along with his pass, should get them both to Carmen, Oklahoma, without a hitch.

Once there, he'd locate the family and turn the rest over to them. He didn't fancy do-gooders much and didn't consider himself to be one. As far as he was concerned, this task fell in the line of duty, and while at it he just might turn up something that could explain Samuel Ash's death.

After turning north on Main, Hook headed out of town. He checked on the casket through the rearview mirror. He could see the last of town disappearing on the horizon. While he had nothing against Carlsbad, his luck hadn't been the best there, and leaving it behind suited him just fine.

As he rounded the corner, the road dropped away to the intersection below. With the added weight of the casket, the road-rail gathered up speed. Hook stepped on the brake, but the pedal sank to the floor. His stomach knotted and his mouth went hot. He pumped the brakes again and again but the road-rail continued to charge downhill. The front end shook and rattled as the intersection rose up in front of him.

Hook aimed for the center of the road, praying the while that no one was coming. He clenched his jaw and gripped the steering wheel as he shot through the intersection at breakneck speeds.

When at last he'd rolled to a stop, he leaned back and waited for his heart to stop pounding. Only then did he notice the patrol car that had pulled in behind him, its red light spinning.

Officer Joe climbed out. He walked around the road-rail and then back again. He came to Hook's window.

"Small world, ain't it?" he said.

"They just don't make brakes like they used to," Hook said.

Officer Joe pushed his hat back. "Maybe you'd like me to pull the patrol car around front here, so you can tear off the other fender? That way we could save everyone a lot of time."

"No, no," Hook said. "That won't be required."

Officer Joe looked back at the casket.

"What's in the box? You running guns, hooch?"

"It's a body," Hook said.

A smile pulled up the corner of Officer Joe's mouth. "Sure it is," he said. "And I'm Robin Hood, and this is merry ole England."

"I'm shipping it home," Hook said.

"Maybe it's something duty-free out of Juárez?"

"It's just a body, like I said."

"If my memory is correct, you owe money to the city of Carlsbad for the destruction of public property, namely the fender on my patrol car."

"The company will be picking that up," Hook said. "Now, I'll just be on my way, if it's alright with you."

"Step out of the vehicle, Runyon. I think we best have a look in that box."

Hook stepped out. "I wouldn't if I were you."

"I'll bet you wouldn't." He paused. "Why not?"

"That box is hermetically sealed."

"You being a smart-ass, Runyon?"

"Sealed, you know, like a canning jar. Keeps the disease from spreading."

"What disease?"

"Cholera."

"Cholera? What's that?"

"You shit rice water until your skin turns to paper and your blood dries to powder. If you're lucky, you die fast."

"That so?"

"Look, suppose I make an advance payment on that little fender accident, you know, to show my good intentions?"

Officer Joe looked at the casket and then at Hook. "How much good intentions did you have in mind?"

Hook reached for his billfold and counted out the bills. "Fifteen. Cash."

"Well, now," he said. "Far be it from me to expose the citizenry of Carlsbad to a dreaded disease. I'll see this money goes for repairs. Now, move on out of here, Runyon, and get those goddang brakes fixed before you kill someone."

Hook bounced up on the sidewalk outside the Clovis depot and shut down the road-rail. Popeye awaited with his hands spiked on his waist.

"Hook, you can't be parking that road-rail on the sidewalk."

"Popeye," Hook said. "If I hear any more complaints, I'm going to park it on top of your desk."

"You lose your badge again or something, Hook?"

"Did that Junior Monroe show up?"

"Well, last I checked I didn't get paid to watch him, but he's back. In fact, here he comes now. I swear he bawls like a weaning calf when you ain't around."

Junior Monroe stepped in the door and adjusted his tie. "The road-rail's up on the sidewalk, Hook."

"That machinist helper couldn't put on his overalls without instructions," Hook said.

"What's that on the back?" Junior asked.

"It's that wigwag boy, if it's any of your worry," he said.

Junior looked over at Popeye.

Popeye shrugged and sat down at his desk. "He's got his shorts in a wad, Junior, so there ain't no fixing it."

"I thought that someone hung the boy," Junior said.

"Well, they did, but that's him nonetheless."

"What are you going to do with him, Hook?"

"I'm shipping him home where he belongs soon as you loan me fifteen dollars for a ticket."

Junior turned his pocket out. "I paid the last of my check to that chef. I don't have enough left for food."

Hook turned to Popeye. "Oh, no," Popeye said. "I'm still three dollars down from last month."

Junior peered out the window. "Is that really a body out there?" he asked.

"No, I made the whole thing up for your entertainment, Junior. Hell, yes, it's a body, and I intend to see it gets home."

"Well, you can't put it in here," Popeye said. "It's against regulations."

"I've never seen a dead man before," Junior said.

"Well, there's one sitting right there behind the desk," Hook said. "And where is my dog?"

"He's out there relieving himself on the road-rail tires," Junior said.

"Go catch him and take him to the caboose. Wait for me there. I've got calls to make."

Hook dialed Eddie Preston and waited through a half-dozen rings.

"Security," Eddie said.

"Eddie, Hook. I've uncovered some important information on those pickpockets."

"You get that thing in Carlsbad taken care of?"

"Yeah, Eddie. They were thrilled, though there's some question yet as to the final costs for repairs."

"The company's paid those bastards all they're going to get, Runyon. You can just tell them that."

"Sure, Eddie. Listen, I've tracked down those pickpockets. They've moved their operation to the Amarillo-Wellington run. I've got them right where I want them." He paused. "Just one thing."

"What one thing?"

"I need an order cut to move my caboose to Avard, Oklahoma. There's a good siding there, and it's about halfway along the line. I could work both ends from there."

"I can't be dragging that caboose all over the country."

"It would be a hell of a lot cheaper than putting up in a hotel somewhere, Eddie. Frenchy's shuttling steamers to salvage. Have him pick me up. It won't cost the company a damn thing."

"Maybe I ought to send that boy instead," Eddie said. "Someone I can trust."

"He's working a hoptoad out of Lubbock. Anyway, I doubt he studied pickpockets in college. Look, I've got those bastards on the run, but I need to get in the area fast."

"Alright, Runyon, I'll see what I can do, but I expect to see some results."

"You're the one I always turn to when there's nothing else left, Eddie."

Hook found Junior waiting on the steps of the caboose. Mixer, stretched out under the steps, lifted his head and then went back to sleep.

"Come on in, Junior. We have some figuring to do."

Junior stood, took off his hat, and held it in front of his lap.

"I don't care for more Beam and water, Hook."

"Well, that's good because you're not getting any. Drinking on the job will get you canned in a hurry, Junior."

"I sure won't be drinking on the job anymore. I can promise you that."

Hook opened the door, and Mixer bound up the steps. He ran between his legs and into the caboose.

"Sit down, Junior, and tell me what you found on that hop-toad."

Junior moved books to the side and took up a place at the table.

"Four cars jumped the rail not far from the north crossing. The engine broke loose and traveled on down the track. The cars jack-knifed, tearing out a quarter mile of track before they came to a stop. I should think it's going to be a while before they get the mess cleaned up, Hook."

Hook lit a cigarette, and Junior slid to the side.

"And what do you figure caused her to jump the rail?"

"Well, at first I thought maybe they hit the curve too fast, but the engineer swore he didn't break the speed limit, not so much as a mile over. So, I walked the tracks back and forth to see if I could find where it had first jumped off the rail. I'm telling you, Hook, it looked like it had been dug up with a bulldozer."

"And?"

"Pretty soon I found where the inside rail had sprung up from the ties, and the cars had shoved it twenty feet into the air."

"Had someone tampered with it?" Hook asked.

"Not that I could tell."

Hook squashed out his cigarette and walked to the door of the caboose.

"Junior, I want you to snoop around the signal department here in Clovis and see if you can find out if any of those boys were in the area of that hoptoad the day it happened. It's best you keep it under wraps for now, so don't go making a big deal out of it."

"Okay, Hook."

"Some of those boys can play pretty rough. You understand what I'm saying?"

"I'll be careful, Hook."

Hook sat back down and tapped his prosthesis on the table.

"You have a shoelace, Junior?"

Junior looked up at him. "Sure, Hook. They're genuine leather. They can be polished right along with your shoes."

"Give me one."

"It's how I keep my shoes on, Hook."

"I'll give it back, Junior. Jesus."

Hook took the shoelace and held it out in front of him. "I want you to watch how I tie this."

"I learned how to tie my shoes in the first grade, Hook."

"Just watch, Junior. Make an overhand loop like this. Bring the tail around and over like this. Got it? Then tighten here."

"What is it?"

"That's the question."

"It's a loop," Junior said.

"That's good, Junior. It sure as hell is. But what kind?"

"A loop is a loop, isn't it?"

"That's what I want you to find out."

"Where?"

"I don't know, Junior. That's why I have an assistant. If you can't find a goddang knot, how you going to solve crimes?"

"May I have my shoestring back now, Hook?"

"Here. And keep it in your pocket; otherwise, you'll forget how it's tied."

Junior dropped the shoestring into his pocket. "May I go now, Hook?"

"No. I need some help."

"I'm not able to take care of your dog anymore, Hook. He followed me into the lobby of Hotel Clovis and sprayed on the luggage cart. They threatened to remove me if he ever showed up again."

"We'll talk about that later. Right now I want you to help me lift something."

"Lift what?"

"Dead weight, Junior. Follow me."

16

JUNIOR AND HOOK groaned as they slid the coffin off the road-rail and onto the caboose platform. Mixer circled and sniffed before curling up in the shade of the coffin. Hook tied it off with ropes and cinched the whole thing up tight on the caboose railing. Afterward, they pulled the road-rail back around to the front of the depot. Junior looked at him from the passenger's seat.

"Creepy," he said.

"I'm moving the caboose to Avard to hunt pickpockets, Junior. I don't see why that boy can't ride along."

"But he's dead, Hook."

"Everyone will be sooner or later, including you. Anyway, he'll complain a hell of a lot less than some folks I know."

"When will you be returning?"

"Soon as I get here. In the meantime, you look into that business I told you about. If you find out anything, let Popeye know. I'll check in with him now and again."

"Yes, sir."

"And remember, Junior, you're smack in the middle between management and labor, and both of them are going to hate you before it's over. It won't make a damn difference what you do."

"And what about the derailment? I mean the hoptoad."

"For now, we'll call it an accident. There's no need to ratchet up the tension just yet."

"Hook?"

"What?"

"Do you think you could obtain a pass for me now?"

"I'll take care of it. In the meantime, you can use the road-rail, but don't go getting on the line without clearance."

"But you did, Hook."

"Experience, Junior, like a professional high-wire acrobat walking over Niagara Falls. Not everyone who comes along can just do it."

"I see."

"Then what you hanging around for? There's work to be done."

Hook watched Junior limp off toward the depot, his shoe clopping up and down on his heel. Junior turned at the door and waved back.

That evening Hook went through his books before storing them away under the bunk. Soon enough he'd have to find somewhere else to keep them, either that or trade out his caboose for a boxcar.

Mixer snored under the table as the moon rose over the cupola. Hook couldn't sleep, so he slipped on his britches and went outside for a smoke. The depot had emptied, and the moonlight cast off the casket in an ivory glow. The night smelled clean and fresh. He leaned against the railing and considered what he knew about the death of Samuel Ash.

Someone had wanted the boy dead badly enough to follow him into the middle of the desert and hang him. Union men hated scabs, no secret there, and Samuel Ash had been just that. He'd been killed on railroad property, too. Whoever did it had to know his location.

Moose Barrick, a guy just dumb and mean enough to kill someone, couldn't be ruled out. And Slope Hurley was just smart enough to put him up to it. But Slope, if telling the truth, had made an effort to defuse the situation by sending the boy on the road. On the other hand, he'd made it a hell of a lot easier for Samuel Ash to die without witnesses.

Hook flipped his cigarette away, and it spiraled out into the darkness.

He opened the caboose door and paused. "Night, Samuel Ash," he said. "Tomorrow, you go home."

Frenchy coupled in while Hook put Mixer into the caboose, after which Hook climbed the ladder to the engine cab and took up his perch behind Frenchy.

Frenchy didn't say anything as he bumped out the slack. The fireman shoved the boiler door shut with his foot and dabbed at his face with his bandanna. Frenchy opened up the throttle, and the old teapot churned and huffed as she stepped out onto the high rail.

Frenchy lit his cigar, smoke swirling about his head. "Okay, Hook," he said. "What's in the box?"

"What box?"

"The one cinched up on your caboose deck. What the hell box do you think?"

"It's a body," Hook said.

"You ain't drinking Runt Wallace shine again, are you?"

"It's a body, Frenchy."

"You running tequila or something?"

"Jesus, Frenchy, it's a dead body."

"Holy hell," he said. "You got to have a permit to haul a dead body around?"

"So, I have one."

"Then you wouldn't mind showing it to me, I guess?"

Hook handed him the permit. Frenchy rolled his cigar to the other side of his mouth as he looked it over. He handed it back. Just then the crossing outside of Clovis loomed up, and Frenchy lay in on his whistle. He glanced back at Hook.

"So, you finally did it," he said.

"Did what?"

"Killed Eddie Preston."

"Eddie Preston is alive and well, I'm sorry to say."

The old teapot leveled out, and her drivers drummed as she shot into the prairie.

"If you didn't kill Eddie, who *did* you kill?" he asked.

"If I was to kill someone, it would most likely be an engineer," Hook said.

The fireman turned and grinned. "I know one you could kill right off, Hook."

Frenchy flipped the ash of his cigar out the window. "I can't be hauling a body around without knowing who it is. It might be the president or a railroad official."

"His name is Samuel Ash, if you got to know. He's that boy I found hanging off the potash wigwag."

Frenchy studied Hook. "It's mighty peculiar for a dead man to be riding around on the back of a caboose, even for you, Hook."

"This is a different situation, Frenchy. Suffice it to say that I'm taking this boy home for a proper burial, providing this tin can ever gets us there."

"This ain't the *Super Chief,* Hook, as you know, and I've got engines to pick up along the way. Them blast furnaces been running twenty-four hours a day. You'd think the world would come to an end if they left one of these old sweethearts running. Anyway, I've got a 2-10-2 sitting just outside of Tulia and an old engine in Borger, north of Panhandle."

"Tulia and Panhandle? Hell, Frenchy, I need to get on to Carmen."

"Maybe you should have thought this out before putting that dead man on your caboose."

"I did think it out. He's hermetically sealed up for the trip, even one with this old galloper at the lead."

The fireman thumped the pressure gauge with this finger. "Joe Stinson said he saw one of those hermetics in an Amarillo cathouse once. I never did see one myself, though."

Hook leaned back. "Lord, help me," he said. "Side me off at Canyon, Frenchy. I'll grab something to eat and catch some shuteye. Maybe I can figure out what the hell this bakehead is talking about."

As soon as Frenchy's engine had disappeared down the Canyon spur, Hook fed Mixer and let him out of the caboose for a run. As a rule, Mixer no longer strayed far off when they traveled, having been left behind to fend for himself on more than one occasion.

Hook double-checked the ropes on the casket before stretching out on the bunk for a nap. When he awoke, the sun had nearly set, and he decided to strike out for town in search of a café. Within a short time, he located Roscoe's Diner, which lay within earshot of the Canyon depot.

Smelling of smoke and grease from Frenchy's engine, Hook cleaned up best he could in the restroom before taking up a booth near the back of the diner. He ordered the pork chops he'd spotted bubbling away in a black iron skillet in the kitchen. Such bounty required sides of mashed potatoes, white gravy, corn on the cob, and fresh oven biscuits with sweet butter. After he'd finished, he ordered the apple pie, which smelled of brown sugar and cinnamon. He topped the meal off with a cup of chicory coffee black as roof tar.

Pushing back his plate, he checked for the waitress before wrapping the bone in a napkin to feed to Mixer later on.

Outside, he counted his money. The meal had cost him too much, but if he starved to death tomorrow, it would still be worth it.

From there, he could see the lights of the depot and decided to cut by for a quick look before going back to the caboose.

The depot, though small, was packed with passengers waiting for the arrival of the eastbound train. Hook took up a seat near the door and watched the crowd gather.

When the train whistle blew in the distance, Hook followed the crowd outside, where they lined up to board. Soon, the train arrived, her wheels screeching as she slid in next to the platform. The engine bell clanged, and kids hopped about on the ends of their mothers' arms.

Seeing nothing suspicious, Hook turned up line for the caboose. He'd nearly reached the passenger train's engine when he glanced over his shoulder for a last look back.

That's when he spotted the girl in the pink dress. In that same instant, she saw him, and she moved away into the crowd.

Air shot from the brakes of the passenger train, and the engine whistle blew. Hook moved toward the crowd, picking up his pace as the cars creaked and edged past him. People waved from the deck as the train accelerated, its engine thundering underfoot.

The car windows flicked by like snapshots of another world. Hook stopped to catch his breath, and when he looked up, the girl in pink watched him from the window of her car as it raced off into the darkness.

Hook walked down the tracks toward the caboose. Frenchy, providing he'd had no trouble, should be arriving anytime. The sounds of the desert lifted from out of the darkness, the distant yip of a coyote, the call of a whip-poor-will. He paused and lit a cigarette.

The moon slipped from behind the cloud, and in the distance, he could see the coffin under the moonlight. For a moment, he thought he saw something move, and a chill swept through him.

He dropped the cigarette into the cinders and reached for his side-arm. A light flashed from somewhere beyond the caboose, and the whine of a bullet ricocheted off into the night.

Hook threw his arm up just as the second round slammed his prosthesis into his chest. His lungs emptied and pain settled in his jaw. His legs liquefied under him, and he gasped for air.

When he collapsed onto the tracks, his head struck the rail, and a light, bright as noon, flashed behind his eyes. His ears rang, and a fire raced its way through his brain. The light in his head turned to red and then disappeared.

Something wet bathed his face, and he struggled to orient himself. Blackness enveloped him, covered him like a thick, dark syrup. Somewhere a voice rose up, delicate and mournful like a woman sobbing. He could smell creosote and iron and the dust of the desert, and he knew that he should know where he was. He moved his head, and heat pooled in his stomach.

A spot of light no larger than a match head blinked on in the darkness. He tried to concentrate, to make sense of its existence. Again, something wet on his face, bathing away the confusion, and the light grew brighter. The voice lifted and fell and lifted again. He knew the sound. He knew it like his own heartbeat, but what could it be?

And when night turned to day, he stared into the approaching light. Mixer stood over him licking his face. Hook pushed him off and sat up. The light roared toward him, and the whistle of the engine ripped open the night.

"Good God!" he said, grabbing Mixer around the neck. "It's Frenchy."

He rolled off the tracks with Mixer in tow, spilling down and into the right-of-way. The engine's whistle screamed, and her bell clanged in alarm as she thundered past. Heat and steam shot from her sides and debris blew into his face. Mixer squirmed free from

Hook's grip and bounded off down the tracks to greet Frenchy, who had climbed down from the cab and was making his way back.

Frenchy knelt at Hook's side and looked at the lump on his head.

"Hell, Hook," he said. "You out to derail me?"

Hook rested in the engine cab while Frenchy and the bakehead loaded Mixer into the caboose and connected up the coupler. The knot behind his ear throbbed, and his ribs, bruised from the bullet's impact on his prosthesis, complained with every breath.

Frenchy pulled out onto the high rail and brought her up. He lit his cigar and turned to Hook.

"Okay, what the hell is going on?"

"Someone took a shot at me," he said.

"A damn poor shot, lucky for you."

Hook turned to the fireman. "Hand me that screwdriver, will you?"

"I was just funning about killing the engineer," he said.

Hook laid his prosthesis across his lap and dug at the wrist mechanism with the screwdriver. He popped out the spent bullet that had lodged there and held it in the light of the boiler furnace for them to see.

"A quarter inch to the side, and this bullet would have made a hole through me the size of Johnson Canyon Tunnel," he said.

"And a second later, this engine would have turned you into a hookburger," Frenchy said. "It's a good job that dang dog brought you around. I guess you could call him a hero."

"You could, 'cept he was just looking for that pork chop bone in my pocket," Hook said.

Frenchy lit his cigar stub and hung his elbow out the window.

"Who do you figure would do such a thing?" he asked.

"Might have been strikers," Hook said. "They're pretty riled up."

He settled back against the cab. The moon, having escaped the clouds, hung outside the window like a yellow lantern as the old steam engine labored under the dead weight of the 2-10-2 at her back.

"Frenchy," he said. "I think I spotted one of those pickpockets back there at the depot."

"Maybe *they* shot you up, Hook?"

"Maybe," he said. "But picking pockets is a misdemeanor. Carrying a weapon to do it is a felony. They're thieves, but they aren't stupid."

"Eddie Preston's stupid," Frenchy said. "Maybe he did it."

"The only thing I'm sure about, Frenchy, is that some son of a bitch is out to get me, and I better get him first before it's too late."

17

B<small>Y THE TIME</small> they pulled into the Amarillo yards, dusk had fallen. The lights of the roundhouse shone dim through the smoke-laden panes. Both steamers and diesels rumbled about like spring thunder, and the smell of smoke and heat filled the evening. Frenchy pulled onto a siding and sat silent for a moment.

"She's running cold, boys," he said. "I think the oil jets are plugged. Wait here while I talk to the yardmaster. This old girl needs a checkup."

Hook let Mixer out for a run and stretched his own legs as they waited for Frenchy to return. He rubbed the sore spot on his chest where the prosthesis had slammed into it and considered how things could have been a hell of a lot different.

When Frenchy came back, he hiked his foot on the rail and torched up his cigar.

"They're going to take a look at her," he said. "That means a layover. I figure at least twenty hours. The yardmaster wants the

2-10-2 and the caboose set off on that spur next to the sand house over there."

"Why didn't you just put me in the machine shop?" Hook said. "That way I couldn't get any sleep at all."

"Ain't it too bad the railroad don't provide you with a private car instead of a caboose, seeing as how important you are. Now, me and the bakehead will put up in the sleeping rooms. I reckon you could bunk there if you've a mind to."

"Thanks, Frenchy, but I have property to protect. Anyway, I'd as soon bunk in the machine shop as listen to an engineer and bakehead snore all night."

"Suit yourself," he said. "The yardmaster thinks we will be ready to roll by seven tomorrow evening after the line's cleared."

When they'd sided the caboose and the 2-10-2 steamer, Hook checked his store of food, finding several cans of Spam shoved to the back of the larder. He ate half of one on dry crackers and fed the rest to Mixer, who had been sitting at his feet watching him eat.

He'd no sooner let Mixer out, with a warning about the dangers of loitering under the cars, when the yardmaster showed up.

"Don't be making camp," he said, pushing back his hat. "I might have to move you around if something comes in."

"This isn't my idea of a permanent residence," Hook said. "You happen to know what time the *Super Chief*'s due?"

The yardmaster looked at his pocket watch. "Four ten and on time," he said. "She don't stay long. Them celebrities ain't big on exploring Amarillo. Can't figure why."

"Thanks," Hook said.

"What's in the box?" he asked.

"Dead body."

"Right," he said. "You know you ain't supposed to haul nothing on that deck, don't you?"

Hook showed him his badge. "Security matter," he said.

"We got boys shooting windows out of the roundhouse. I don't suppose there's anything you can do about that security matter?"

"I'll check it out," Hook said. "And that dog there is my tracker. Try not to run him over, will you?"

The yardmaster squinted an eye. "He don't look like much to me."

"If looks mattered, the railroad would be in a hell of a shape," Hook said.

The yardmaster grinned. "You sure got that right," he said.

The next day, after listening to the bump and haul of engines all night, Hook made his way to the depot. The Texas heat quivered up from the brick platform outside. He sat on the bench next to the baggage room to watch the passengers.

He'd awakened in the night thinking about the pickpockets and had concluded that a definite pattern could be identified. First came the distraction, and then the lift, and then the handoff. The culprits involved in the actual heist never had the goods on them except for a brief moment. Everything came down to a set of preplanned maneuvers.

So far, he figured he'd come up short on the distraction and the lift. Given another shot, maybe he could pin down the handoff and redeem himself.

When the *Super Chief*'s glimmer broke downline, folks stirred on deck and proceeded to pick up bags and check their tickets.

Hook moved to the end of the baggage wagon for a better view. The *Super Chief* blew her whistle as she came sliding into the platform. The crew stretched the fuel hose across the tracks and buckled into the engine. The conductor dropped down and set up his steps that led into the car.

Hook worked his way around the end of the train and came up to the other side door. He knocked, and the porter, who had been clearing the aisle, peeked out the window. Hook flashed his badge, waited for him to open the door, and then hoisted himself up.

"Pickpockets," he said, holding a finger over his lips.

The porter nodded and moved off. Hook found a window where he could see the platform. And within moments he spotted her, the girl in pink walking through the crowd. She carried a diaper bag in one hand and a baby's milk bottle in the other.

Determined not to be distracted himself, he concentrated on the people surrounding her. A man wearing a hat stood off to the side. Suddenly the milk bottle crashed onto the platform. Milk and glass sprayed everywhere, and the girl covered her mouth with her hand.

An old lady with a purse over her shoulder reached out to help, and the man behind leaned in. Just as quickly he turned and made his way to the back of the line where another man, who carried a leather suitcase, waited to board. The exchange happened so fast, Hook wasn't sure he'd seen it.

By then the girl in pink had recovered and was on her way to the restroom, while the man in the hat had moved into the crowd. Hook waited at the top of the steps for him to work his way to the conductor. The conductor punched his ticket and then reached down to load the steps into the car.

Hook stepped out, blocking the man's way. The man's nose had been shoved to the side like a boxer's nose, and he smelled of beer and cologne.

"One moment," Hook said.

The man's face blanched, and the conductor, having overheard, hurried on past. The man turned to descend the steps, and Hook caught him by the arm.

"Who the hell *are* you?" he said, yanking his arm away.

"Railroad security," Hook said. "You're under arrest."

The man's eyes narrowed, and when he doubled his fist, Hook caught him across the bridge of his nose with the prosthesis. The blow cracked like gunfire, and the man stumbled back, his eyes filling with water. Hook shoved him in the chest with his foot, spilling him out the door. Dazed, the man squirmed on the platform.

Hook dropped down next to him. The passenger train's whistle blew, and the cars edged off. The man shook his head, pulled onto all fours, and struggled to stand.

"You son of a bitch," he said. "I'll kill you."

Hook caught him across the ear with a short punch. He grunted and rolled onto his back. His eyes flipped white, and his lungs sucked for wind. Blood oozed from the bridge of his nose.

Hook picked up the leather suitcase, which had fallen onto the platform. He caught the man under the arm and lifted him to his feet.

"Like I said, you're under arrest."

Hook pulled him into the baggage room and closed the door. The man dabbed blood from his nose and cursed under his breath. Hook dumped his leather bag onto the floor and scattered the cash and jewelry and wallets about with his foot.

"Who's working with you?" he asked.

"I'm not talking to no one-armed dick," he said, snorting.

Hook snapped him again across the bridge of his nose, and he melted onto his knees.

"Someone took a shot at me," Hook said. "I figure it might have been you. Frankly, my feelings are hurt."

"I don't need a gun to pick a pocket," the man said, sniffing. "Why would I chance a felony?"

"Because you're a brainless shit?" Hook said. "And that girl looks underage to me. I'm going to find out, and when I do, the charge won't be a misdemeanor anymore. In the meantime, I'm turning you over to the Amarillo police. You're going to love it."

By day's end Hook had given his statement to the locals and had the pickpocket booked in the city jail. He went back to the depot to use the operator's phone.

"Yeah," Eddie said.

"I'm in Amarillo," Hook said. "I nabbed one of those pickpockets. He's cooling out."

Eddie said, "They don't work alone, you know? You only get the one?"

"So far, but I'm hot on their trail. Course, Frenchy's dragging in every stack of rust between here and Kansas City. All the pickpockets in the country will be retired and living on the lake by the time I get there."

"So Carlsbad City Hall calls me, see," Eddie said. "They're pissed because they haven't been paid for that cop car. What the hell you do with that money, Runyon?"

"I gave it to the cop. You can't trust anyone anymore."

"Those bastards aren't getting a penny more from the company," Eddie said.

"That's how I feel about it, too, Eddie. Everybody thinks they can squeeze the railroad."

"You need to wind this pickpocket thing up. There's talk of a general strike, and Truman's got his steam up. The unions could shut down the whole line."

"I'm pretty good, Eddie, but I don't know if I can stop a general strike."

"What about that Lubbock hotload?"

"Just another derailment far as I can tell so far. Poor switch maintenance, probably."

"Call me if you find out anything."

"Right, Eddie, and I don't care who says otherwise, I like your style."

Hook hung up, thought for a moment, and then dialed Popeye's number in Clovis.

"Clovis depot," Popeye said.

"Hook Runyon. Has Junior checked in?"

"He's standing right here eating my peanuts," he said.

"Let me talk to him?"

Junior picked up. "Hook," he said, "have you arrived in Carmen?"

"Not yet. What did you find out about that hoptoad?"

"Slope Hurley wasn't forthcoming about where his men were working. He said that *he* ran the signal department, not Hook Runyon."

"So?"

"So, I told him we'd be looking into the signal department's overtime and sending in a report."

"Threatening someone is against the rules, Junior. What did he say?"

"He said that Moose Barrick and his boys moved their crew car to Pampa several days ago."

"And?"

"I believe it's possible that they could have gone on to Lubbock and sabotaged the track."

"I want you to catch the next train to Panhandle. I'll be laying over there while Frenchy goes to Borger to pick up an old smoker. While you're waiting, keep an eye out for a girl in a pink dress."

"Yes, sir. I will. Have you acquired a pass for me yet?"

"I'm working on it. In the meantime, hop something going through."

"But it's so irregular, sir, hopping a train, and really rather embarrassing."

"You want to learn to walk that tightwire, don't you?"

"Yes, sir, I do but . . ."

"When I get to Panhandle, you and me are going to have a talk with Moose and his boys."

"Hook?"

"What?"

"About that knot."

"What knot?"

"The one you asked me to identify?"

"Oh, yeah."

"It's a honda knot."

"A what?"

"A honda knot. It's like a lasso knot that cowboys use."

"How do you know?"

"I asked a Mexican coming out of the beer joint downtown. He told me and then he called me a stupid gringo."

"Honda. Yeah, I knew that," Hook said.

"Hook?"

"What?"

"May I put my shoestring back in my shoe now?"

The lights of the yards gathered up in the low-hanging clouds as Hook made his way back to the caboose. When he arrived, Frenchy had already coupled in and had brought up steam.

Hook climbed the engine ladder and stuck his head in the cab. He found Frenchy checking the boiler pressure.

Frenchy turned. "Well, it's about time," he said. "This old sweetheart's humming and rearing to go."

"Let me go find my dog, Frenchy."

"The bakehead's already found him and put him in the caboose."

The bakehead stuck out his boot to show Hook the teeth marks. "That son of a bitch tried to bite me."

"He's just spirited," Hook said.

"John Perez says he's the antichrist," Frenchy said.

"If you bastards are going to belittle my dog, I'm going to ride in the caboose. I could use some rest, anyway. Even a yard dog can't work all the time, you know."

Back at the caboose, Mixer jumped up and placed both paws on Hook's chest.

"Go lay down," Hook said. "I swear I'm going to give you to Eddie Preston."

Mixer crawled under the bunk, his tail clumping against the floor. Hook took off his prosthesis and put it on the table. He stretched out on the bunk and pried his shoes off with his toe. Catching pickpockets had proved to be a tiring activity.

Frenchy finessed the old steamer out of the yards, and they were soon churning their way down the high rail toward Panhandle. Hook considered a Beam and water. But weariness overtook him, and he soon fell asleep under the hypnotic cadence of Frenchy's engine.

Sometime in the night he awoke to Mixer scratching at the door. Hook sat up on the edge of the bunk. The caboose clipped along in a high waddle, and steam from Frenchy's engine wafted over the cupola.

"Go back to sleep," he said. "You're just going to have to wait until we get to Panhandle." Mixer whined and dug at the base of the door with his paw. "Alright, alright," Hook said, slipping on his shoes. "Damn dog. You'll have to go on the porch, I guess."

When he opened the caboose door, Mixer darted onto the porch and commenced barking at the coffin. Hook went out to get him. The wind whipped his hair into his eyes, and the clack of the wheels beat out a rhythm. He stared into the blackness and shivered against the night cool.

"Come on," he said, hollering into the wind. "Get back in here."

But Mixer's bark turned pitched and certain. Just then the clouds parted, and Samuel Ash's coffin lit up in the moonlight. Hook moved forward, gripping the rail against the roll of the caboose. And there, squeezed in behind the coffin, the girl in the pink dress looked up at him.

"Oh," he said, reaching for his britches. "What's your name?"

"What's yours?"

Hook turned and zipped his britches. "As long as you're hitching a ride on my caboose, you answer the questions."

"Jackie," she said.

"Jackie?"

"That's right. Short for Jacqueline, if it's any of your business."

"Oh, it's my business. I'm the railroad bull, and you've just made one hell of a mistake."

"I haven't done anything," she said. She pushed her hair behind her ears and stuck her chin out at him. "You going to arrest me?"

"Picking pockets is against the law."

"I don't pick pockets," she said.

"No, you just distract the mark long enough for someone else to do it." He slipped on his shirt. "How old are you?"

"How old are you?" she asked. "A hundred?"

Hook said, "I've been watching you pick pockets for some time now. *You're* likely to be a hundred by the time you get out of jail."

"Seventeen," she said.

"Where you from?"

"Katmandu."

Mixer peeked out from under the bunk, and Hook shot him a hard look. He crawled back under.

Hook dug his handcuffs out of the drawer and said, "Have it your way, Jackie. I'll be turning you over to the police in Panhandle. Until then, we'll need to secure you."

She stood and straightened her dress. He could see the mark on her chin and the chiseled cut of her profile in the dim light of the lantern. She had a natural beauty that had, no doubt, given her trouble with men.

"Kansas City," she said.

Hook laid the cuffs on the table. "You hungry?"

"No," she said, pausing. "For what?"

"Spam and crackers."

18

W HAT THE HELL are you doing?" Hook asked, pulling her out from behind the casket.

She shoved him in the chest with both hands, and he stumbled back against the caboose. Before he could regain his composure, she headed for the railing to jump. Hook leapt forward, catching her by the foot and dragging her back. She whirled about, her eyes lit in the moonlight, and drew back her fist. Hook caught her on the chin, and she wilted onto the deck. Mixer barked and ran in a circle around her.

Kicking open the door, he said, "Get in the caboose, Mixer."

Hook dragged the girl in and closed the door behind him. He lit the lantern. When she opened her eyes, she sat up and drew back her fist again.

"I wouldn't do that," he said.

She lowered her fist. "Don't touch me," she said. "I'll scream rape."

"What makes you think I'm interested in raping you?"

"You don't have any pants on," she said.

"Is that it?"

"That's it."

"I guess I could eat," she said.

Hook opened a can of Spam and cut slices with his pocketknife. He slid the plate across the table and watched as she wolfed it down.

"You a runaway, Jackie?" he asked.

She looked up at him and shrugged. "I left home, if that's what you mean?"

"It's not what I mean."

"My mother's dead. I lived with my father as long as I could."

"Was he mean to you?"

"No," she said, pushing her plate away. "Indifferent. When Barney came along . . ."

"Barney? The man in the hat? The one who took the purse?"

She wiped her mouth and reached into her pocket for a lipstick.

"I didn't say that."

"Barney helped you run away?"

She tightened her lip against her teeth and worked the lipstick back and forth until her lips turned a deep red.

"Barney says not to talk to anyone about anything."

"Barney hasn't been caught by the law, has he? You have. Where is he now?"

She shrugged again. "I don't know."

"So, Barney left you to fend for yourself when things got rough? He's gone, and you're headed to jail. Hardly seems right."

She wet the end of her finger, dabbed the bits of crackers off the plate, and put them in her mouth. Frenchy's whistle trailed off in the night as they came to a crossing.

"Barney's Barney," she said. "I never thought he'd do otherwise."

"Does Barney carry a weapon?"

"No," she said, glancing away.

"Has he used it on anyone, Jackie?"

"It's just a pistol that he puts in his belt. He says it's for an emergency, that working the rails is like walking into a jungle. You never know what's going to come after you."

"Coffee?" he asked.

She wrinkled her nose. "Milk."

"I don't have milk. I have coffee. Jesus, are you related to Junior?"

"Junior who?"

"Never mind."

"Water then, if it's such a big deal," she said.

"So where do you figure he went?"

"Barney doesn't tell me anything. He says the less I know the better off I'll be."

"Don't you have a rendezvous in case you get separated?"

"What's a rendezvous?"

"A place to meet."

She shook her head. "No, but Barney don't give nothing up."

"Including you?"

She shrugged. "Maybe."

"Does he have other people who work for him?"

"You arrested him back there at the depot."

"What about diversions?"

"Barney says that common folks make the best diversion. He picks them up along the way. Some don't even know what they're doing."

"Like old ladies, for example?"

"He paid a kid in Wellington a dollar to throw a tantrum on the platform. He sure got his money's worth."

Hook walked to the door and looked out. The blackness of the prairie engulfed the caboose as it charged into the night. When he turned, she was watching him.

"Barney's got his coming," he said.

She looked at him square on. "I wouldn't mess with Barney."

"Why's that?"

"You can't scare Barney, 'cause there's nothing in there to scare. All you have to do is look in his eyes. He'll be coming for me."

"I'll keep it in mind."

She looked at herself in the window reflection and adjusted her hair.

"What happened to your arm?" she asked.

Hook lifted his empty sleeve. "Wore it off pointing out trouble to smart-ass kids."

"That's silly," she said.

Hook slipped the prosthesis on. "I hadn't expected company this time of night."

"Is that your dog under there?"

"Sometimes," he said.

"He sure is ugly."

"Yeah, but he has a personality to match," he said.

She took a drink of water. "I didn't mean it when I said you were a hundred."

"That's good to know."

"Do you have something I could wear? Barney makes me put on this pink dress. I think it's stupid."

"I have some old stuff."

"I don't care. Anything's better than this."

Hook took out an old shirt and a pair of pants that had shrunk over the years. He turned his back while she slipped them on.

"Okay," she said, sitting back down at the table. "You didn't even look."

"I thought about it."

"Aren't you going to tell me your name?"

"Hook Runyon," he said.

"Because you wear a hook?"

"That's right."

"What's in the box outside?" she asked.

"A body."

"Not either," she said.

"I'm taking him home."

"That's kind of weird, isn't it?"

"So I've been told."

"Did you know him?"

"No."

She fell silent for a moment. "Why would you take a body home if you didn't know him?"

Hook thought about it. "I don't know," he said.

"Sometimes I don't know stuff I do, either," she said.

"Look," he said. "It's late. You can sleep in the bunk. I'll take the bench."

"What's going to happen to me?"

"I'll figure that out when we get to Panhandle. Now, if you're through asking questions?"

"How do I know you won't rape me in my sleep?"

"I'd be disappointed if you slept through it," he said.

"Okay," she said, slipping off her shoes and placing them at the foot of the bunk. "But I'll be watching."

Hook blew out the lantern, rolled up his old coat for a pillow, and stretched out on the bench. The caboose pitched and rolled beneath him, and Mixer snored under the bunk.

He didn't know what to do with her. She was just a kid, but a damn tough one. Kids could be unpredictable, and unpredictability could be lethal. He turned on his side. He'd give it some time. Being a hundred years old, he'd learned that time was indeed the best test.

At some point in the night the caboose lurched to a stop. Hook sat up on his elbow. Jackie slept with her back to him and with her knees pulled up. Mixer had climbed into bed with her and now lay curled at her feet.

Hook checked his watch and looked out the window. He could see the Dumas sign. Frenchy had probably stopped to water the hog. Jerkwaters like Dumas presented ample opportunity for boes to climb aboard in the darkness. What with Barney on the loose, Hook figured it prudent to take a walk to check things out.

He put on his prosthesis and coat and slipped out the door. A light fog had settled over them, and the night sounds were close in the stillness. Frenchy's engine sighed and huffed, and the heat from the boiler drifted back in the fog. The smell of creosote and oil hung in the night.

Hook walked the length of the 2-10-2, an enormous old steamer weighing in over a half-million pounds. She carried two lead wheels, five sets of drivers, and two trailer wheels. She towed a tinder at her back and had considerable age under her belt. Such behemoths, under full steam, caused the hair to rise on the necks of the most hardened railroaders.

He stopped to relieve himself. The creak of iron and heat rippled down the rails, and the thud of the brake compressor chugged off in the distance. Something cold drew in, something unsettled and foreign in the fog. Over the years he'd learned not to ignore such uneasiness. Paying attention to such things had saved his life more than once. Pausing, he looked back.

He turned and walked to the end of the tinder. Lowering his head, he parceled out the sounds one by one. Whatever he'd heard hadn't fit in the context about him: the bakehead hollering up to Frenchy, the beat and throb of the engine, the quarreling pigeons on top of the water tower.

Squatting down, he looked under the 2-10-2, and then crawled over the coupler and checked the other side. And then he looked up, the golden rule of survival on the rails. The ladder to the top of the tinder, wet with the fog, rose into the darkness.

As he climbed the ladder, he could hear the bakehead finishing off the water, and the blow of steam as Frenchy brought up the pressure. Frenchy's bell clanged, and his whistle blew announcing their departure. Hook climbed on up, determined for a quick look before they departed. He'd sleep a hell of a lot better knowing the tinder had been cleared.

Just as he reached the top, the first bump rippled down track, and the old engine creaked forward. He took a quick look, finding the tinder empty. He then hurried back down the ladder. Frenchy's whistle blew, three short blasts, and another bump traveled down track. Nearly to the bottom, he skipped the last two rungs and slid the remaining distance to the ground.

The blow came from behind just as he touched down, and his brain sloshed. He shook his head to clear it. Frenchy's whistle screamed from the darkness, and the train moved forward.

He struggled to turn, to throw himself out and away from the rails, but his prosthesis had caught in the ladder rung overhead. He fought to disengaged it, to free himself from the tangle that now threatened to drag him under the wheels.

Suddenly Frenchy brought her up, and the 2-10-2 lurched forward, flipping him onto his back. Sweat ran into his eyes, and his heels bumped over the ties as the train dragged him down track at an increasing rate of speed.

Frenchy lay in on his whistle again as he powered up for the final run into Panhandle. Hook's head bumped against the ladder rung, and his pant leg tore as it caught on a protruding spike.

Reaching up with his good hand, he worked at the harness that held on the prosthesis. His heart pounded, and his fingers burned as he worked at the harness that now tore into his flesh. The clack of the wheels, steel against steel, pooled like molten lead in his stomach as he struggled to free himself from certain death.

The instant the harness gave way, he pushed off to the side as hard as he could. Rolling away from the wheels, he tumbled down the right-of-way. Jumping up, he watched the caboose paddle on by him. With a burst of adrenaline, he raced after it. Catching hold of the grab iron just in time, he hoisted up onto the steps.

Panting, he lay back on the caboose step as the jerkwater disappeared in the fog behind. Moving out of the wind, he examined the tear in his pant leg and the patch of hide missing from his elbow.

The attempts on his life had gotten too damn frequent and too damn close. Waiting around for someone to kill him just didn't fit his style.

He opened the door to the caboose and found Jackie still asleep. Mixer lifted his head before curling up again. Hook fixed his coat into a pillow, lay down on the bench, and turned on his side. The moon broke through the fog, and moonlight struck through the cupola window, falling on Jackie's shoes, which now sat at the *head* of the bunk.

19

STILL AWAKE, HOOK sat up as the train slowed for arrival into Panhandle. Sleep had eluded him. Every time the train bumped, the knot on the back of his head fired off.

He rose to make coffee, leaning in against the pitch and roll of the caboose. Long ago he'd developed sea legs, and it took a rough ride to set him off course. The girl stirred as Frenchy backed the caboose onto the siding. She sat up, yawning, just as someone knocked on the door.

When Hook opened it, Frenchy stood there with Hook's prosthesis in his hand.

"Jesus," he said. "I thought we'd killed you."

"Not from lack of trying," Hook said.

Frenchy glanced at the coffin. "Death at the door. That thing's just scary, Hook."

"How old are you, Frenchy?"

Frenchy held up the prosthesis. "The switchman found this thing hanging off the tinder ladder. We figured you'd slipped and fell under the wheels."

"Well, I would have if you'd had your way," Hook said.

Jackie stepped up behind and peeked around Hook's shoulder at Frenchy.

"Who's that?" she asked, sleep still in her voice.

"This is Frenchy," Hook said. "He's supposed to be the engineer. Frenchy, this is Jackie, and you can close your mouth now."

"Will you look at that," Frenchy said. "How the hell did you pick up a girl while going down the track?"

"By dangling from the tinder ladder," Hook said.

Frenchy rolled his eyes. "Well, I'm a married man and don't know much about these things, but isn't this girl a little young?"

Hook rolled his eyes. "Like you say, you don't know much about these things."

Frenchy said, "We're headed to Borger to pick up an old Baldwin. We'll be laying over there. I don't know just how long yet."

"Well, I guess we won't be going anywhere until you get back, seeing as how you have the engine."

Frenchy came up on his toes for another look at Jackie. "Right," he said. "See you then."

"You figure on using that yourself?" Hook asked.

"What?"

"My arm."

"Oh, yeah. I mean, no," he said, handing it to Hook. "Just don't leave this thing swinging from my train no more. You about gave the switchman a heart attack."

After letting Mixer out for a run, Hook cooked breakfast, fried Spam, while Jackie made up the bunk. He poured coffee and sat down at the table with her.

"Barney sometimes buys me steak and eggs for breakfast," she said.

"I didn't have time for steak and eggs this morning," he said.

"I'll bet Frenchy's wondering what we're doing right now," she said, pushing back her hair.

"Engineers don't have much of an imagination," he said.

When she'd finished her breakfast, she rolled the sleeves of his old shirt up to her elbows and searched out her lipstick. He watched as she traced the outline of her mouth with practiced skill. A switch engine rumbled by and set the caboose windows to rattling.

"Aren't you curious about where I went last night?" he asked.

She dropped her lipstick into her purse. "Sure, I guess. Where did you go last night?"

"When we stopped for water at Dumas, I went out to check for boes. Thing is, someone hit me on the head and damn near got me killed."

"Is that so?" she said.

"And when I came back here, your shoes had been moved from one end of the bunk to the other. How is that?"

"Could I have a cigarette?"

"No."

"You aren't the only one who has to use the bathroom, you know," she said.

"How do you know I went to the bathroom?"

"Didn't you?" she asked.

"It's a possibility," he said.

"It could have been Barney," she said. "He'll come looking for me. Barney will never let someone take me away. I'd sure hate to tangle with him on a train. Barney's like a cat."

Hook touched the knot on his head. "You'd think Barney could hit hard enough to knock a man out, wouldn't you?"

She shrugged and searched through her purse for chewing gum. She folded two sticks into her mouth and said, "What's the books?"

"They're books," he said.

"So, I *know* they're books."

"I collect them."

"Why?"

"Because I've made a fortune at it."

"I never heard of that," she said.

Hook reached for the handcuffs. "Come on," he said. "I've business to attend to."

"You don't have to cuff me," she said. "I won't go anywhere."

"Right," he said, snapping the cuffs around her wrists.

The Panhandle depot reminded Hook of an old fort with gun turrets on its top. He secured Jackie to the bench outside before looking up the operator, who sat with his feet on the desk reading a Zane Grey novel.

"Must be a slow day," Hook said.

The operator dropped his feet and laid the paperback aside.

"Someone left it in the waiting room," he said. "Was looking for a name. What can I do for you?"

Hook showed him his badge. "I've been expecting my associate to come in, a young fellow with his shirt buttoned to the neck."

"No, sir. Don't see many like that around here."

"When's the next train due in?"

The operator checked the board. "No passengers today."

"Anything else?"

"There's an old peanut roaster with a load of hogs coming out of Clovis. Should be arriving in about ten minutes. Wouldn't be nothing but squealers on that stinker, though."

"Thanks," Hook said. "I better check anyway. This kid's green as they come. If you see anyone looks like he just ate a lemon send him to my caboose. I'm sided north of the stockyard."

"Oh, sure," he said. "But there ain't no hurry."

"What do you mean?"

"A hoptoad just piled up between here and Pampa, half-dozen freight cars. The main line's down until they get a crew out."

Hook looked over at the window. He could see the top of Jackie's head.

"You don't have transportation I could use, do you?" he asked.

The operator shook his head. "I don't think so. Except, there's an old popcar down at the buzzard's roost. The yardmaster's there. You could ask him, I suppose. Course, the track inspector uses it now and then. Guess he won't be coming in with the line down, though."

"Thanks," Hook said.

Hook and Jackie waited on the platform for the freight train to pull by. The smell of hogs, thick as molasses, hung in the air as the train screeched to a stop.

Hook walked the length of the train with Jackie trailing at his side. As he headed back toward the engine, he spotted Junior dropping down from one of the cars.

"Hey," Hook said. "You know it's against the law to hop trains?"

"Hook," he said. "Is that you?"

Looping his arm through Jackie's, Hook pulled her forward.

"What took you so long, Junior?"

His hair had blown into a tangle, and dirt had gathered in the corners of his eyes. He smelled his sleeve.

"My pass didn't come through, Hook, so I jumped on this thing. I came within an inch of being swept over the side."

"This is Jackie," Hook said. "Short for Jacqueline."

"Hi," Junior said. "Why is she handcuffed?"

"This is the girl in the pink dress you were supposed to watch for, Junior, the pickpocket. As you can see, I found her instead."

"I'm not a pickpocket," she said.

"That's true, she isn't," Hook said. "She just works for one."

Junior looked through his eyebrows at her. "She's not wearing a pink dress, Hook."

"It's in the caboose," she said. "These are Hook's clothes."

Junior looked at Hook.

"It's a long story," Hook said.

Junior pushed the hair from his eyes. "I sure would like to have a train pass, sir. I'll never get the smell out of my clothes."

"I'm working on it, Junior. In the meantime, there's a hoptoad this side of Pampa, and the main line's shut down. I've got a popcar lined up to go out there."

"Moose and his crew are not far from there," Junior said.

"I know."

"What about her?" he asked.

Jackie snapped her gum. "Just leave me here," she said. "I won't go anywhere."

"We'll take her along for now," Hook said. "We need to get over there before the work crews show up and destroy all the evidence."

Junior dusted off the knees of his pants. "When do we leave?"

"Soon as you've had a bath," Hook said.

Junior, his hair still wet, waited for Jackie to get in the popcar before he climbed in next to her. Hook removed the cuffs and fastened them to the railing of the popcar. He cranked over the engine and waited for it to level out.

"You get clearance?" Junior asked.

"The line's shut down, remember?"

"I remember nearly losing my life in Clovis," Junior said.

Hook eased out on the high rail, and they were soon clacking downline. Jackie's eyes grew wide as they raced into the countryside. The wind tossed her hair into curls, and she shivered. Junior took off his jacket and gave it to her.

"Thanks," she said, smiling at him.

Junior smiled back as he settled in next to her. He turned to Hook.

"Do you think there's been foul play?"

Hook leaned below the windshield to make himself heard. "Hard to say. Derailments are not uncommon. Takes less to dump over rolling stock than most people realize."

The plains opened up in front of them, an expanse as vast as the ocean. Without landmarks, all sense of direction and distance could give way to confusion. Old-timers had been known to walk in circles for days trying to find their way out.

"Why would anyone derail a train?" Jackie asked.

Hook said, "Railroaders have been caught between the war and the company for a good many years now. The unions agreed not to strike so long as the war was on. In turn, the company agreed to make union membership mandatory. That worked fine for everyone except the employees. Now you've got these wildcats popping up."

"What's a wildcat?" she asked.

"Workers striking without the say-so of the union. Feelings are running high, too high, and there's always someone willing to step over the line. In the end, when no one's in charge, things can get out of hand. People can get hurt."

Jackie searched out her gum, popped a stick into her mouth, and licked the sugar off her lips.

"Do yard dogs strike, too?" she asked.

Hook smiled. "Yard dogs couldn't organize a poker game," he said.

"Look," Junior said.

Hook brought the popcar down to a stop. The sun had descended and cast long shadows from the tumble of boxcars in the distance.

"Jeez," Junior said. "What a mess."

Jackie snapped her gum and buried her hands between her knees. "They look dead," she said.

"They've taken the engine on in so the work train can get through. We better take a look," Hook said. "It's going to be dark soon."

They walked the line, pausing to study the path of the jack-knifed cars. One of them had split open and spilled dozens of boxes of new pliers down the track.

Jackie walked by the side of Junior, their shoulders touching now and again as they examined the condition of the rails. The setting sun cast rays of yellow and orange into the evening sky.

Junior squatted down. "I think it derailed here, Hook," he said.

"Yeah," Hook said. "But it started a quarter-mile back."

"I didn't see any rails damaged until just now, and all the spikes are still intact," Junior said.

"Come on, I'll show you what I'm talking about."

They walked back and were nearly to the popcar again when Hook knelt down.

"See where this rail is popped up at the joint."

"About an inch is all," Junior said. "Would that derail a train?"

"Unlikely. But notice how these rails are laid out like bricks in a wall. Each joint falls at the midpoint of the opposing rail. This makes for strong construction. The wheels never hit more than a single connection point at any given time."

"That makes sense," Junior said.

"There's a crossing about five miles down track from here. That means this train had to slow down, probably below twenty-five miles an hour."

"Slow and with no spikes gone doesn't add up to a derailment, does it?"

"In fact it does," he said.

"I don't get it," Junior said.

Hook studied the rail. "When a wheel hits a joint, it kicks the car to the side. About then it hits the joint on the opposite rail and rocks it back again."

"But how does that cause a derailment?" Junior asked.

"It doesn't unless the cars have spring-loaded trucks under them, which these do. In that case, a thing called harmonic motion can be put into play."

"I can sing harmony," Jackie said. "But Barney doesn't like it."

"This is different," Hook said. "When a car is moving slowly, usually between about twelve and twenty-five miles an hour, and something sets it to rocking, like these loose joints here, it can commence to pitching from one side to the other. As it moves down track the rocking gets more and more pronounced until it finally derails."

"I heard that a cat walking over a bridge can make it fall down," Jackie said.

"Happens all the time," Hook said. "Now see how these connection points have been pried up just enough to set the cars in motion?"

"I believe you're correct," Junior said.

"Once a car is tipped, the forward motion takes care of the rest.

"Did those cars in Lubbock have springs?"

"I think so," Junior said. "How do you know all this, Hook?"

"By walking tightwires," he said.

"So, what do we do now?" Junior asked.

"We'll turn about up at that crossing. This old speeder should manage the track past the hoptoad without a problem if we take it easy. Then we'll head back to Panhandle and catch up with Moose and his crew later."

Hook stood on the back bumper of the popcar while Junior spun her around and dropped her down onto the track again. As they headed back toward the derailment, the moon, orange as a pumpkin, rose on the horizon, and the first stars of the evening clicked on. The night had begun to cool under the clear sky, and Jackie scrunched into Junior's coat against the chill. Now and again, Junior would glance over at her.

As they approached the hoptoad, Hook slowed down. The track, while still intact, snaked about, and the wheels of the popcar complained.

Suddenly, Hook cut the motor, and they drifted to a stop. Ahead, the derailed hulks loomed in the darkness like dinosaurs.

"What is it?" Junior asked.

"I think I saw something," Hook said. "A light flash."

"Maybe it's Barney come for me," Jackie said.

"No one comes for you unless we permit it," Junior said.

"I'm going to take a look," Hook said. "You two stay here."

Junior shook his head. "I'll go with you."

"Just do as I say, Junior. Make certain this girl stays put."

Hook worked his way down track. As he approached the derailed cars, he moved into the shadows, keeping low as possible. From there, he could see a truck in the distance and men loading the boxes of pliers onto the back. He heard Moose Barrick's voice, deliberate and low, and he could smell tobacco smoke drifting in the stillness. So Moose's greed had gotten the best of him, and he'd come back to make a little money off his handiwork.

Hook moved behind the end car, which had skidded down track and landed with its wheels in the air.

"Get them boxes loaded," Moose said. "That damn work crew could get here at any time."

Hook drew his P.38 and stepped out of the shadows.

20

D ROP IT," A voice said from behind him.

Hook let the P.38 fall to the ground. He turned to see a figure standing in the shadows. When he heard the click of the hammer and saw the moonlight glint off the barrel of the weapon, he charged full bore into the darkness, striking the assailant in the chest with his head. The man grunted and dropped his weapon.

Hook stuck him in the belly, and the air whistled through his teeth. The man, honking like a goose, stumbled back against the side of the car.

Hook could hear men running down track toward him, their voices pitched, and his assailant was pulling himself up in the darkness. Hook squared off, prepared to sidestep. For a one-armed man, clinches could be deadly.

Suddenly, the man shook his head, snorted, and charged. Hook spun to the side and drove his fist into his opponent's ribs. The man crumpled at the waist, and drool strung from his lips.

Smelling of sweat and sick, the man leaned over, his fight having flagged. Hook shoved his knee up into the man's chin; his teeth clacked; his head snapped back, and he spilled onto the tracks.

Hook searched in the darkness for his weapon, finally spotting it lying next to the rail. Just as he reached for it, arms snared him and crushed him to a standstill. He struggled to free himself, but the absence of leverage left him caught like a bear in a trap.

Blood rushed to his head, and his eyes strutted in their sockets. His breath rushed away, and he fought for oxygen with fast, shallow pants. The whiskers of his assailant scrubbed against his ear.

With each second, Hook's strength faded. His ears rang, and his nose dripped onto the predator's arms. Lights swarmed behind Hook's lids, and his knees trembled under him.

"I'll squeeze your guts out like a tube of toothpaste," the man said, his breath stinking of tobacco.

Hook recognized Moose Barrick's voice, in it the sum total of stupidity and cruelty one could expect. Hook's blood coursed in his ears, and his veins knotted in his neck.

Jackie came from out of nowhere, from out of the darkness like a cougar. She landed on Moose Barrick's back, gouging and shrieking and tearing chunks of gristle from his ear with her teeth. Blood, stinking of heat and iron, rained down on Hook with each pump of Moose's heart.

Moose squealed like some ancient creature from the high reaches of a rain forest, and the second his grip loosened, Hook broke away. Oxygen, sweet as life, filled his lungs.

Jackie rode Moose to the ground, all the while punching and ripping and cursing.

Down track, Junior, his arms propped up like a prize fighter, squared off with one of the thieves. He circled and punched, each time stunning his foe with precision blows to the head.

Hook dove for his P.38, brought it up, and fired into the air. The shot split open the night, and Junior's man dashed off. Hook spun around to find his man, too, had escaped into the darkness.

Junior came downline, straightening his tie, and Jackie, exhausted from beating the life out of Moose, stood and wiped the blood from her face. Moose whimpered on the ground and held his hand against what remained of his ear. Junior sat down on the track and wiped the dust from the toes of his shoes.

Hook lit a cigarette and looked about. "Jesus," he said. "For a minute there, I thought you two were going to kill them all. Where the hell did you learn to fight like that, Jackie?"

"Barney," she said.

Hook looked at Junior. "College," he said. "Varsity boxing.

"So what do we do about the others?" Junior asked.

"We've cut off the head of the snake," Hook said. "That's enough for now. Get the cuffs off the popcar and secure our boy here. Then I want you to take Jackie and the truck and deliver Moose to the Panhandle jail. Between here and there, I want you to think up every possible charge against him that you can."

"What about you?" Junior asked.

"I haven't done anything," Hook said.

Junior rolled his eyes. "I mean what will you be doing?"

"I'll take the popcar back. Meet me at the depot when you're finished."

"And Jackie?" Junior asked.

"Bring her to the depot with you."

"You aren't going to turn her over to the police, are you?"

Hook looked at Jackie, who had found her lipstick and was busy applying a new coat.

"Not yet, Junior. But you remember she's here because of her involvement with pickpockets. Do you understand what I'm saying?"

Junior ducked his head. "Yes, sir."

"And I'd be damn careful about picking a fight with her, if I were you."

Hook found the operator reading the last chapter of his Zane Grey novel. He looked up when Hook came in and then slipped the book into the drawer.

"Haven't found the owner's name yet?" Hook asked.

The operator grinned. "Pampa called, and they've got a crew working on that hoptoad. They said it wouldn't take long to clear it enough for slow traffic."

Hook nodded. "The rail's still intact, more or less."

"I heard they found blood everywhere, but they couldn't find nobody, dead or alive."

"What time does the eastbound *Super Chief* come through?" Hook asked.

"Ten."

"Anything else coming in?"

The operator checked the board. "Eastbound cattle train about three in the morning."

"Mind if I use your phone?"

"Go ahead," he said.

Hook dialed Eddie and waited through several rings.

"Security," Eddie said.

"Eddie, this is Hook."

"Runyon, have you left the country? The main line's shut down, and the big boys are on their hind legs."

"It's all taken care of, Eddie. Turns out Moose Barrick tampered with the tracks, and then he made the mistake of coming back to steal freight."

"How do you know that?"

"Crack detective work, Eddie. Moose is cooling in the Panhandle jail as we speak."

"Are you sure it was Moose who did it?"

"Start the paperwork, Eddie. We got him dead to rights."

"Were there others?"

"Hard to say."

"Is that it, Runyon?"

"I could use an advance on my paycheck."

"Don't try to be funny, Runyon. Security work ain't funny."

"Look, Eddie, I've got these pickpockets on the run. But I think the main man is working out of Kansas City."

"Surprise us all and arrest him, Runyon."

"It's not that simple. Trains don't stand still, you know. I need someone herding him this way, someone to help box him in."

"Can't you keep it simple, Runyon?"

"I'll try for your sake, Eddie. Look, I want to send that green-horn on ahead to Kansas City, so we can squeeze those bastards from both ends."

"So, send him."

"You'd think the company could come up with a goddang pass by now, wouldn't you? It's important I get him up there tonight. I want to put him on the *Super*."

"Taking up a seat on the *Super* costs the company a lot of money."

"If the word gets out that she's crawling with pickpockets, it will cost a hell of a lot more."

Eddie fell silent and then said, "What is it exactly you want?"

"Arrange with the operator here for a ticket. I'm pretty sure we can nail these bastards if we move on it now."

Eddie thought for a while before answering. "Alright," he said. "But why do I feel like I'm getting screwed?"

"It's just a passing fantasy, Eddie. You'll get over it."

Hook, Junior, and Jackie waited on the platform for the *Super Chief* to slide in. Hook handed the *Super Chief* ticket to Jackie.

"This will get you back to Kansas City," he said.

She looked up at him. "You mean you're not going to arrest me?"

"Lack of evidence," he said. "But if I catch you on my trains again, it will be a different story. Do we understand each other?"

Jackie went forward to give her ticket to the conductor. She waved her fingers at Junior before turning to Hook.

"Barney wears a gander feather stuck in the brim of his hat," she said. "You can't miss it in a crowd."

Hook and Junior waited on the platform as Jackie searched out her seat. She folded a stick of gum into her mouth and watched them from the window as the *Super Chief* pulled away.

Junior sighed. "Real nice of you, Hook."

"Nice had nothing to do with it, Junior. Had I the evidence, she'd be sitting in jail with Moose Barrick this very minute.

"I saw you ogling that girl, Junior. A detective has to keep his head clear at all times. You start getting all involved, and you're likely to get into trouble."

Junior looked at his feet. "I didn't mean anything by it, Hook. Anyway, you're the best yard dog I know."

"I'm the *only* one you know, Junior."

"Are we going back to Clovis now?"

Hook pulled at his chin. "There's still a pickpocket on the loose. I want you to go on ahead to Kansas City and start working your way back. Lay over at the depots along the way. Wander around like as if you don't know what the hell you're doing."

"Sure. I can do that, Hook."

"If you come up with something, call Popeye or Eddie. I suggest you call Popeye since Eddie doesn't like things to get complicated."

"The *Super* goes to Kansas City, right?"

"That's right."

"So you've a *Super Chief* ticket for me, too?"

"It's rare to find boes and pickpockets riding in the *Super's* dining car, Junior. It's important to get out amongst them if you claim to be a real yard dog."

"Then how am I supposed to get there?"

"There's a stock train coming through at three A.M. I asked the operator to call in a slow for you, seeing as how you haven't mastered the skill of hopping a train yet."

"Aw, jeez, Hook, again?"

"And keep it a little more tidy, Junior. Poor hygiene reflects on the company."

Junior looked down the track. "So, what are you going to be doing?"

"I've got a casket to deliver."

"Couldn't you just send it on the train?"

"Someday you're going to make prosecutor, Junior, and when that day comes, no matter where I am, I want you to give me a call."

"Why's that, Hook?"

Hook turned and walked off down the track. "'Cause that's the day I'll be killing myself," he said over his shoulder.

21

MIXER, BUSY WORKING a burr out of his paw, looked up at Hook and then lay back down next to the casket. He'd taken a fancy to the spot and had refused to come into the caboose lately, even to eat. Hook, understanding that Mixer lived by a set of rules known only to him and God, had started leaving food and water outside the door.

Once in the caboose, Hook lit the lantern and checked out the remains of his pants. Having been dragged downline on the tinder ladder and scrubbed through the cinders by half the signal gang, his pants were now torn and ragged.

He fixed himself a Beam and water and lined his collection of books across the table. The 1902 *Hound of the Baskervilles* slid into its slot like a new brass bushing, the final piece that turned the parts into a whole.

Hook liked things completed, finished. He liked knowing that nothing remained to be done. Finding the final piece to the puzzle, the last remnant of a life's work, provided pleasure unparalleled in the world of collecting.

Hook sipped his whiskey and ran his finger down the spine of the purloined book. Left on its own, it would most likely have ended its life in a landfill. No doubt the library didn't even know that it had been taken, that a lesser book now reigned in its place. In any case, who would care? No one understood its value like him. No one appreciated its place in the world like him.

He drained his glass and poured another, shorting the water, which had grown tepid in the hot caboose. Walking to the door, he opened it and looked out on the casket. Mixer lay curled in the same spot.

Junior had a point. He could have sent the casket on by train or, for that matter, left it to be buried in the pauper's grave in Carlsbad. The body he'd taken down from the wigwag would return to dust no matter where it lay.

For Hook, death had always been a companion, a friend of the most serious kind, one who visited sometimes in the wee hours. Often, he waited for it in the darkness to share his secrets. How could he now abandon it for the sake of convenience? What compelled him to take this stranger home, he didn't know. Perhaps death, like his purloined book, deserved its place in the scheme of things. He needed the boy returned to where he belonged, and he needed to do it personally. He needed it finished.

Closing the door, he fixed another Beam and slid the bottle to the side. He thought about the events of the last few weeks. For days he'd been unable to shake the feeling that someone followed his every move.

Twice now he'd been attacked by unknown assailants: once dangling from the tinder ladder and another when someone took a potshot at him. It could have been Moose, a man capable of violence, or it could have been the allusive Barney, who, according to Jackie, carried a firearm and had no qualms about using it. Even Jackie herself could not be left out of the equation, though she may well have saved his life at the hoptoad.

Finishing off his drink, he hung the glass upside down on the bottle neck, took off his prosthesis, and crawled into bed. Mixer's leg thumped on the platform outside as he dug at an ear. Hook put the pillow over his head and closed his eyes. It had been a trying few days all around. But tomorrow, being payday, promised to be better.

Frenchy arrived at sunup and had coupled in before Hook could get his coffee made. When Hook opened the door, Frenchy stood there about to knock.

"We're pulling out," he said. "You got any girls in there, you better send them home to their mommas."

Hook rubbed the sleep from his face. "I haven't had my breakfast yet, Frenchy. What the hell is the rush?"

Frenchy lit up his cigar and pushed back his hat. "Engineers run on a fast clock, unlike some folks I know. You riding with me or sleeping your life away in here?"

"Alright. I'm coming."

"And do something with this dog. The son of a bitch tried to bite me."

"Jesus," Hook said. "I wonder why?"

Hook poured coffee out of Frenchy's thermos and took up his perch in the back of the cab. The old engine bore down as she hauled at her load. By the time they hit the limits of Panhandle, she churned along at a top speed of forty miles an hour.

Frenchy lit his cigar and leaned back in his seat. "We'll be laying over in Canadian, Texas, Hook. I think this old gal's sprung a leak somewhere, and she won't hold pressure. I'm taking her into the roundhouse to see the pipe fitter."

Hook lit a cigarette and shook his head. "This old clunker spends more time in the hospital than she does on the rails, Frenchy."

"Wait 'til you get as old as her and see how hot you can run, Hook."

Frenchy slowed as they approached the hoptoad. The engine bumped and rolled when she hit the loosened rails. Only one of the derailed cars now lay on her side in the right-of-way. The crew, still working to upright her, stepped back and waited as they idled by.

Hook stepped to the door and looked through the faces. Recognizing none, he returned to his perch and stretched out for a nap.

"Keep an eye out for trouble," he said. "There's been a lot of derailments of late."

Frenchy pushed back his hat. "Don't you worry about that. I've been running these old smudge pots for nearly forty years, and I ain't tipped one over yet."

A few hours later, Frenchy lay in on his whistle as they approached Canadian. Hook got up and stretched out the kinks.

"Leave me off at the depot, Frenchy. I need to find the paymaster."

"It's a rare yard dog what puts a dime away for tomorrow," Frenchy said.

"And it's a rare engineer what takes it with him beyond the grave," Hook said. "I'll catch up with you at the roundhouse."

After collecting his check, Hook made for the Harvey House to eat breakfast. The smell of bacon cooking greeted him at the door, and a Harvey girl, fresh as the morning, guided him to his table.

He ordered three eggs, sunny-side up, sugar-cured ham, scratch biscuits topped with white gravy, hash browns, tomato marmalade, and a cup of Chase and Sanborn coffee.

"Anything else?" the waitress asked, lifting her brows.

Hook thought it over. "A rack of bacon, crisp."

After breakfast, he went to the reading room, where he caught up on the news. President Truman was still threatening to nationalize the railroad because of all the wildcat strikes. Hook folded the paper and lay it aside. "And he thought the *war* was tough. Wait 'til he tries to run a railroad," he said to himself.

Afterward, he went to the depot and called Popeye, who said he hadn't heard from Junior yet, thank the Lord, and then he reminded Hook that today, being payday, might be a good time to settle up on that three dollars he owed.

Hook walked to the roundhouse and found the caboose and the salvage engines sided a short walk from the turntable. Like a giant cat, Frenchy's engine straddled the work pit in the third stall of the roundhouse. Hook could hear voices emanating from underneath the engine.

He leaned over and could just see the pipe fitters, like mine mules, at work in the dimness of the pit. Grease and soot covered their faces and brightened the whites of their eyes.

"How long?" Hook asked.

"Have lots of work in the shop here," one of them said. "Most the day, maybe longer."

"You seen Frenchy?"

"Yeah," one of them said. "He's even uglier than I remembered."

"Know where he is?"

"Sleeping rooms. Said he'd check back later."

"Thanks," Hook said.

Unwilling to spend the day roaming the yards, Hook went back to the caboose, where he found Mixer still curled up alongside the casket. Mixer whopped his tail against the floor and then turned back to his sleep.

Inside, Hook sat at the table and read for a while. Between the heat and the size of his breakfast, he soon grew sleepy. Slipping off his shoes, he crawled into his bunk and fell sound asleep.

———

When he awakened, the sun had set, and the yard lights winked through the windows of the caboose. He put on his shoes and went out on the caboose porch. Mixer had disappeared. Given several weeks had elapsed without a scrap, he'd probably set out to hunt strays.

Hook leaned against the casket and watched the moon rise.

"Well, Samuel Ash," he said, "another delay, but, don't worry, we're going to get there one way or the other."

He walked to the roundhouse to check on the engine, only to find the second shift on.

He leaned over the drive wheel. "How long?" he asked.

"What the hell difference does it make?" someone said. "She'll be melted into washing machines by summer's end, anyway."

Hook didn't answer but picked his way over the maze of tracks and out into the yards. Steam rose up into the lights, and the chug of engines filled the evening.

The hostler had sided a diesel next to the machine shop and had planted a blue stop-flag in her nose. Her engine thumped and throbbed in an idle. The smell of sulfur and oil drifted down track on waves of heat, and insects swarmed in the yard light overhead.

Hook had turned to go when he noticed a man, large and slightly bent, standing at the front of the engine. He had a gander feather stuck in the band of his hat.

"Barney," he said quietly to himself.

Hook moved back into the shadows of the engine, uncertain as to whether he'd been spotted or not. Barney had probably come for the girl like she said he would, to take her back or to silence her, or maybe to silence him as well.

Barney moved behind the nose and out of sight. Hook checked the area for places he might escape. The yard light lit the distance between the engine and the machine shop, and no other cars or engines were close enough for cover. Barney's only escape would be to follow along the other side of the engine, wait until it was clear, and then make a run for it.

Hook slipped toward the nose, the rumble of the engine quaking underfoot. He pulled his P.38. If this guy was half as stealthy as Jackie claimed, he didn't want to take any chances.

Nearly to the front, he paused and tried to listen through the drone of the engine. He squatted down, leaned against the wheel, and peered into the darkness under the engine. There was only a couple feet of crawl space, but as long as that blue flag remained in place, the engine would not be moved, clearing the way for him to maneuver under and take Barney by surprise.

Tucking his sidearm into his belt, he lay down on his back and worked his way under. The rail ground into his spine and the cinders scrubbed against the back of his head and shoulders as he scooted under inch by inch. Water dripped from the maze of pipes and cables that ran overhead, and the stink of diesel drifted down on the engine heat.

He tried not to think of the colossal weight above, the steel and iron, the raw power that crushed everything in its path.

With barely enough room to breathe, he pushed and wormed his way farther under the engine. Leaning his head back, he could just see the other side. And then he saw a foot, a boot the size of a journal jack. Barney, the son of a bitch, was waiting for him to come around the nose. And then just as quickly the boot disappeared.

Hook shoved his shoulders under the bracing that cut at an angle across the undercarriage. If he could just get out far enough to draw his weapon, he had this bastard right where he wanted him.

Halfway under, he realized he couldn't move. The harder he pushed, the tighter his body wedged itself beneath the bracing. Hot water from above dripped into his face and eyes. He couldn't move forward or backward or to the side.

Gritting his teeth, he forced himself to lie still, to think it through. The engine had been flagged, and as long as that flag stayed put, the engine wouldn't be moved. He had plenty of time to work himself free. If he got under, he could get out. Simple as that.

This time he'd relax, lower the height of his torso, which had gone rigid from adrenaline. He had plenty of time. Blue-flagged engines sometimes sat for weeks in a state of disrepair.

He let the tension go, worked it from his jaws, down his spine, and out the bottoms of his feet. He dug his heels into the cinders and inched back a fraction. The bracing rode up on his rib cage, tearing at his shirt and his skin. Pain, like an electrical current, pooled in the glands under his arms.

He turned his head to the side, the stink of creosote in his nose. Hot water dripped into his ear and ran down his neck. He could see the faint glow of the yard light seeping under the front of the engine, a thousand miles of steel waiting to crush him into a gore ball.

At first he thought it no more than the thump of his heart, but when it came again, he recognized it as footsteps moving down the length of the engine. He started to call out for help, but then it might be Barney returning to kill him.

When the footsteps stopped nearby, he turned his head up once more. He shoved his chin as high as possible, but he failed to see anything.

The footsteps turned then and moved off toward the rear of the engine. Hook lowered his head and struggled to catch his breath. Once again, he pushed his chin up in an effort to see. This time he did see, and what he saw froze his heart into a block of ice. The blue stop-flag had been tossed under the engine only feet from where he lay.

22

THE VOICES DRIFTED in from a distance and then grew louder. Someone coughed, and the smell of cigarette smoke wafted in. Hook called out just as the brake compressor thumped on, his voice fading beneath the racket.

He pushed against the bracing, his ribs firing off waves of pain into his neck and jaw. And when the diesel engine revved up, the ground under him shuddered. His scalp tightened, and once more he shoved against the bracing, his flesh tearing beneath his shirt.

Air shot into the night, releasing the brakes, and Hook clenched his jaw. He held his breath and waited for the disemboweling, the stringing of body parts down the track.

Suddenly the engine bumped, and the wheels screeched, iron against iron as the engine backed up a few inches. White lights flashed in his eyes, and the engine howled in his ears. The engineer paused to gather up power, and in that moment Hook realized that the brace had loosened.

If only he could make it between the wheels in time, life lay but a few feet away. Reaching up, he caught the frame with his prosthesis and pulled with everything he had. He slid between the wheels and rolled out onto his side. Muscle spasms jerked up his body as he scrambled into the shadows. The engineer's profile lit against the cab instrument lights as the engine growled off down track.

For several minutes Hook waited in the darkness, his life returning with each gulp of oxygen. Barney could not have gotten far. He had to be somewhere out there in the yards.

From there, Hook could see the roundhouse, the machine shop, and the turntable cabin. When he spotted a shadow slipping past the dingy window of the machine shop, he cocked his P.38.

Holding his arm against his ribs, he slipped through the darkness. Ducking low, he moved into the machine shop and squatted in the shadows to wait for his eyes to adjust. Empty of employees, the building creaked and settled in the coolness. Great lathes and grinders lined the walls. Belts shot down from the maze of overhead pulleys mounted in the high reaches of the ceiling. Driver wheels and trailing trucks stretched down the walls, along with smoke boxes, boilers, and mammoth-sized tools. Babbitt and lead vats smoldered, their smells acrid in the still evening air.

He stepped into the light just as Barney came from behind a drill press. He came with murder in his eyes, the full force of his weight, and hit Hook in his midsection. Pain exploded up Hook's rib cage, and his lungs emptied. His P.38 spun out onto the machine-shop floor.

Barney, stinking of sour and whiskey, buried his head into Hook's belly. His hat fell away as he struggled to tip Hook off-balance, shoving him back again and again with his legs. Sweat soaked the collar of his shirt and glistened on his neck.

Hook squared off to counter the attack. Barney fought to encircle him, to crush him into submission, but the booze had taken its toll.

Hook thrust Barney back on his heels. "It's time for a fishing lesson," he said.

Barney snarled, and he charged in again and then again. But with each failed attempt, his strength lessened, and his determination waned. He gasped for air, and his eyes rolled as he struggled to focus on Hook.

Each time, Hook countered the attack, sidestepping, moving just out of reach, forcing him to expend his energy even more. Water dripped from Barney's nose, and his face reddened in the yellow lights of the shop.

Gathering up his resolve, Barney rushed Hook full bore. But this time Hook came in straight and yanked his prosthesis up into Barney's crotch. Barney's eyes widened, and his scream reverberated within the confines of the machine shop. Hook leaned in close to Barney's ear.

"First, bait the hook," he said.

Hook cuffed Barney and rolled him onto his back. Barney pulled his knees into his stomach and issued strange barking noises. Spittle drooled from his mouth, and his face churned with blood.

Hook searched him for a weapon and found a pistol tucked in his belt. He wondered why carry a firearm and not use it? But when he held the weapon under the lights, he understood why. No *sane* man draws a Roy Rogers cap gun in the middle of a fight.

When Frenchy coupled in, Hook rolled out of the bunk, his ribs protesting. He'd spent the better part of the night getting Barney situated in the local jail. The cops pointed out that anything more serious than resisting-arrest charges would probably be in vain, since toting a Roy Rogers cap pistol failed the attempted-murder charge even in Texas. They further advised that blaming the incident on some blue flag, or even a red flag for that matter, would most likely result in a jury laughing off its collective ass.

Hook declined Frenchy's invitation to ride in the engine cab, deciding instead to stay in the caboose. Frenchy shrugged and lit up his cigar.

"I ain't stopping for that dang dog, Hook. If he falls off, it's just good-bye Mixer."

"Mixer's been riding this caboose damn near as long as you've been railroading and without half the complaining."

"And I ain't hauling dead bodies up and down the line no more either," he said. "You want to ride my train, you have to be alive."

"Tell that to the bakehead," Hook said.

"And this here train don't go into Carmen, as you know."

"Side me off in Avard. And while you're at it, maybe you can arrange for the Frisco to take me on into Carmen. I hear they're less particular about helping a man out."

"That's 'cause hauling wheat cars back and forth fifty miles a day with a bobtail don't make for a real railroad."

"Right," Hook said. "When you coming back through?"

"You wanting a free ride home, too, I suppose?"

"I don't know yet how long this is going to take. I'll check in with Popeye from time to time. In the meantime, maybe you can side me off someplace quiet in Avard."

Frenchy puffed on his cigar. "There ain't no other kind of place *in* Avard," he said.

Hook slept for a couple of hours, secure in the clack of the wheels as Frenchy's steamer lumbered through the night. When he woke, he climbed into the cupola to see if he could make out their location. The sky spilled over with stars, and the moon sat on the horizon like a fat pumpkin, but not a sign or light to place him in the world.

He rubbed at the soreness in his ribs and made a mental note to never climb under another engine for any reason whatsoever.

He wondered if Jackie had made it home, and if she had, whether she would stay there. Her infatuation with Barney's big talk might well draw her back into a life of crime.

He figured that Barney, too, would soon enough return to business as usual. But unlike some crooks Hook had encountered on the rails, Barney's taste for violence didn't extend much beyond moving stop-flags and brandishing his Roy Rogers cap gun.

Even though moving that flag could have been lethal, he figured Barney's actions stemmed more from panic than intent to murder. After all, no one carried a cap pistol for anything more than a prop. In the end, the more disturbing proposition for Hook lay in the likelihood that whoever took that potshot at him still remained at large.

There'd been no shortage of enemies for Hook over the years, and they never made life easy. But at least he'd known who they were and what their motivations might be. In this case, he knew neither.

When they'd stopped at Avard, Frenchy said, "A Frisco switch engine comes in for those wheat cars over there in the mornings. Without an order the engineer can't legally run you into Carmen. Been my experience that it's hell seeing past the third hopper car, though."

"There's a rule against hopping trains, Frenchy, or didn't you know?"

"I got to go before this gets any deeper," Frenchy said. "I'll be in touch."

Hook stood on the platform and watched Frenchy's engine disappear. Mixer jumped down and headed off into the weeds. He circled wide, marking his territory as he went. The afternoon sun beat down, and heat waves quivered up from the tracks.

Mixer soon returned, his tongue hanging out. Hook filled his food and water dishes and set them outside near the casket. Mixer lapped his water before curling up in the shade.

From the siding, Hook could see the wheat elevators, concrete fortresses rising into the sky. Beyond them sat the sparc buildings of Avard, a town failed from the Depression and the ravages of tornadoes, hell-bent screamers that bore in with regularity to destroy everything in their paths. Each time, the residents rebuilt the town, only for it to be torn asunder once again. Now, no one any longer cared.

Hook dug the Bronze Star out of the shoe box he kept pushed behind the coal stove. Dropping it in his pocket, he headed for town. Main Street, being no more than a dirt road a couple blocks long, had a general store at its end. A small hotel stood across the street, a structure built so close to the tracks that the railroad mounted its mail hook just outside the back door. By not making a full stop, the railroad saved both fuel and time for more important stops farther along the way.

Next to the hotel, a tin shed leaned to the south, the remains of a once-active blacksmith shop. The door hung at an angle from the top hinge, and a streak of light shot through the hole in the roof.

Hook peered into the blackness and could see the anvil still mounted on a walnut stump and the forge with remnants of cinders in its hearth. The smell of heat and sweat still resided in the soot and in the packed-earth floor.

A sign on the front door of the hotel read EAT. Hook dusted off his britches and went in. A single light shone from the kitchen, and a fan hummed from an opened window. He found a booth, its vinyl cover cracked with age and wear, and sat down.

A little girl in the back booth, ten or eleven, he calculated, sucked on a straw to make noises with her drink. Her yellow hair lay in matted curls about her face, and a wad of bubble gum clung to the side of her empty plate.

Bobbing her foot, she relocated her straw in the ice and sucked up the last of the contents. She wore oxford slippers with scuffed toes, and her socks drooped from weakened elastic. A scab on her knee, the size of a half-dollar, testified to some recent mishap. She watched Hook through her hair.

The cook, a woman in her fifties, ducked her head under the serving window.

"What will you have?" she asked.

"Burger and fries," Hook said. "Coke."

She turned to her stove without answering. Hook looked around for something to read, finding an auction bill lying on top of the high chair next to the front door. He searched in vain for books.

Pretty soon the little girl got up, went into the kitchen, and came back with her glass refilled. She sat in the booth, her chin in her hand, and nursed the straw.

The cook arrived with his burger, a mountain of fries, ketchup, and a bottle of Tabasco. Lines drew at the corners of her eyes, and her hands shook with tremor.

"Anything else?" she asked, writing out his ticket.

"No, thanks," Hook said. "What's going on in town tonight?"

She tore off his ticket and dropped it on the table. "Oh, just the normal things, a parade at six and then a ball after. We're expecting the king and queen to show up about seven."

"Right," Hook said, turning to his burger, which tasted as good as anything he'd eaten in a month, including the Harvey House fare.

By the time he tabbed out, the sun had slipped lower on the horizon. He paused outside to watch a westbound thunder by. It rattled the front windows of the hotel and sent dust spiraling off down Main.

He walked toward the caboose, taking his time to enjoy the quiet and peace. Iron-red hills jutted into the sunset, and a flock of blackbirds banked away like kamikazes. He stopped and lit a cigarette, and that's when he noticed her standing back a hundred feet or so behind him. She still carried her drink and had transferred her bubble gum from plate to mouth.

Hook went on to the caboose and sat down on the steps. She stopped at a distance, but when Mixer joined him, she idled on up to the caboose.

"Hello," Hook said.

"Hello."

"You live here?"

She nodded. "My name's Bet Haimes. That was my daddy's name. I live with my grandma at the hotel. Sometimes I'm the waitress when she gets sick."

"That so?" he said.

"What's your name?" she asked.

"Hook."

"Oh. Is that your dog?"

"His name's Mixer."

"That's a funny name," she said. "I had a cat named Felix, but the train ran over him. I found his tail."

"That's too bad," he said.

"Yeah. Did a train run over your arm?"

"No."

She stretched her bubble gum out and ate it back to her fingers. "What's in the box?"

Hook turned. "That?"

"Yeah."

"Well, that's a body," he said.

"What's its name?"

"Samuel Ash."

She took Mixer's ear and felt the scars in it.

"His ears are icky."

"He likes to fight," Hook said.

She sat down next to Hook on the steps and bobbed her legs.

"You smoke a lot, don't you?" she said.

"It's a bad habit."

"Yeah. What are you going to do with Samuel Ash?"

"I'm taking him home to Carmen soon as I find his people."

"One time I hid in the culvert under the tracks when the train went over," she said.

"That's dangerous," he said.

"Yeah."

She climbed up on the caboose porch and looked at the casket.

"Does Samuel Ash want to go home?"

"Everyone wants to go home," he said.

"I don't," she said. "That's why I live with my grandma." She wiped at her nose. "How do you know Samuel Ash is in there?"

"Why wouldn't he be?"

She climbed down. "I don't know. I got to go now and help Grandma with the dishes."

"Listen," he said, "I'm going on to Carmen tomorrow and will be gone a few days. Do you think you could feed and water Mixer for me?"

"For a dollar," she said.

"Okay, for a dollar. I'll leave the door to the caboose open."

"Are you taking Samuel Ash?"

"Not yet. You don't have to be afraid."

"I'm not," she said, turning. "Bye, Hook. Bye, Mixer. Bye, Samuel Ash."

23

Hook WAITED BY the grain elevator until the next to the last hopper car rolled by before he swung up on the ladder. He crawled into the opening over the trailing wheel truck and secured a place to sit. While not the most comfortable spot to ride, he didn't have that far to go.

The old switch engine chugged downline at a slow clip. Within a few minutes, they'd moved into the countryside, an expanse of wheat fields reaching to the horizons. The wheat, nearing harvest time, rippled off in waves of gold from the train's turbulence. Soon combines would move in like giant insects and chew their way across the landscape.

Within the hour, the short haul approached Carmen, and the engineer blew his whistle. From where Hook sat, he could see the elevators rising into the blue sky. The train slowed, and Hook maneuvered to the side of the hopper car to bail off.

A great building rose up to the north, a grand and elegant structure isolated from the town proper. A sign out front read, SPIRIT OF AGAPE ORPHANAGE.

Hook counted four floors, including the basement, and, sitting atop of it all, a turret with windows encircling its circumference. Steps, bolstered by Greek columns, ran from ground level to the first floor, where a carved wooden door awaited entry.

A picketed balcony rested atop the columns, with the entire structure repeating itself and extending yet again to the next floor. In spite of the building's splendor, no life moved about in the yard, and the windows lay darkened and gloomy.

Behind the house, a dairy barn stretched the length of the grounds. Its cedar roof sported two cupolas, and a half-dozen bay windows ran down its length. Two silos with conical tops rose from the barn's east end, and the entire southern exposure opened onto a maze of corrals churning with matched Holstein cows.

As the short haul slowed to uncouple the hoppers at the grain elevator, Hook jumped off and headed into town. A filling station sat on the corner across from the newspaper office, and down the street, a small grocery store touted sale prices in its window. A cobbler's shop, with weathered sign, huddled near the back of the end lot. The town café, funeral parlor, and a beer joint with painted windows made up the remainder of downtown. A block over, three church steeples all rose up within shouting range of heaven.

Hook found the proprietor of the filling station sitting out front on a bus seat that had been bolted to the concrete drive. His hat bill, covered with greasy fingerprints, stuck out over one ear. He clamped an RC Cola between his legs and poured a package of peanuts into its neck.

When he looked up, he said, "Toilet's around back. There ain't no paper, though. Damn kids plug up the stool."

"Thanks, anyway," Hook said. "I thought you might give me some information."

He tipped up his RC and maneuvered some of the peanuts into his mouth. He chewed, pushed his glasses up onto his nose, and took a long look at Hook.

"What happened to your arm?" he asked.

Hook held up his good hand, which still bore cuts from his scrap with Barney.

"A little misunderstanding," he said.

The proprietor took another swig of his RC and said, "The other one."

Hook turned over his prosthesis. "Hardly skinned it up at all," he said.

"Say, you ain't one of them goddang carnies from the state fair, are you?"

"I'm the Santa Fe railroad bull, which comes mighty close to the same thing," he said.

"The hell?"

"Have you lived in these parts long?" Hook asked.

"Long enough," he said.

"You ever know a fellow by the name of Samuel Ash?"

He took another pull of his RC and set the bottle next to him on the bench.

"I knew a Samuel Newsome, 'fore he died of the lockjaw. They fed him gravy with an eyedropper, but it didn't make no difference."

"Do you know anyone who might know?"

"Well, there's Patch Hunter, the cobbler over there. He's lived here since the parting of the sea. According to Patch, there ain't much he doesn't know.

"Then there's Juice Dawson, the digger. In the end, no one gets by him. And course you got Doc Tooney. Doc's probably pulled a couple thousand squealers into this world over the years. In the day, wasn't nothing for a woman to shell out ten, fifteen kids for helping out with the harvesting and chores."

"Thanks," Hook said.

The proprietor ducked his chin. "Name's Bill," he said.

Hook held up his prosthesis. "Hook Runyon."

"You come sit in the afternoon anytime you take a notion, Hook. My oil changing's in the mornings."

"Thanks, maybe I will."

Hook found Doc Tooney's office, a remodeled bungalow, two blocks down from the funeral home. Unwilling to complicate matters just yet, Hook passed up the funeral home until a later time. Once he'd identified Samuel Ash's kin, then he'd contact the mortician. At this point, getting a professional involved could only tangle things.

"Doc Tooney's not in," the nurse said. "Is it an emergency?"

"I'm trying to find the relatives of a Samuel Ash," Hook said. "I thought the doctor might be able to help me."

"Sorry," she said. "The doctor's not feeling well, so he went to see the doctor over in Cherokee. Should be back after lunch."

"Second opinion?" Hook asked.

She frowned. "Excuse me?"

"Have *you* ever heard of Samuel Ash?"

She clicked her pencil against her teeth. "No. No Samuel Ash. We had a Samuel Newsome, but he's dead now."

"Maybe I'll come back later," he said.

"Hang on," she said. Going to the file cabinet, she thumbed through a few of the folders and then shook her head. "No. You might try Patch down at the shoe shop. Patch is an expert on about everything."

"Thanks," Hook said.

Patch Hunter's cobbler shop looked like something out of the nineteenth century. There were pinchers and pliers of every imaginable shape lined on the wall over the workbench. On the other wall hung awls, hammers, knives, and wooden shoe stretchers. Great treadle sewing machines, hole punchers, and buffing wheels sat about everywhere. There were balls of thread, piles of tailings, and sheets of cow leather, calf leather, and sheepskin. There were buffing wheels, vises, nippers, tacks, pots of glue, waxes, and saddle soaps. The smells of leather and shoe polishes permeated the air. An artist's easel sat near the back of the shop with a partial pencil sketch propped on it.

A tall man stood at the high workbench pounding nails into the heel of a shoe. He wore a leather apron that hung to his knees. The apron shined where his ample belly had rubbed it smooth against the workbench over the years. The tacks in his mouth were nearly hidden in the thick of his handlebar mustache. He pushed his glasses up and took out the tacks one by one and laid them on the bench.

Hook waited until he'd finished. "Are you Patch Hunter by chance?"

"That would be me," he said, laying down his hammer. "You must be that feller rode in on the grain hopper."

"How'd you know that?"

"Saw you jump off the train on my way in to the shop. I hear you're looking for someone by the name of Samuel Ash?"

"Right again," Hook said.

"Bill at the filling station said a one-armed man had been asking about a Samuel Ash. Not hard to figure. There's rare few one-armed men in Carmen riding in on a grain hopper."

"Can you help me out?"

Patch ran his hand into the shoe to check for nail points.

"There's no Samuel Ash in Carmen," he said. "Never has been. Now, we had a Samuel Newsome, but he died of tetanus when a rat bit him on the finger while he scooped wheat out of his granary into that old Chevy truck of his. He paid too much for that truck, you know. It had over a hundred thousand when he bought it. That's a hell of a lot of miles for a wheat truck. They sit most the year, so you got to figure how old that damn truck must have been.

"Anyway, Sam had a son named Roy, or so he thought, but everyone figured Roy's real father to be Ben Clemson, the veterinarian over to Cherokee. Ben cut Samuel's bore hogs every season. But squealing pigs gave Samuel migraine headaches, so he always came to town to shoot pool when Ben showed up. Some say Samuel got more services than he paid for, if you know what I mean.

"So when Samuel Newsome died from lockjaw, Roy went off to vet school like his real father had, but then he flunked chemistry three semesters in a row. He's the city plumber now and a damn poor one.

"But there's no Samuel Ash in Carmen and never has been."

"Maybe I'll check the cemetery," Hook said.

"You can do that, I suppose. There's two of 'em you know, the city cemetery and the orphanage cemetery outside of town. Putting that orphanage cemetery out there just wasted good wheat land if you ask me. Guess they didn't approve of them kids being buried with the town folks. But either way, you ain't going to find no Samuel Ash.

"Course, you could always talk to Juice Dawson, the undertaker. Juice figures himself to be an important man in these parts. He sits on the orphanage board and the school board and any other board he can find will take him. Picks up a little business that way."

"He's on my list," Hook said.

"Know why they call him Juice, don't you? He drinks a quart of apple juice every morning for breakfast. Says it keeps him regular. What he don't tell you is he eats a half-pound of cheddar cheese for lunch every day, sharp cheddar he gets over to the grocery and at a dang high price. Lord knows what would happen if he'd miss a dose of juice someday."

"Right. Well, thanks for the help."

"Guess you'll be needing a place to stay. The Frisco don't make that Avard run but once a week, you know. Course, you could always stay with Mamie Stokes. She rents her upstairs out, but she won't take less than a month's rent. I figure you ain't interested in staying in Carmen any longer than necessary."

"Well, I haven't thought that far ahead," Hook said.

"I got a room in the back, five a week. Course, there's no bathroom, but the city park's just across the street. They don't lock the bathroom up anymore since Samuel Newsome died. He used to peek through the exhaust fan and watch the girls. And there's a shower, too, though it don't have hot water since the harvest crews left it running and cost the city two hundred and fifteen dollars in electricity and water bills."

Hook walked to the window. From there he could see the line of hoppers waiting to be unloaded at the elevator.

"I'm going to take you up on that, Patch," he said, reaching for his billfold. "Here's a week."

Patch folded the fiver into his pocket. "I'll leave the back door unlocked. I got a boy, Skink, opens up for me, so you might not want to shoot him with that gun you're carrying there. He cleans the shop early. Skink's an apprentice, I guess you'd say, though all he thinks about is girls and eating. Grew up out there in the Spirit of Agape Orphanage. He's turning eighteen, and they're fixing to kick him out. Says he wants to be a cobbler, but mostly there just ain't nothing else around here, and he's too dang skinny for the army."

Hook started at the west side and worked his way to the wheat field on the east. Just like Patch had said, he could find nothing to suggest that Samuel Ash or any other Ash had ever lived in Carmen. The whole process took longer than he'd anticipated, since the epitaphs turned out to be an unexpected distraction for him. Something about them drew him in.

After picking up a couple of candy bars at the grocery, he walked to the north side of town and then out on the road leading to the orphanage cemetery. SPIRIT OF AGAPE CEMETERY had been painted on the metal archway leading into the grounds.

Inside, the road made a full circle. Headstones, adhering to the road's shape, formed a ring. Modest stones cropped from the grass, while yet others bore only brass markers. On the far side, he found no graves at all. One area had been recently dug for dirt, which served as fill for dressing out settled graves.

Unlike most of the headstones in the city's cemetery, the orphanage epitaphs contained no personal messages, no LOVING DAUGHTERS, or GONE BUT NOT FORGOTTEN, or OUR LITTLE ANGEL. Instead, they touted the perils of a misguided life: NOT MY WILL BUT THINE BE DONE; LET HIS OWN WORKS PRAISE HIM AT THE GATES; LIFE IS NOT FOREVER.

Afterward, Hook stood at the gate and looked out over the landscape. The evening settled in, and the buzz of locusts rose and fell from the cedars that had been planted along the drive. Patch had been right. Nothing in either cemetery suggested that Samuel Ash had ever lived in Carmen.

He clicked on the light in his room. The space, not much larger than a closet, had been furnished with a bunk, bedside table, and a single straight-backed kitchen chair. Absent of windows, the room had only a single door at the back, which led into the shoe shop.

He undressed, laid his clothes across the chair, and slipped under the covers. The candy bars he'd eaten had long since disappeared, and his stomach now growled in protest.

For some time he lay awake in the darkness considering the possibilities. If Samuel Ash never lived here, why did he list it as his hometown when he joined the army? If he never lived here, where *did* he live? And why would he lie about it in the first place?

Pulling the blanket up around his neck, he listened to the cricket that had tuned up outside his door. He hoped that little Bet had fed Mixer as she'd promised. He hoped that the caboose and casket were still secured. But most of all he hoped he'd not hauled Samuel Ash to a place where he didn't even belong.

24

Hook CRAWLED OUT of bed and rubbed the sleep from his face. He needed to shower, but without windows in the room, he couldn't be certain of the time. In any case, he wanted to scour the town again, see if anyone knew of Samuel Ash.

After dressing and putting on his prosthesis, he checked the door to the shop, finding it unlocked. He could see a boy at the front of the shop sitting at Patch's desk with his head on his arms.

Hook made his way through the network of machines and said, "Hello."

The boy jumped straight up out of the chair.

"Holy shit," he said, wiping the drool from his chin. "Who are you?"

"Hook Runyon. I'm renting the room back there. Didn't mean to startle you."

"Just resting my eyes," he said. "Patch didn't tell me he'd rented out the room."

The boy appeared shorter than he was, slumping at the shoulders and burying his hands under his arms. Though he had ample hair on his head, he'd slicked it back with oil to form a helmet.

In the absence of body hair, his skin shined under the light, and his eyes, little more than black dots, stared out from under hairless brows. A weak chin failed to separate his neck from his face, and his mouth stretched in a thin line beneath a spade-like nose.

"You must be Skink," Hook said.

"How'd you know?" he said.

"Just a guess."

"Yeah," he said. "I'm Patch's apprentice. Mostly I just listen and clean up."

"It's steady work, I suppose," Hook said. "You out of school?"

He nodded his head. "Graduated in May. The orphanage's going to kick me out come my eighteenth birthday. I'd figured on joining the army, but, what with the war over, they're a bit more particular now. So I'm thinking maybe I can open up a cobbler shop somewhere."

Hook said, "How long you been at the orphanage?"

Skink licked his lips and rubbed at his elbow, which looked like the business end of a navel orange.

"Long as I can remember," he said. "A drunk found me in a trash can a few hours after I was born. At first, he thought to kill me with a stick, thinking I might be a rat or a blind kitten, but then I started mewling.

"Anyway, the police brought me to the Spirit of Agape Orphanage. They took me in, figuring I'd die soon enough anyway, but Miss Eldridge, the matron, put me in a shoe box, set it on the oven door, and fed me goat's milk. I lived, as you can see, though Miss Eldridge died of the tick fever last summer."

"Sorry to hear that."

"They have a new matron now, Miss Feola. She don't look like Miss Eldridge. I seen her come out of the shower one day, by mistake, and my heart nearly stalled."

"I know the feeling," Hook said, taking out a cigarette. "Care for a smoke?"

"I only smoke Cuban cigars," he said.

"You like it at the orphanage?" Hook asked.

"That's sure a funny-looking arm," he said. "Does it work?"

"In a fashion," Hook said, picking up a pencil off the desk. "It doesn't do so well for holding hands."

Skink picked up his broom and leaned forward on the handle. "They got a rule out there for everything," he said. "A body can't breathe without a rule, and, if it's broken, the superintendent don't let it pass."

"What's his name?"

"Bain Eagleman."

"What kind of punishment does he hand out?"

"Walking the circle, mostly."

"The circle?"

"The road in the orphanage cemetery, round and round until Mr. Eagleman says stop. I've wondered how many of those graves out there were kids who just fell over dead from walking the circle.

"And then there's Buck, the farm foreman. He's got a room out in the barn. Mr. Eagleman says it's good for kids to raise their own food, especially kids living off the public dole. Makes 'em respect what's given to 'em free of charge.

"The boys do the milking and mucking out the barn. The girls do the gardening and canning. Bessie Roper canned a green frog one time. When Miss Eldridge opened a jar of jam for breakfast, she wet her pants. I think Bessie's still out there walking the circle.

"There's no pleasing Buck, though, no matter. He yells and cusses and cracks his cow whip all the time. He popped Jim Stoop's earlobe off with that whip. The cook sewed it back on with catgut, so it didn't hurt nothing, I guess.

"Buck said Jim Stoop got between him and a contrary milk cow, and he didn't see that earlobe until the whip had already left the station. I never believed it."

"What's an orphanage doing with a foreman?" Hook asked.

"He ain't no real foreman, though he sure thinks so. He milks the cows, mows the grass, and hauls out the trash. Sometimes he spies on the kids who are walking the circle and then tells Mr. Eagleman if they don't finish. One night he spied on me, but I saw him. So when he left, I followed him back. He went into Mr. Eagleman's office just like I thought. When he came out, he had Mr. Eagleman's trash can."

"You said he took care of the trash."

"Yeah, but then he went through it and stuck something in his pocket. I think he takes stuff doesn't belong to him sometimes."

Hook searched out a chair. Dusting off the toe of his shoe, he said, "Did you ever know a Samuel Ash, Skink?"

Skink got up and made a couple swipes at the floor with his broom.

"Knew a Samuel Newsome. He used to watch the girls in the park shower."

"I mean at the orphanage."

"Kids come and go at the orphanage. Lots of them were just left behind by folks. Sometimes the parents start feeling guilty or sober up and come back to claim their young. Sometimes kids just run away, I seen lots of that. And the orphanage don't go looking that hard, 'cause of the expense, Mr. Eagleman says. Says it takes food right out of the mouths of everyone else. Says runaways deserve whatever happens to them, even if they wind up dead in a bar ditch. Says they didn't care what their running away did to hurt everyone else so to hell with them."

Skink pushed the trash can to the side and swept under Patch's desk. "I never heard of no Samuel Ash, though," he said.

The next morning, after yet another lost day, Hook looked up Skink, who had fallen asleep in the channel of light that shot through the front window. He woke him up and inquired about a shower.

Skink found him a towel and a bar of soap. "Park's over there," he said.

"Thanks," Hook said.

"You going to shower with your arm on?"

"A man's got to keep clean, doesn't he?" Hook said.

"Don't it rust up?"

"Not if the oil's changed regular."

"Samuel Newsome showed me how to look at the girls through the exhaust fan one time. I didn't see nothing but Mildred Bonfield's big butt." Skink shrugged. "It's cold water, you know, and there's roaches big as yard gophers. They say one carried off Ben Hosier's wiener dog. He never did find him."

"I carry a sidearm," Hook said.

Skink stuck his hands in his pockets. "You going to tell Patch about me sleeping on the job?"

"Patch strikes me as hard to stop once his button's pushed," Hook said. "I guess I won't push it."

Skink grinned. "You want help finding that Samuel Ash, just say so. I know every hiding place in this town."

After his shower, Hook headed for the Spirit of Agape Orphanage. The sun lit the treetops and set the sparrows to skittering from limb to limb. From there, he could see the orphanage looming at the end of the road like an old fortress.

He planned to talk to the superintendent, who might have records that would help him locate Samuel Ash. If he could get no help there, he'd check in with the town cop. Small-town cops often knew the ins and outs of family histories, who was cheating on whom, who owed whom money, and who nurtured what grudges over the years.

Hook had no reason to believe that Samuel Ash had ever been in trouble. And it struck him as unlikely that a Bronze Star recipient would wind up on the wrong side of the law. But then again, exceptions to the rule were not all that exceptional when it came to lawbreakers. Some of the orneriest bastards he'd known on the rails could show uncommon courage when things turned hard.

Hook stopped at the bottom of the steps leading up to the main landing of the orphanage. A pickup pulled out from the rear of the building and backed up to a brick incinerator that had been constructed near the fence line. A man in a cowboy hat got out and threw several bags of trash into it.

After taking a chew, he climbed back in and pulled off down the drive, turning to look at Hook as he went by.

Hook rang the doorbell twice before an older woman opened up. Her hair had been lifted into a high bun on the top of her head, and a food-spattered apron covered her from neck to knees.

"Yes," she said.

"My name is Hook Runyon. I wonder if I might speak with the superintendent?"

"I'm just the cook around here, as you can see. There's a board meeting starting up, I'd guess, given Mr. Eagleman ordered food on top of everything else I've got to do. You never know how long it's going to last, do you? I never knew men had such important business to tend to."

"I'm the Santa Fe bull. This is an official call."

"Come on in," she said. "You can ask him yourself. His office is upstairs, second door on the right."

"Thanks," he said.

She stopped at the bottom of the stairs. "If those men had to fix meals for all these kids, with nothing but lovesick girls for helping out, they'd be a little more considerate about what they ask for."

"Thanks, again," Hook said.

When she'd gone, Hook climbed to the landing and looked down over the railing. The dining area had an oak table that stretched the length of the room. Wooden, straight-backed chairs lined the table on both sides. Large windows, bare of curtains and mounted high up on the wall, shed little light into the dimness of the room.

He found the office door ajar and a man pouring a glass of water from a pitcher that sat on top of an old safe under the window. A row of filing cabinets ran the length of the office wall. Hook knocked, and the man looked at him over his shoulder.

"Mr. Bain Eagleman?" Hook asked.

"Yes," he said.

"My name is Hook Runyon. I'm the Santa Fe railroad bull. Could I speak to you for a moment?"

Eagleman set his water on his desk, an enormous flattop desk with nothing on it but a telephone, an opened calendar, and a wide-brimmed fedora.

Transparent eyes, like blue glass, leveled in on Hook. A strand of hair dropped down on Eagleman's forehead, and he pushed it aside with his fingers.

"There's a board meeting in progress, Mr. uh . . ."

"Runyon."

"Mr. Runyon, if this is about a child, you need to speak with Miss Feola, our matron, at the end of the hall."

"No. It isn't that," Hook said. "Another time then."

Eagleman stepped from behind the desk, much larger and older than Hook had first thought. He wore a spare black suit with notched lapels, white shirt, wide tie, and highly polished wing-tip shoes. His weak stomach suggested a man well into middle age.

"We operate by appointment here at Agape. Perhaps a call first would save you a trip."

"Right, I'll be sure and do that," Hook said, closing the door behind him.

He stood for a moment to let the heat in his neck dissipate. He had a low tolerance for pompous bastards, even when they came wearing suits. Being dismissed by one didn't rank high on his feel-good list. But then maybe Eagleman's job required a high degree of self-importance. Running a place like Agape couldn't be easy.

The hall stretched off in both directions with only a single window at each end to light it. Buildings, like people, had a way about them. This one struck him as too clean and too organized. Given children lived here, it lacked life: no toys, no clothes left about, no arguments in progress.

Hook decided to take a quick look around before heading back to town. Perhaps he could find out about Samuel Ash from someone else, someone in authority like Miss Feola.

He had just lifted his prosthesis to knock, when the door opened, and a young woman stood foursquare in front of him with a hammer in her hand.

"Oh," she said.

"I may look like Captain Hook, but we're only namesakes," he said.

"Oh, my," she said. "You startled me. I was just going to hang my office sign."

The secretary looked up from her desk, checked out Hook's prosthesis, and returned to her papers.

"I'm Hook Runyon," he said. "Are you Miss Feola?"

"Yes, Celia Feola," she said. "I'm the matron here."

"I'm the Santa Fe railroad bull and would like to visit with you about a case."

She laid her hammer and sign on the chair next to the door and straightened her skirt.

"What kind of case would that be?"

"Could we talk in private, Miss Feola?"

She placed a finger at the corner of her mouth as if to accentuate the curve of her lip. Her auburn hair, nearly the exact color of her eyes, lit in the sunlight that struck through the hall window. A small cupped scar interrupted the sweep of an otherwise perfect widow's peak. For a woman so tall and willowy, ample breasts were evident beneath her blouse, and her skin, as transparent as candle wax, had somehow escaped the harshness of the prairie sun.

"I'm sorry, Mr. Runyon. I'm expecting an appointment at any moment. Perhaps you could come back another time?"

"I'm trying to locate the relatives of a Samuel Ash. Maybe you've heard of him?"

She lifted her chin. "No, but then I've just arrived myself, you see. If you could come back, say, tomorrow afternoon around two, I'd be happy to speak with you."

"One question," Hook said. "Where are all the children?"

"Most of them attend the public school," she said. "They won't be back for several hours yet."

"I see," he said. "Tomorrow, then."

Without reading material or company, Hook decided a little Beam might be in order to pass away the evening. The package store, tucked away behind the filling station, turned out to be a little building no larger than a bathroom. He bought a half-pint of Beam, ignoring the owner's stare as he counted out the change with his prosthesis. On his way out the door, he flipped a penny up, snatched it from the air with his prosthesis, and dropped it into his pocket.

The shoe shop had yet to close, so he went in the front and found Patch gluing on half soles to a pair of work boots.

"There you are," Patch said. "I thought maybe Eagleman had run you off."

"How'd you know I went there?"

"Bill over to the filling station saw you walking down the road. Ain't nothing out there except the orphanage and the cemetery. You likely went to the cemetery already so that left the orphanage; besides, Skink said you showered over to the park. A man doesn't just up and shower for no reason."

Hook watched Patch run the boot sole through the sewing machine with accomplished skill.

"I couldn't get in without an appointment," Hook said.

"Well, I could of told you that if you'd asked. Bain Eagleman wears wing-tip shoes."

"Excuse me?"

"Wing tips ain't casual, but they ain't formal; they ain't neither or both, and the word of a man who wears them can't be much trusted."

"I'm going to bed on that one, Patch."

"And in the morning, you can tell Skink to stop sleeping on the job if he wants to work here."

"How'd you know that?"

Patch turned back to his shoes. "I didn't 'til just now," he said.

Hook found a paper cup in the bedside table and fixed himself a Beam. Having no water, he drank it neat, which in turn emptied the half-pint in short order.

Turning out the lights, he lay in the darkness and considered the day's events. This much he knew: if in fact Samuel Ash had lived here, there might be one or two people who hadn't heard of him. But when no one in town had heard of him, then the mistake had to be his own.

Tomorrow, he'd make a final run at it, check in with the town cop, and then out to the orphanage and Miss Feola. If that didn't pan out, he'd hop the next short haul back to Avard and figure out from there what to do with Samuel Ash.

25

Skink laid down his broom and pointed out the window to the sheriff's office.

"It don't look like it," he said. "But that's where he is when he ain't painting houses. Even when he's on duty, he don't drive around that much. Says the city don't pay enough for him to use his own car and buy his own gas for cruising up and down the street."

Hook pulled up the stool to Patch's workbench.

"By the way, Patch says he doesn't want you sleeping on the job. Says he'll be watching."

Skink picked up his broom and swept at the dirt that had fallen off someone's shoes at the door.

He paused. "I thought you weren't going to say anything about that, Hook."

"Well, I didn't, not exactly. Patch figured it out on his own."

Skink shook his head. "There ain't nothing gets by Patch. He's like a spirit flying over and looking down on everyone all the time."

"Patch doesn't strike me as spiritual, Skink."

Skink pulled at what passed for his chin. "Sometimes in the night, I think I see him standing over my bed. 'Skink,' he says. 'I'm telling Mr. Eagleman about what you're doing under them covers.'"

"Maybe you ought go to sleep when you go to bed, Skink. That way you could stay awake at work."

"It's the only attention I get," he said.

"I'm sure you've had girlfriends, Skink."

"Not so many as you might think," he said.

"Don't you worry, Skink. Someone will come along."

"I sure hope so. I'm dead sick of Patch standing over my bed."

Hook found the sheriff sitting on the steps, leaning back with his legs crossed. He wore cowboy boots with holes in the bottoms.

Shielding his eyes against the sun with his hand, he said, "Yeah, I'm the sheriff. What can I do for you?"

"I'm the Santa Fe bull," Hook said. "Suppose we could talk?"

"Sure," he said. "Come on in. Talk don't cost nothing."

His office and the city utilities office sat side by side in the same building. The jail, no more than a cage, actually, had been welded up from angle iron and fitted into the back room. A thunder pot had been shoved under the bunk.

The sheriff pointed for Hook to sit down.

"So what's the problem?" he asked.

"I've been trying to locate the kin of one Samuel Ash. It's my understanding he once lived here."

The sheriff took off his hat, revealing a sunken place in his skull.

He looked at Hook. "I won't ask about your arm if you don't ask about this hole in my head."

"Deal," Hook said.

"Is there a warrant out on this guy?"

"He's dead. I'm trying to find his people."

The sheriff tossed his hat on his desk. "No Samuel Ash that I ever heard of. We had a Samuel Newsome. Died of tetanus. I got called on that one. Dead as a carp he was, and he had this grin pulled up nearly to his ear, all from that lockjaw, I guess. Just froze up that way. Damndest thing I ever saw."

"Ash," Hook said. "Samuel Ash, a young guy."

"Had to watch old Sam Newsome every minute, you know. He'd stand out there in the park and take a leak where all the girls could see him. If there was ever a son of a bitch what deserved to die with the lockjaw, it had to be Samuel Newsome. But no Samuel Ash ever lived here, that much I can tell you."

"Well, thanks anyway, Sheriff. Guess I have the wrong information."

"You hear of anyone needs their house painted, let me know. This goddang job don't pay squat."

"Right," Hook said.

When the phone rang, the sheriff picked up. "Yeah. No shit," he said. "I'll be on out. Take me about twenty minutes."

When he'd hung up, Hook said, "Problem?"

The sheriff plunked on his hat. "Old lady Engle fell out of her porch swing and broke her leg. I better get on out there. Might have to shoot her."

Hook watched the sheriff pull off. Through the door window, he could see an old man paying his utilities in the adjoining office. The old man adjusted his crotch before leaving.

While he shouldn't be using the sheriff's phone for long-distance calls, Hook supposed it *was* all law business. Might even say he was doing the legwork for the sheriff himself, saving the city money.

He dialed Division and leaned back in his chair. When Eddie answered, Hook said, "Eddie, Runyon here."

"You been on vacation or something, Runyon? I ain't heard a word out of you."

"I've been kind of busy, Eddie. I pulled Moose Barrick in for

derailing cars and stealing freight. Caught the head honcho who has been running the pickpocket scam, and listened to Frenchy bitch for three hundred miles. Other than that, I haven't been doing a damn thing."

"I need you in Wellington. Someone's breaking car seals out there."

Hook ducked down to check the window.

"Someone's always breaking car seals somewhere, Eddie. It's not exactly an emergency. Anyway, I have a hotbox on that junker caboose. I need her towed in and repaired."

"Goddang it, Hook, how come you're always where you ain't needed?"

"I'll have Junior check it out when he comes through Wellington. He's clearing the line back from KC, making sure we've rounded up the last of those pickpockets."

"He's not there to do your job, Runyon. You were supposed to keep him out of trouble, teach him something."

"It will be great experience for the kid."

"I don't want nothing happening to that boy, you hear."

"Why don't you pay off that loan to his old man, Eddie? He's got you by the balls, and you can't stop dancing."

"What loan? What the hell you talking about?"

"I'm not one to preach, Eddie, but there's a rule I live my life by: never a lender nor borrower be. I suggest you think about that. Got to run now, Eddie. There's work to be done."

Hook checked the window once again before dialing Popeye.

"Clovis," Popeye said.

"This is Hook, Popeye."

"When did you get back in town?"

"I'm in Carmen."

"I heard you nailed old Moose."

"That's right."

"The son of a bitch," Popeye said.

"Listen, Popeye, you heard from Junior Monroe?"

"I never did get that money, Hook. Guess you misplaced the address."

"I'll pay you soon as I get back. Jesus, you'd think it was a lot instead of just two dollars, and I always pay you back, don't I?"

"I think it's three, Hook, and mostly you just wait until I forget altogether. You probably owe me a couple of thousand, truth be known."

"About Junior Monroe?"

"Yeah, he called in."

"Well?"

"Says he's thinking about giving up yard dogging after that ride on the stock train to Kansas City. Says he's thinking about not being a persecutor, too."

"Prosecutor," Hook said.

"Whatever. So, I says, 'Yard dogging is less work for the money than about anything else you can do, Junior.'"

"When he calls in, tell him someone's busting car seals over in Wellington. I need him to check it out."

"I'll tell him."

"And I'll get that two dollars to you soon, Popeye. Don't you worry about a thing."

Miss Feola's secretary looked up. "Mr. Runyon," she said. "Miss Feola is expecting you. Please go on in."

A crucifix hung on the wall behind Miss Feola's head, like the rising sun, and a Roman missal lay open on her desk.

Her hair, pulled back in a bun, highlighted the perfection of her widow's peak. The room smelled of incense, sandalwood maybe. She stood and reached for his hand.

"Mr. Runyon, my apologies for not being able to see you yesterday."

"I should have called," he said.

"Please, sit."

He pulled up a chair and dropped his prosthesis below the rim of the desk.

"You've only just arrived at Agape, then?" he asked.

"Yes. I'm from the East, actually, Italian, as you probably have surmised from my name. I'm still trying to find my way around."

Hook reached for his cigarettes and then put them back into his pocket.

"And did you work for an orphanage back East?"

She smiled, a smile that lit up her eyes. "I lived in a nunnery there. I found I didn't have the temperament for such a life. This work struck me as a logical alternative, though I failed to imagine how different living in a small town could be."

"I'll be damned, a nunnery."

"And you're the Santa Fe railroad bull?"

"That's right," he said.

"And have you always been a railroad bull?"

"No, I was a baby for a while, but folks don't much take to babies with hooks."

She looked at him, her brow furrowed. "Really."

"So I took up bumming on the rails. Had the temperament for it alright, but the pay didn't work out."

"So that's how you became a railroad bull?"

"It was either that or being the president," he said. "And that job had been taken."

"I've never known a railroad bull," she said.

"We don't hang out at nunneries much."

She folded her hands in front of her. "Are you ever serious, Mr. Runyon?"

"It's Hook," he said. "And I'm dead serious about finding Samuel Ash's people. I had been led to believe he lived here in Carmen at one time. So far I have found no one who ever heard of him. I thought to come here on the outside chance of a lead."

"Well, I took the opportunity to speak with Mr. Eagleman, the cook, and Buck, the farm manager. None has heard of a Samuel Ash. I'm sorry we can be of no help."

"Have they all been here awhile?"

"Why, no. The cook came on just before me. It's my understanding that Mr. Eagleman and Buck have been here for many years."

"Skink tells me the turnover in children is considerable."

"Yes, you could say that. It *is* an orphanage."

"It's possible they may have forgotten this Samuel Ash, then?"

"Possible, I suppose, but it hardly seems likely."

"Perhaps there are records we could check?"

She placed her chin in her hand and dropped a finger across her lips.

"There are records, of course, but confidential. Mr. Eagleman secures the files in his office. The records are private, as you must appreciate. Like I said, this is an orphanage, Mr. Runyon, and these children have been placed here for many reasons, some of which are quite sensitive. While under our care, their privacy has to be protected. Even *my* access is limited to certain background information."

She looked at her watch. "I'm sorry we were unable to help. Now, if you'll excuse me, I have an appointment in Avard and need to get there before dark."

"Avard?"

"That's right. Do you know it?"

Hook stood. "I'm living there, temporarily, I mean. In fact, I'm hopping a short haul back today, providing there's one headed out."

"Short haul?"

"An engine with a few cars in tow going a short distance."

"You jump on them?"

"Something like that."

"But isn't it dangerous?"

"Only if you fall off," he said. "Thank you for your time, Miss Feola."

She came around the desk. "Celia, please. Mr. Runyon, Hook, I'm taking the orphanage car over now. Perhaps you'd like a lift? I'd hate being responsible for you falling off a short haul."

"I'd hate that myself," he said. "You mind telling me why you're going there? There's not much happening in Avard as I recall."

"Well, I suppose I could say since you *are* with the law, aren't you?"

"More or less," he said.

"Welfare is meeting me there with a young girl who has been orphaned. She lived with her grandmother who died a few days ago from a stroke. She has no place to go. They've asked that we take her in until things can be sorted out. I'm picking her up and bringing her back here to the orphanage."

Hook stood. "Do you know her name?"

"Why, yes," she said. "It's Bet, I believe. Bet Haimes."

26

CELIA ADJUSTED THE car seat and stretched a trim leg for the gas pedal and sighed. "Why is it men think it's their privilege to leave the toilet seat up and the car seat back?"

Hook rolled the window down. "It's a problem I haven't given much thought," he said. "Consider the toilet seat. There's two choices as I see it: it's either left up or it's left down. Leaving it up could result in a certain amount of distress and effort for those who follow, I suppose. However, knowing the poor aim of most men, leaving it down might well have a less desirable outcome than putting it up."

She reached for the key and started up the car, looking over her shoulder as she backed out.

When they'd pulled out onto the main road, she said, "There's a third solution here."

Hook looked at her. "I can't figure what?"

"Put the toilet seat up. When finished, put it back down."

Hook pulled at his chin. "I concede to the logic but object to the unfairness of the proposition, given men would have to both put it up and then put it down, while women wouldn't have to do either."

Celia rolled her eyes. "You haven't been married, have you?"

"No, I haven't."

"Well, now we know why."

"I admit some compromise is called for, though the overall significance of the issue is in question. It boils down to no more than a point of view, as I see it."

"That's because it's not happening to you."

"Riding on top of a moving railcar behind a whizzer puts the whole situation into perspective, I can assure you," he said.

Celia laughed and brought the car up to speed.

"I don't mean to be nosey, Celia, not entirely anyway, but what makes a girl decide to hide away in a nunnery in the first place?"

Hanging her arm over the steering wheel, she said, "It's hard to explain. I wanted to live purely, I suppose, with singular purpose. I wanted the path of my life to be straight and clear. I thought I could do that in the nunnery."

"And that didn't happen?"

She shook her head. "All of my confusion and doubts and weaknesses followed me right through the gates."

"Life's rarely clear *or* pure, no matter where you put it," he said. "And the only straight line I know is that one that leads from birth to death."

She pushed her hair from her face. "A philosophical yard dog? Really?"

"Don't underestimate a yard dog's sensitivity. I never busted a man in my life what it didn't give me pause."

"I see, and what exactly does a yard dog do?"

"Solves crimes on the go, catches boes and pickpockets and renegade strikers. It's all fine blow at the pool hall, but, fact is, most hoboes are just looking for that purpose you talked about, knowing it's not where they been, hoping it's where they're going. Yard dogs are more or less on the same hunt, difference being it comes with a salary.

"Course, there are a few here and there who are escaping what they couldn't face and walking over what gets in their way in the process."

"And they are the dangerous ones?" she asked.

Hook turned to the window to let the sun warm his face. "The danger is in not knowing which ones are which."

They turned onto the dirt road leading to Avard. The white elevators towered on the horizon.

Celia grew quiet. "I've not picked up a child for the orphanage before," she said. "I'm a bit nervous. She is all alone now and probably terrified."

"I know Bet, some at least," he said. "I'm thinking she's a tough kid and in the end will do what has to be done."

"You know her?"

"I owe her money. It's a sure way to seal a friendship," he said. "There, turn down the tracks to that caboose."

"Excuse me?"

"The red caboose just down there. It's where I live."

"You live in a caboose?"

"If you call it living. Bet's been taking care of my dog, Mixer. I had no idea about her grandma being sick."

Celia pulled into the shade of the elm that grew along the right-of-way.

"But this is railroad property."

"And under my watch," he said. "Your car will be just fine here."

Hook got out and stuck his head back in the window. "Would you care to come in?"

She checked her watch. "I've an hour before she's due to arrive. But . . ."

"You needn't worry, Celia. When I lost this arm, I stopped taking anything or anybody for granted."

"Well," she said. "For a bit then. I admit to being curious."

Mixer bound up the tracks as they approached the caboose. Hook gathered him up and pulled his ears.

"This is Mixer," he said. "He's a purebred son of a bitch."

Celia stepped back. "Is he safe? I mean, he won't bite?"

"I watched him whip a pack of mongrels to a standstill in Amarillo a while back. He'd rather fight than eat, and there's nothing he likes better than eating. But he's got a soft spot for pretty girls. You couldn't be safer."

She knelt and stroked his head. Mixer sidled in. "He's a love," she said.

"Bet's been taking good care of him by the looks of it."

Mixer circled Celia's legs and then headed for the shade under the caboose.

Hook swung up on the steps and took her hand to help her up.

"It's a bit of a reach," he said. "Frenchy doesn't give a whole lot of thought to where he parks me, but the more I complain, the worse it gets."

When she reached the top step, her hand dropped over her mouth. She looked at the casket and then at Hook.

"Oh my god," she said. "That looks like a casket."

"That's 'cause it is. It belongs to one Samuel Ash."

Her face paled. "I don't understand. This is just too eerie."

"I've been riding with Samuel Ash all the way from Carlsbad, and we've not had a cross word. If Bet isn't afraid, you shouldn't be either. Come on in, and I'll explain."

Celia looked around the caboose before taking up a seat at the table.

"It feels like a home," she said. "And all these books."

"I'm a collector," he said.

"But books?"

"I'd explain it if I could, but it's like Beam and water. There's no explaining why a man drinks what shortens his life and increases his enemies. He just does, that's all.

"Speaking of which, I'm all out of tea. Would you care for a drink?"

"Well," she said, "I don't normally drink."

"I'm not much of a normal drinker myself," he said.

"No, thanks, a water."

Hook fixed her a water, and handed it to her. He poured himself a Beam.

"You may think this is all a bit strange," he said.

"You mean having a casket with a body in it strapped on the porch of the caboose that you live in? Why would I think that?"

"I found Samuel Ash hanging from the potash wigwag signal outside of Carlsbad."

She shuddered. "Oh, dear."

"Things like that can happen on this job," he said. "Over the years, I've gathered up more bodies than I care to remember. But this one's different."

She sipped at her water. "How, different?"

He reached into his pocket and laid the Bronze Star on the table. "For one thing, he had this around his neck." He turned it over. "The name Samuel Ash has been inscribed on the back."

"A war hero?"

"He'd been scabbing on the railroad, probably broke and needing money to get back home. Strikers don't favor scabs, hero or no hero. I thought I'd nailed who might have done it, more than once in fact, but too many unexplained things have happened since."

"What do you mean?"

"Someone took a shot at me, for one thing. I don't know who, and I don't know why. It could have been random, but I'm not much on coincidences, not when my life's at stake. I've pretty much ruled out every other possibility."

"And do you always bring these bodies home with you?"

"On rare occasion, I admit, but they were going to bury this boy in a pauper's grave back in Carlsbad, a war hero. I just couldn't let that happen. I need to find his people."

She locked her fingers, long and white as chalk, in front of her. "But why Carmen?"

"When Samuel Ash enlisted, he named Carmen as his hometown."

"And you think he may have come from the orphanage?"

"Thought it possible since on that same form he indicated that his parents were deceased."

Hook finished off his drink and slid the glass aside. "No one in the entire town has heard of him. Either everyone is lying, or I've been wrong about the whole thing."

Mixer scratched on the door, and Hook got up to let him in. He jumped up on the seat next to Celia and lay down.

"Get," Hook said.

"No, it's alright," she said. "What are you going to do now?"

"The mortuary in Carmen is expecting a body to be delivered to them from Carlsbad. If I don't find his people soon, I'll have no choice but to turn him over. He'll be buried without friends or family in a strange town. And the worst of it, his killer might still be on the loose."

"His killer?"

"It's a possibility," he said.

"Oh, it's time. I must go. I'm sorry about Samuel Ash. I wish I could have helped."

"Wait," he said, reaching for his billfold. "I owe Bet a dollar."

"I'll see she gets it."

As she left, she paused at the casket and made the sign of the cross. She turned to Hook, who watched from the door.

"You're right about that straight line," she said. "Good-bye, Hook, and good luck."

After she'd gone, Hook shaved and put on a clean shirt. He lined his books across the table and pulled out his newly acquired American first edition of *The Hound of the Baskervilles*. She had perfect boards, not a smudge or dent, and the "Published 1902" appeared on the reverse of the title page, indicating a first state. Had it not been for the library marking, it would have been a mint copy indeed, yet one more reason for him to rescue it from an indifferent public.

The sun struck through the cupola, warming his head and shoulders. Weariness rose up in him as if it had waited for this exact moment for him to get home. He lay down on the bunk and soon fell asleep.

He dreamed of blue flags and disembodied parts, and when a rap came at the door, he sat straight up, his heart pounding. Mixer crawled from under the bunk and commenced barking. Again, the knock came, louder this time.

"Alright, alright," he said. "I'm coming."

When he opened it, Celia and Bet stood side by side in the moonlight.

"What is it?" he asked, rubbing the sleep from his face.

"May we come in?" Celia asked.

"Oh, sure. Hi, Bet," he said.

Bet's lip quivered, and Mixer moved in next to her. Hook glanced at Celia.

"I'll fix something to eat," he said.

"No, thanks anyway," Celia said.

"What's the problem?" Hook asked.

"I don't want to go to an orphanage," Bet said.

"I see," Hook said. "I'm sorry about your grandma, Bet."

"They burned her up," she said. "'Cause we didn't have any money."

"Bet says she'll go if Mixer can go with her," Celia said. "You know, until she gets adjusted."

Hook took out his handkerchief and wiped the tears from Bet's cheeks.

"Well," he said, "how would the orphanage feel about that, I wonder?"

Celia pursed her lips. "The orphanage has a farm, so I don't see what a dog would hurt. Anyway, it wouldn't be permanent."

"I'll give your dollar back," Bet said.

"No, you earned that for taking such great care of Mixer, and I'm sure he'd like to take care of you for a while."

"Will you go, too?" she asked.

"Me? Well, I don't know."

"It would make things easier," Celia said.

"I do have some time left on my rent with Patch, and Frenchy hasn't called in yet. Sure, I'll go back, and Mixer can stay with you. How would that be?"

Bet nodded and looked at Celia. "Can Mixer sleep with me?"

"Of course," she said.

Hook turned out the lamp and secured the door, while Celia and Bet waited in the car with Mixer. He climbed down the steps and looked up at the casket, which reflected the moonlight back like giant cat eyes. He slid in next to Bet.

"Aren't you going to take Samuel Ash home now?" she asked.

"Not yet. I haven't found his people."

Celia pulled away, and Bet leaned against Hook. "I don't have people either," she said.

"You have Mixer and Miss Feola," he said. "They are your people now."

"And you," she said.

Hook glanced at Celia, who looked at him through the darkness.

"Yes," he said. "And me."

27

Hook THOUGHT THE tapping noise must be Celia Feola knocking at his caboose door again. He opened it to find her standing there, smiling and stark-naked, except for the bouquet of roses she held in front of her. When the noise came again, he sat up, remembering that he had returned to the shoe shop and that the noise had to be Patch or Skink instead.

Slipping on his prosthesis and clothes, he opened the door to find Patch busy nailing new heels onto a pair of engineer boots.

Patch looked up from his work. "Benny Hoffsteader bought these engineer boots in the city. Now he thinks he's a goddang motorcycle rider. Truth is he ain't nothing but the garbage man and a damn sorry one at that."

"We all have our illusions," Hook said, searching out the coffeepot.

"How'd that talk go with the sheriff?" Patch asked.

"You mean you don't know?"

"Well I know the sheriff," he said. "I'd as soon call out the quilting club if serious trouble set in."

Hook pulled up to the workbench and sipped his coffee. "You got a newspaper around here, Patch?"

"Over there," he said. "No charge."

Hook opened the paper and searched for sales. "Looks like the Methodists are having a rummage sale today," he said.

"Guess you didn't notice that pothole in the sheriff's head, seeing as how you didn't bring it up?"

"The sheriff and I have an agreement," Hook said. "Wonder if there'd be books?"

"I don't think the sheriff's given to reading, 'less you want to count comic books and the Sears catalog."

"I mean the rummage sale, Patch."

"Never know what you'll find in a rummage sale around here," he said. "But finding books ain't as likely as finding almost anything else."

"The sheriff said he'd never heard of Samuel Ash," Hook said.

"I could have told you that," Patch said, setting the boots aside. "Samuel Ash never lived here. If he did, I damn sure would know it, 'cause I lived here my whole life."

Hook scanned the rest of the paper and folded it up. "So, are you going to tell me how the sheriff got that dent in his bumper?"

"You'll have to ask him, though there's been plenty of rumors."

"Come on, Patch. I know you're going to tell me."

"Some say he got in a dustup with that Buck Steele who works out to the orphanage. Wouldn't surprise me. Buck Steele wears Justin boots with riding heels, and he wouldn't know a horse from a jackrabbit. You just can't trust a phony like that.

"First thing we hear, the sheriff's gone to the city, laid up in the hospital. The Watkins salesman said the hospital cook told him they were going to put a steel plate big as a hubcap in the sheriff's head, but he wouldn't have it."

"Well, it's his business," Hook said.

"Not so long as I have to look at it. A pig could make a wallow in that thing. We never heard another word about it back here in Carmen."

"About this coffee," Hook said.

Patch laid down his hammer. "Now, if you are fixin' to complain about my coffee, you just keep in mind how much you paid for it."

Hook dumped the coffee in the sink and rinsed out his cup.

"I'm off to the rummage sale, Patch. If anyone's looking for me, tell them to go to hell."

"I'll tell them *you* said to, Hook. I don't need no dent in my head."

Hook found the rummage sale in the auxiliary building of the Methodist church. The room, dimly lit, smelled of old clothes and scented candles. An old lady with watermelon breasts sat at the door paring her nails. She wore a man's wedding band on her thumb. She looked at Hook over her glasses when he came in.

"Twenty percent off on everything today," she said. "There're some nice overalls on that back rack."

"Thanks," Hook said. "Just looking."

Hook worked his way around the room, checking the boxes that had been pushed under the table. Being less convenient, they were more often overlooked by bargain hunters. He dug his way through mountains of pots and pans, scented candles, matchbooks, and strings of Christmas lights.

A young woman with a kid in tow came in and made for the clothes section. Pregnant, she wore a large shirt buttoned only at the top. Her shoes, overrun and oversized, made sucking noises on her feet as she pulled the kid along by his arm.

Every now and again, the kid whimpered and wiped his nose on his sleeve, which caused the woman to jerk him up short and fire off an array of threats, none of which had any impact on the boy's whimpering.

After an hour of hunting, Hook had found only a small stack of Jehovah's Witnesses pamphlets and three Gideon Bibles for his trouble. He'd nearly given up, when he spotted a book with a sewing box sitting on top of it. The book, with red covers, turned out to be Lewis Carroll's *Alice's Adventures in Wonderland*, not the 1869 edition, but an American first in very good condition.

He paid up and headed back to the shop, satisfied that his time spent had been worthwhile. He'd gone only a couple blocks when he spotted the sheriff up on a ladder painting the eaves of a white bungalow.

"Hello, Sheriff," Hook said.

The sheriff looked under his arm. "Oh, it's you," he said, climbing down. Taking off his hat, he wiped the sweat from his head with his sleeve.

"Damn it's hot," he said.

"How's old lady Engle?" Hook asked.

"Didn't have to shoot her," he said. "Not yet, anyway. You find out anything about that Samuel Ash?"

"Not a thing," Hook said.

The sheriff laid his paintbrush across his paint can and searched out his cigarettes. Hook retrieved a match with his prosthesis, struck it on his zipper, and lit him up.

"You're pretty good with that thing," the sheriff said, blowing smoke into the air.

"Thanks," Hook said.

"How'd you lose it, anyway?"

Hook smiled. "Car wreck. My girlfriend didn't drive so well."

"She still your girlfriend?"

"She turned out to be a bit squeamish," he said.

"The world's a shithouse, ain't it?" he said.

"Pretty much. How about you?"

"What do you mean?"

"We had a deal. If I showed you mine, you had to show me yours."

"You mean this?" he said, pointing to his head. "That ain't nothing."

"Nonetheless."

"Stupid argument over a pool game," he said.

"I heard that Buck Steele did it, but then you know rumors in a small town. I heard he is a pretty nice guy."

"Well, he ain't all that nice by my count," he said. "The son of a bitch waylaid me in the alley."

"The hell? Why didn't you file charges?"

He flipped the ashes off his cigarette and peeled the dried paint from his fingernail. "Off duty. You know how it is. Town like this won't let a guy have a life of his own."

"Still, assault and battery isn't something a man ought get by with."

"This is between us, you being the law and all," he said. "I did file charges against that bastard. But here comes old man Eagleman all fired up and with a high-priced lawyer, saying as how he'd sue me for all I was worth, and how he'd have me fired for drinking and brawling, and how I'd never work anywhere again."

"It's hard to take on the big boys," Hook said.

"Damn right. Said he'd pay for patching up my head, and we'd just let the whole thing go. I could keep my mouth shut, and so would they."

"So that's what you did?"

"Damn straight."

"Can't say I blame you, Sheriff."

"And then that bastard Eagleman refused to pay for the plate they wanted to put in my head. Said he hadn't agreed to cosmetic surgery. Now, I gotta walk around looking like a flat tire."

"Least you can wear a hat, Sheriff. I got this hook hanging out of my sleeve for everyone to gawk at."

"You got a point, I guess. Thing is, I never understood why Eagleman got so stirred up in the first place. Buck Steele doesn't hold much for working, 'cept for bossing those kids around, and there's not a day goes by what he doesn't make it to the pool hall. Eagleman could have replaced him with a real hand and for half the trouble. Never understood why he didn't."

"Well, I'll be letting you get back to work, Sheriff."

The sheriff picked up his paintbrush. "What you doing with the book?"

Hook turned it over. "Found it laying on the sidewalk. Some kid, probably. You take care, Sheriff."

"Yeah," he said, climbing onto the ladder. About halfway up, he turned. "You might try the newspaper," he said. "They got obits and stuff like that."

"Good idea," Hook said.

Hook stopped at the café before going back to the shop, a small place with only a few booths available. He ordered up the calf fries, cole slaw, mashed potatoes and gravy, and hot rolls with butter and honey.

When he'd finished, the waitress tallied up his bill. Unsure about the prosthesis, she smiled and laid the money on the table instead.

Hook took a shower in the park bathroom, cold water and all, and shaved best he could in the broken mirror. Back at the room, he lay in bed and read some from the Carroll book. He'd no sooner turned out the light when a soft knock came at the door.

Slipping on his britches, he said, "Who is it?"

"Celia. I need to see you."

He opened the door to find her standing there with Mixer at her side.

"No roses?" he said.

"Excuse me."

"Never mind. Did Mixer kill someone?"

"Not that I know about. May I come in?"

"Oh, sure," he said, looking for his shirt.

Mixer circled the room to catalog the smells before jumping up on Hook's bed.

"Please, have a chair," he said to her, taking up his place next to Mixer.

"I'm afraid Mixer can't stay at the orphanage," she said. "Mr.

Eagleman wouldn't permit it. He said that no pets were allowed and that exceptions could not be made."

"I see."

"I told him that the arrangement was temporary until Bet adjusted, but I failed to persuade him. I'm afraid he's quite strict about the rules."

"And how's Bet?"

"Disappointed, as you might guess. I could hear her sobbing after lights-out."

"Poor thing," Hook said. "Maybe if I talked to him."

"I don't think that's a good idea, Hook."

"I'll come out to see her soon."

Celia looked away and then turned back, her eyes damp. "I'm sorry, but I'm not very good with this. I promised her, you know, and now I've gone back on my word."

"It's not your fault, Celia. Bet's a pretty game kid. She'll be okay. I'm sure of it."

"Yes, you're right, of course. Well," she said, "I'll be on my way. I've an early start in the morning, paperwork at the courthouse over in Cherokee."

"Wait," he said, reaching for the book. "I found this today. Perhaps you could give it to her for me."

"Oh, yes. Of course," she said, opening the door. She paused. "I've been thinking about Samuel Ash, about that Bronze Star, about him being buried all alone with his people not even knowing where he is. It's a sad thing," she said.

"Yes," he said.

"Mr. Eagleman is leaving for the city tomorrow evening for a meeting," she said. "Something about funds from the state. I guess I'll be in charge of things for a few days."

"You'll do fine," he said.

"Yes," she said. "I'll do my best."

28

Hook FOUND SKINK asleep with his head down on Patch's workbench. Mixer circled the shop before lifting his leg on Skink's foot.

"What the hell," Skink said, looking around, his eyes bleary. He turned to look at his foot. "Oh, shit," he said.

"Meet Mixer," Hook said.

"He peed on my foot, Hook."

"He's just saying I love you."

"Maybe I'll just say it back," Skink said.

"Love begets love in the dog world," Hook said. "By tonight, every dog in Carmen will have said I love you on that very same foot."

"Sure not the way to start my day."

"I've got some dry socks back there. Go change, and I'll fix coffee."

Hook poured water in the coffeepot and put in an extra helping of coffee grounds. Mixer wagged his tail and went back into the room for a nap.

"I could use a cup," Skink said, gimping back into the shop.

When the coffee had finished, Hook pulled up to the workbench across from Skink and handed him his cup.

Skink sipped at his coffee. "This tastes better than Patch's," he said.

"That's 'cause it has coffee in it," Hook said. "Listen, Skink, you know Patch is going to catch you sleeping on the job again if you keep doing it."

"It's like trying to hide from a ghost," Skink said. "He could be listening this very minute for all I know. Anyway, I've been thinking maybe I don't want to be a cobbler."

"Oh?"

"I'm thinking I might want to be a yard dog instead, carry a gun and shoot people."

"Being a yard dog requires singular intelligence," Hook said.

"I got Cs in school."

"And integrity."

"All except algebra. I took it over, though."

"A hundred percent integrity," Hook said.

"I took it over twice and still flunked it, and once I stole Mildred Bonfield's underwear out of the gym."

"Railroad bulls have to have lots of courage, too, Skink."

"Like yourself?"

"That's right. It's like being a full-time hero, and there's no time off and no sleeping on the job. In fact, there's hardly any sleeping at all."

"Do you shoot people?"

"Now and then, but I'm particular about who I shoot."

"What about girls?"

"I don't shoot girls."

"I mean do you get lots of girls?"

"That's the biggest problem. Sometimes I think if one more girl climbs into my bed, I'll just go into the shoe-repair business and forget about it."

Skink sucked at his coffee and looked off into space. "And you don't have Patch watching all the time, do you?"

"I got Eddie Preston, which comes to the same thing. Speaking of which, does Patch have a phone?"

"Back there in the supply room. He don't ever use it, though. Says he doesn't know anybody worth calling. Says he only has it in case of fire or his heart gives out."

"I guess you wouldn't mind then if I make a call or two?"

Skink dumped his grounds and picked up his broom. "I don't mind at all, Hook. Make all the calls you want."

Hook found the phone buried under a stack of calfskin pelts. He wrote Patch's phone number down on his prosthesis and dialed Popeye.

"Clovis," Popeye said.

"Hook here, Popeye. Has that boy called in yet?"

"Junior Monroe?"

"That one," Hook said.

"He's in Wellington. Said he spotted an old man and his wife breaking the boxcar seals and stealing cases of macaroni. Said he tried to arrest them, but they got away."

"When he calls in again, tell him to stop by my caboose in Avard and check on things."

"What things?"

"Everything things. Jesus, Popeye. He can call me at this number."

Hook read him the number.

"Got it," Popeye said.

"And tell him to call the yardmaster, too, and get those cars off that siding. The railroad needs its macaroni."

"Right," Popeye said. "About that money, Hook?"

"What money?"

"The two dollars you owe me."

"I paid you back already."

"Well, I don't remember it."

"Jesus, Popeye, I'm going to have to stop borrowing it if you can't remember when I pay it back. You're downright disconcerting."

"Downright what?"

"Disconcerting."

"I ain't disconcerting, Hook. Everybody knows that."

"Eat fish, Popeye. It's good for your brain."

"This is New Mexico. There ain't a fish within five hundred miles."

"Try Beam and water. It keeps your brain pressure up and finetunes other important body parts.

"Look, I got to run now, Popeye. Remember, this is Hook, Hook Runyon, your old friend."

"It's the one thing I can't forget," Popeye said, hanging up.

Hook dialed Eddie Preston. "Division," Eddie said.

"Hook here, Eddie."

"Did you get those car seals checked out in Wellington?"

"Goddang boes, I figure. I'm having the cars moved into the yard."

"Did Junior Monroe get in on it?"

"More or less. Kid has a lot to learn, though."

"I need you back in Clovis, Runyon. These wildcat strikes are popping up everywhere."

"Right, Eddie. Soon as I get these seal busters rounded up and the bushings replaced on this worn-out caboose. I'm waiting on Frenchy to tow her in. I don't want to leave her sitting out for somebody to break into."

"And what about that wigwag hanging?"

"Guess you were right on that one, Eddie. I haven't found a thing."

"Baldwin Felts training," Eddie said. "That's why I'm supervisor, and you're chasing seal busters."

"Good information, Eddie. I've been wondering a long time why you were supervisor."

Hook, leaving Mixer asleep under the bed, hoofed his way through town. As soon as he made the corner, the orphanage, with its turrets and flights of stairs, loomed up at the end of the road like an English castle. He stopped and listened to the stir of leaves in the elms before heading on down the road. Climbing the steps of the orphanage, he knocked on the door.

"Oh, it's you again," the cook said, drying her hands on her apron. "Miss Feola isn't here, and Mr. Eagleman told me appointments only."

"I'd like to speak with Bet Haimes," he said.

"Bet who?" she asked.

"The new girl."

"She's not here."

"Where is she?"

"She wouldn't eat her shepherd pie last night. You'll find her walking the circle, I expect."

"Who put her to walking the circle?"

"That would be Mr. Eagleman. He does all the discipline here at Agape."

Hook made his way to the bottom of the steps and turned. "Did Mr. Eagleman eat *his* shepherd pie?"

"Mr. Eagleman don't eat with the children. I take his plate up."

"And what was it?"

The cook folded her big arms over her bosom. "Steak, rare, with baked potato."

Hook found Bet walking the cemetery circle just as the cook said. As she came around the far corner, he gave her a wave. She paused, uncertain as to whom he might be, and then came toward him. Her cheeks were flushed, her eyes red, and dust covered her white socks.

"I got to keep walking," she said. "Or I'll have to do it all over again."

Hook took her by the arm. "It's alright, Bet. Now what's going on?"

"How's Mixer?" she asked.

"Mixer's fine. You'll see him soon."

"I couldn't eat it," she said. "It had cold mashed potatoes, and the meat swelled up in my mouth. Mr. Eagleman said if I didn't eat it, I'd have to walk the circle. He said I wasn't at home anymore, and I'd eat what everybody else ate. I better walk now."

"Come on, Bet. We're going back, and I'm having a talk with Mr. Eagleman."

Hook found the cook sweeping up the entry. "I'm going to talk to Eagleman," he said. "Fix this girl something to eat, and it damn well better not be shepherd pie."

"You can't go up there without an appointment," she said.

Hook walked to the bottom of the staircase and shouted up to Eagleman. "This is Hook Runyon, and I'm making an appointment. I'll be up there in about one minute." He turned back to the cook. "Anything else?"

"No, sir," she said. "I'll fix something."

By the time Hook made the upstairs hallway, Eagleman had opened the door to his office. He stuck his head out.

"What the hell is going on?"

Hook pushed past him. Eagleman followed him in. "What do you think you're doing?" he asked, his face red.

"Sit down," Hook said.

"What did you say?"

Hook shoved him into his chair. Eagleman's cheeks puffed in and out, and he made strange whishing sounds.

"You can't come in here," he said. "I'll have you arrested."

"I've got an appointment," Hook said.

"This is outrageous. Who do you think you are?"

"That little girl just lost her grandmother, and you put her to walking the circle?"

"Discipline is essential in a place like this," he said. "The girl has to learn to eat what everyone else eats."

"Except you?"

"I'm an adult."

Hook reached over and snared Eagleman's tie with his prosthesis. He pulled him halfway across the desk. Buttons from Eagleman's white shirt popped and rolled across the floor. He stank of fear and cologne, and his ears lit red in the sunlight that streamed through the window behind him.

Hook spoke into his face. "If I ever hear of you not eating what you serve those kids, I'll be back, and without an appointment next time."

Hook shoved him into his chair and went to the door. He opened it and turned.

"Bet's taking the day off," he said. "Any objections?"

Dabbing his forehead with his handkerchief, Eagleman shook his head.

"Good, then."

Hook stopped in the kitchen to get Bet, who had just finished her peanut butter sandwich.

"She's coming with me to see Mixer," he said to the cook. "Here's my number in case Miss Feola wants to talk to me when she gets back."

The cook stood motionless. "What about Mr. Eagleman?"

"He says that from now on whatever you fix for the kids to eat will be fine with him, too."

The cook smiled. "We're having potato soup," she said. "Mr. Eagleman hates potato soup."

Hook and Bet spent the afternoon in the park playing with Mixer, who insisted on digging a hole under the foundation of the bathroom.

When they got back to the shop, they found Patch just closing up.

"This is Bet," Hook said. "She's a friend of mine. She's living out at the orphanage now. And this is Mixer, whose friendship is less clear."

"Hello, Bet," Patch said. "Your heels are run over. Stop by sometime, and I'll put new ones on for you."

Bet said, "I only got a dollar."

"Well," he said, looking over at Hook. "We've got heels enough to spare around here. No charge."

"Okay," she said.

"I better be getting home," Patch said. "Nice meeting you, Bet. See you tomorrow, Hook."

"Yeah," Hook said.

"Course that dog will be sleeping outside, won't he?" Patch asked.

"Mixer? Most likely."

"Good night, then, and you might tell Skink he can just stop using my phone. It's not here for his private business."

"What makes you think Skink is using your phone?"

"Someone moved those pelts. It had to be either Skink or you. I figure a lawman would know better."

"The law is a sacred trust with railroad bulls," Hook said. "I'll tell him what you said."

Hook walked Bet back to the orphanage and turned her over to the cook at the back door that led into the kitchen.

"I don't know what you did to Mr. Eagleman," she said. "But he left for that conference with steam coming out of his ears."

"We just had a little misunderstanding," Hook said. "Is Miss Feola back yet?"

"Not yet. She called and said she'd been delayed."

"See you soon, Bet," Hook said, winking at her. "Maybe I'll bring Mixer around by the school sometime, and he can walk you home."

Hook walked back in the dark. He could smell smoke from the orphanage incinerator, and as he cut toward the drive, he spotted a dim light coming from the barn.

He cut back toward the corral and climbed up on the fence. Below, a dozen Holstein cows circled and moved about in a vast whirlpool. In the center, a bull twice the size of any cow in the lot, and with gallon-sized balls, stirred them about. Mounting at will, he rode them around the corral on his hind legs. The cows' ankles, too delicate for their burden, cracked and popped as they struggled beneath his weight.

Though fenced off from the corral, the entire south side of the barn opened to the outside, and Hook could see the light from somewhere deep in its interior.

He found the top half of the side door open. Reaching in, he unlatched the bottom half, stepped into the darkness, and secured the door behind him. Stanchions stretched the entire length of the barn, and the air smelled of manure and alfalfa. He moved forward to where he could see that the light seeped from under the door of a room at the back side of the barn.

He'd turned to leave when he heard the corral gate swing open, and he crouched down. The bull entered first, a black shadow in the moonlight. He swung salvia onto his back, and flies lifted in a swarm from his shoulders.

Hook crept into the corner, his heart tripping. And then the others followed behind the bull, a wall of flesh filling up the remaining space. They snorted and blew liquid from their noses as they closed in about Hook.

Hook kicked and shoved and hit, but the animals, impervious to his blows, crammed in ever tighter. Suddenly, the bull, intent on getting to the trough first, pinned Hook against the wall. Pain settled into Hook's chest, and he panicked under the crushing weight. Unable to breathe, and his strength waning, he leaned forward onto the bull's neck as far as he could reach and hooked him in the nostril with his prosthesis.

When he yanked, the bull snorted, shook his head, and backed up a few inches, enough for Hook to snare the stanchion railing above him and pull himself up. He worked his way along the stanchion, kicked open the side door, and dropped onto the ground. Leaning onto his knees, he waited for his breathing to level off. He checked his leg, which had taken the brunt of the weight, and it appeared to still be working.

He walked on toward town, pausing at the end of the orphanage drive. He looked back. The light in the barn was off.

Once at his room, Hook let Mixer out and fixed himself a Beam and water, and then doubled the Beam. He checked his leg again, his knee now swollen and red. Mixer scratched at the door, and he let him in.

Hook drank his Beam and fixed another before turning in. The cricket took up its nightly chirping, the sound moving and elusive in the darkness. Hook thought about his day, about his close call in the barn, and he thought about all the mishaps that had plagued him ever since Samuel Ash had come into his life.

Sometime in the night, he awakened to Patch's phone ringing in the shop. He slipped on his shoes and groped his way through the darkness.

"Hello," he said, clearing his throat.

"Hook?"

"Yeah," he said.

"Celia," she said. "I heard about what happened today with you and Eagleman."

"Yeah," he said. "I hope it doesn't cause you a problem."

"Do you think you could meet me tomorrow night?"

"Where?"

"At your place, about ten, after everyone's gone to bed."

"Is everything alright, Celia?" he asked.

"I'll talk to you then," she said.

29

Hook TURNED ON the small porch light just before ten, and within moments Celia knocked on the door. She wore a black beret with a gold medallion pinned on the side. When she took off the hat, her auburn hair spilled onto her shoulders. She pushed her hair back with her fingers, revealing her widow's peak.

"Celia," he said. "Come in."

Mixer leapt off the bed to greet her, and she reached down to pet him.

"I hope I'm not keeping you up," she said.

"No. I've been reading. May I take your things?"

She slipped out of her jacket, which smelled of green scents, and Hook arranged it on the back of the chair.

Sitting down, she crossed her legs. She wore tan slacks and black pumps. Hook wondered what significance Patch would assign to their short heels.

"You caused quite a stir at the orphanage," she said.

"I'm sorry about that, Celia. I let my temper get the best of me."

"No apology necessary," she said. "I've been having second thoughts about things myself."

"What do you mean?"

"Intuition, I'd guess you'd say. Even though the Spirit of Agape facility is rather nice as orphanages go, there's something not right. I'm just not certain what."

"Kids will be happy if given half a chance," Hook said. "Bet isn't."

"Few *are* out there," she said. "The question is why."

"Even kids can spot a phony," he said. "And in my opinion that's what your Mr. Eagleman is."

Celia leaned forward on her knee. "I can't stop thinking about Samuel Ash," she said. "About him being out there on your caboose, a war hero, and not having a resting place with his own people."

"Samuel Ash haunts us all," he said.

"Maybe we should take a look at those orphanage records. I have the key to Eagleman's office while he's gone. I mean, who knows if there's something there that might help."

"It could cause trouble for you, Celia, and there is no guarantee we will find anything."

"No," she said. "But you can at least rule it out."

"When?"

"Tonight. Now. Everyone's in bed."

"We'll need a flashlight," he said.

"I brought one. We can go in through the kitchen."

Mixer jumped off the bed, his tail wagging.

"Alright," Hook said to him. "But you'll have to keep it quiet."

The streets of Carmen were vacant and the night still as they made their way toward the orphanage. The moon, full and bright, ducked behind the clouds that raced along as if in an invisible river.

As they approached, they could see the turrets of the orphanage reaching up into the sky. The barn lay in darkness, and smoke from the incinerator hung in the evening air.

Hook waited as Celia unlocked the back door to the kitchen, and then he stepped in behind her. He eased the door closed. Celia climbed her way up the staircase with him close at her heels.

Once they reached Eagleman's office door, she paused and listened before unlocking the door. Clicking on her flashlight, she panned the office.

"There," she whispered.

They started with the top file drawers, looking through the folders one by one.

Soon, Celia said, "There are so many. We'll never get through them all."

"No pictures either, but I think they're organized by date and gender," Hook said. "There's no point in going through all the girls' records or even the more recent males'. Let's start with these down here."

They searched through the records, but there was no evidence of Samuel Ash. Hook sat down on the floor and leaned against the desk.

"Dead end," he said

Celia, scanning one of the files with the light, glanced over at him. "Take a look at this one," she said.

"Bruce Mason? Who is Bruce Mason?"

"I don't know, but look. His parents are listed as deceased."

"Most of them are, Celia."

She came over and knelt next to him. "Here," she said. "His father's name was Samuel Mason. His mother's was Ruth Anne Mason. But check out her maiden name."

Hook focused the light on the folder. "I'll be damned," he said. "Ash. Ruth Anne Ash. Do you suppose he used his father's first name and his mother's maiden name when he enlisted in the army?"

"The age is right, too," she said.

Hook closed the folder and looked over at Celia. "That would mean I've been searching for the wrong guy all along."

"Exactly," she said.

"But why hide his real name?"

Celia slipped the folder back into the file. "There could be any number of reasons, I suppose."

"You should have been the yard dog," he said.

"And you the matron? I don't think so, Hook. Come on, let's get out of here."

Hook checked out the window before opening the back door. He turned to Celia. "Thanks for this."

She nodded. The moon slipped from behind a cloud and lit the red in her hair.

"Let me know," she said.

"Celia," he said, "intuition only whispers, but it often speaks the truth. You're wise to have listened to it. Be careful."

As Hook made his way down the drive toward town, his knee protested, and his head reeled at the new information. Involved in his thoughts, he failed to see the pickup sitting in the middle of the road with its lights out. The door opened, and a man in a cowboy hat climbed out. His jaw bulged with chew.

"What are you doing on Agape property, Runyon?" he asked, coming in closer.

He wore a belt buckle made of Indian Head nickels, a shirt buttoned to the neck, and a white beard in need of a trim. When Hook saw the riding heels, he said, "You must be Buck Steele?"

Buck rolled his chew and spit to the side. "That's right. What you doing on Agape property?"

Mixer, his head lowered, stepped up next to Hook.

"Seeing Miss Feola home," Hook said.

Buck smiled somewhere beneath his beard. "It just might be worth dying for at that," he said.

"Miss Feola and I are friends," Hook said. "I suggest you keep this out of the gutter."

Buck stepped in closer, and Mixer, growling, laid his ears back.

Buck stopped. "My advice to you is to stay off Agape property.

A man could get mistaken for a coyote and get his carcass hung up on a fence post."

Hook started to answer, but Buck got back in his pickup, turned on the lights, and pulled away.

Back at his room, Hook fixed himself a drink and slipped off his shoes. Everything he thought he knew about Samuel Ash had vanished. Nothing fit anymore, and he didn't know how much longer he could stall Eddie Preston.

And then there was Samuel Ash, or Bruce Mason, or whoever the hell lay in that casket on the porch of his caboose. And why hadn't Eagleman gone to the sheriff about their encounter in his office? And how did Buck know his name when they'd never met before?

This much he did know: a full right turn had to be made in his thinking, and he figured to start it by talking to Skink first thing in the morning.

30

WHEN THE PHONE rang at four in the morning, Hook thought of Celia. He stumbled through the darkness and dug the phone out from beneath a stack of shop receipts.

"Hello," he said.

"Hook?"

"Yeah."

"Junior Monroe."

"Why the hell you calling me this time of morning, Junior?"

"I'm in Avard, Hook. I caught a train out of Wellington. We sat for four hours on a siding outside of Kiowa. I'm exhausted, and I can't feel my hands."

"Neither can I, but you'll get used to it," Hook said. "Anyway, that's no reason to wake a man up at four in the morning."

"But you said you wanted me to check on things."

"And?"

"So I did."

"Jesus, Junior, can you just get on with it?"

"It's gone."

"What's gone?"

"Your caboose."

Hook reached for his cigarettes and then remembered he didn't have his clothes on.

"That's not funny, Junior."

"I'm serious, Hook. It's gone and Samuel Ash with it."

"Jesus," Hook said.

"I'm calling from the general store here in Avard. The owner almost shot me for knocking on his door. He said he thought I was a hobo."

"Well, maybe it just got sided off by the elevators when they were loading hoppers."

"I looked, Hook, and I walked up and down the tracks. I couldn't see anything, eastbound or west. Why would anyone want to steal that old caboose with Samuel Ash tied on the porch?"

"I don't know. Why was I ever born?" Hook said.

"What do you want me to do? I'm running up this guy's phone bill, and he doesn't look too happy."

"Wait for me. I'll catch a short haul over soon as I can."

"Where do you want me to wait?"

"What the hell difference does it make, Junior? It's Avard, not Chicago."

By the time Hook got dressed, fed Mixer, and headed down the street, he could hear the switch engine bumping in a line of empty hoppers at the crossing. Just as he got there, the short haul rolled out. Running alongside, he caught the grab iron and pulled up.

After catching his breath, he leaned back and watched the morning break. The fields had all been harvested now, and a lot of the farmers were already plowing up stubble.

Within the hour, the Avard elevators grew ever larger on the horizon. Junior Monroe had a way of getting things wrong. He hoped to hell he'd done it again.

The short haul slowed as they came into town. Hook crawled out on the ladder and hit the ground running. Junior sat on the steps next to the scale house waiting on him. His Panama, having borne the brunt of his travels, hung limp over an ear. He stood as Hook approached.

"Did you find it?" Hook asked.

"It's gone, Hook. I asked around, and nobody's seen it."

Hook scanned the horizon. "It can't just be gone, Junior. It's a caboose, for Christ's sake, a red caboose."

Junior took off his hat. He looked older than Hook remembered.

"It has to be either eastbound or westbound," he said.

"I guess you learned that in college?" Hook said.

"I came in from the east, and I didn't see any caboose. I guess that leaves westbound."

Hook stood in the middle of the tracks and looked westbound.

"Well, now, that narrows it down," he said. "It's got to be between here and San Francisco somewhere, providing you didn't overlook it in the middle of the night."

"Is there a siding?" Junior asked. "Maybe they moved the caboose out of the way for other cars."

Hook wet the end of his finger and rubbed Patch's phone number off his prosthesis.

"There's a siding about halfway to Waynoka, but how the hell we going to get there?"

"We could walk," Junior said. "If you're up to it, I mean."

Hook looked at Junior. "I walked rail when you were sucking sugar tit, Junior. I think I can manage."

The sun bore down on their backs as they walked along the track. Hook led, with Junior bringing up drag. Hook waited for him to come up.

"Did you ever catch Barney?" Junior asked, adjusting his hat.

Hook walked on. "Course I did."

"Really? Did he carry a weapon?"

"A pistol, but I took it away from him. I never let a weapon interfere with enforcing the law."

"That's quite brave, actually," he said.

"Some might say that," he said. "And did you deliver Jackie to KC?"

"Yes," he said. "I felt sorry for her, you know. I don't think she understood the implications of her actions."

"Well, who does? By the by, Popeye said you let those seal busters get away over to Wellington?"

"They were spry for their age," he said.

Hook stopped and looked up at the sun. "The siding is just around that curve. If there's any shooting, you jump in the bar ditch, and let me take care of things."

"When do *I* get a weapon, Hook?"

"When you start shaving, Junior. Now stay low."

Hook edged around the curve, knelt, and held his hand above his eyes against the sun.

"Do you see anything?" Junior asked.

"The goddang railroad track," Hook said. "But there's no caboose and no Samuel Ash. You got any more bright ideas?"

Somewhere behind them, the whistle of a train sounded.

"Maybe you should call Division?" Junior said.

"You got a phone in your pocket?"

"No, but you could call him from Waynoka."

Smoke from a steamer crawled up into the blue behind them.

"Here's what we're going to do," Hook said. "That's a freighter coming back there. When she slows for the curve, we're going to hop her, ride her into Waynoka, and find out what the hell is going on."

"I'm not skilled at jumping on trains, Hook."

Hook took another look down track. "Just follow me, Junior, and pay attention. I'll show you how it's done."

Hook squatted in the bushes to wait for the train. Junior waited behind him, his Panama pulled down against his ears.

"When I say go, start running," Hook said. "She's moving pretty fast, so don't tarry."

Just then the train's glimmer popped up downline. Hook hunkered down and waited. Just as she charged by, her drivers thudding and steam blowing a hundred feet into the air, he said, "Now, Junior. Run."

Hook charged down track in high gear, checking back over his shoulder now and again in search of an approaching grab iron to latch on to. Junior, holding his Panama on with one hand, ran full tilt behind him.

Hook timed his move, reached out, and snared a grab iron, his legs dangling inches from the ground. He glanced back to check on Junior, who had started to fade. The train's engine, having already made the curve, gathered up speed down the straightaway.

"Get hold, Junior," he yelled back. "Now."

Junior bore down, his Panama spinning off down the right-of-way, and in a last-second effort, he leapt forward and caught hold of Hook's leg.

Hook, hanging on with everything he had, yelled, "Goddang it, Junior, you're dragging me off!"

The whistle blew, and the engine throttled up yet more. Steam and smoke raced down the side of the cars, and the ties clicked away in a blur beneath them.

Hook's pants slipped low on his hips from Junior's hold, and his arm went dead with fatigue. When he could hang on no longer, he shoved off hard, his pants now around his ankles, and they tumbled off down the right-of-way in a cloud of dust.

Hook lay on his back in the bar ditch, blinking up into the blue sky, and listened to the train whistle disappear. Junior sat a hundred feet down track with Hook's pants in his hands.

Hook struggled to his feet, walked to Junior, and took his pants. He put them on and headed off down the track.

"Jeez, Hook," Junior said from behind. "I'm really sorry."

"Just don't say another goddang word, Junior, not if you want to live."

31

As HOOK AND Junior walked into the Waynoka yards, Hook suddenly stopped, and Junior, who had his head down, ran up on his heels.

"I guess you didn't get me finished off just yet," Hook said.

"Sorry, Hook."

"If I'm not mistaken, that's a red caboose sitting inside that roundhouse stall," Hook said.

"I believe it is," Junior said.

"And if I'm not mistaken, it looks a hell of a lot like my caboose."

"It does, though all cabooses look pretty much the same when you think about it," Junior said.

"You might notice that this particular caboose has a casket tied on the porch, Junior, an uncommon feature, and strong evidence suggesting that it's *my* caboose we're looking at and not someone else's caboose."

"I guess that's what makes you such a good yard dog," Junior said.

"That's a fact, though modesty keeps me from saying it, Junior.

Now, I'm going to go in there and check this out. If they got questions, I'll answer them. If you got something you want to say, just keep it to yourself. Understood?"

"Right, Hook. Understood."

"Good, then let's go."

The front wheel truck was gone on the caboose, and three machinists sat on the porch with their lunch boxes lined up across Samuel Ash's coffin.

"What the hell you doing up there?" Hook asked.

The three of them looked down at Hook and Junior. The tall one pushed his hat back and said, "Boes ain't allowed in here, mister. You move on before I call the railroad bull. This is private property."

"I *am* the bull," Hook said, pulling out his badge.

"I'll be damned," the tall one said. "Where's your arm?"

"Up the bum of the last guy who towed my caboose," Hook said.

"No need to get sore," he said.

"What the hell you doing with my caboose?" Hook asked again.

"A work train towed it in here with an order to refurbish the journals. That's what we're doing, though I've seen a hell of a lot worse in my day."

"Who ordered it?" Hook asked.

The tall one dug the order out of his overalls pocket. "Eddie Preston, Southwest Divisional Security Supervisor."

"Eddie Preston can't keep his nose out of nothing. You boys been snooping around in my house, have you?"

"Just eating lunch," the tall one said. "Seemed a good place to set a table."

"You might ask Samuel Ash about that," Junior said.

"Samuel Ash? Who the hell is Samuel Ash?"

Hook jabbed Junior in the ribs. "Never mind," Hook said. "How long 'fore she's ready to roll?"

"Week," the tall one said. "Longer if they pull a passenger in ahead of her."

Hook turned to leave, when the tall one said, "What's in this here box?"

"Say what?"

"This here box?"

"Dead body," he said.

The tall one looked at the others and then laughed. "You can't get a straight answer out of none of these sons of bitches."

"Well, you got me on that one," Hook said. "It's perishables. I'll be making arrangements before I leave, so you boys just leave it be. Is the yard office open?"

"It's open," the tall one said. "Yardmaster's probably gone to lunch, though."

Hook made Junior wait outside the yard office while he called Eddie.

"Preston," Eddie said.

"This is Hook, Eddie."

"It's about time you called in, Runyon. What the hell is going on?"

"I've been looking for my caboose. Maybe you've seen it?"

"You've been bitching about those bushings for weeks now. I had a work train tow it in. Now maybe you can get something done."

"Well, that's fine, Eddie. But don't you think it would have been a good idea to tell me first?"

"That would require me knowing where the hell you were, Runyon."

"I've been chasing seal busters like you asked. Then when I get home, my home it isn't there, and I don't know where the hell it is."

"There ain't no pleasing some people," Eddie said. "Where are you now?"

"Standing here talking to you, trying to figure out why you'd take my caboose and not tell me."

"I need you in Pampa, Runyon. B&B has had a bridge down for too damn long. They claim they're waiting on supplies, but I smell a rat. These union bastards will do anything to slow down the company."

"I'll check it out," Hook said. "Next time, you might let me know before you tow off my caboose."

"Next time, I'll tow the damn thing to salvage," Eddie said. "But I'll damn sure let you know about it first."

Hook found Junior sitting on the steps picking burrs out of his socks. Hook propped his foot up on the step.

"Alright, Junior," he said. "Here's what I want you to do: Eddie thinks B and B is sitting on their hands and holding things up on a bridge over to Pampa. I want you to go check it out."

Junior stood. "You mean by myself?"

"If you're going to be a prosecutor, you need to learn to take on responsibility, Junior."

Junior looked at Hook. Somewhere along the line, he'd torn his shirt, and his elbow stuck out the hole.

"You said you'd obtain a pass for me, Hook."

"I'll do some checking on it. In the meantime, hop something westbound out of the yard. Your running ability isn't worth a damn."

"What are *you* going to be doing, Hook?"

"It's bad form for a lawman to reveal his whereabouts and agenda to just everyone who comes down track, Junior. You never know when someone might derail your investigation."

"I hadn't thought of that," he said. "You sure have a way of figuring things out, Hook."

"Experience, Junior. Now, there's one other thing."

"What's that?"

"After you're done in Pampa, run on over to Clovis and pick up the road-rail."

"You want *me* to pick up the road-rail?"

"That's right. Bring it back here and call me at that number I gave you."

"But can that road-rail make it on the road all the way from Clovis? What if it breaks down?"

"Sometimes lawmen have to make sacrifices, like we talked about before, Junior. Anyway, it's the only way to get it back here. And watch those brakes. We don't want to be tearing up railroad equipment."

Hook watched Junior walk off toward the main line, his hands buried in his pockets. Hook turned to go back to the roundhouse just as the yardmaster pulled in. Hook waited for him to get out of the pickup.

"You the yardmaster?" he asked, showing him his badge.

"That's right," he said, checking his pocket watch. "Is there a problem?"

"My caboose is getting new shoes over there, and there's a crate of perishables strapped on the porch. Wondered if you could have someone take it to the icehouse until I can get back?"

The yardmaster dropped his watch back into his pocket. "What kind of perishables?" he asked.

"I'm not at liberty to say," Hook said.

The yardmaster took off his hat and rubbed at his bald head. "Well, it's against company rules to be handling personal goods. A railroad bull ought know that. The big boys would raise hell if they found out."

Hook said, "I'm aware of that, alright. The thing is, and I wouldn't want this to go any farther, it's the big boys who have a personal interest in seeing this is delivered, if you understand my meaning."

"Oh," he said. "Well, I guess it wouldn't hurt nothing. I'll have the boys store it in the back of the plant."

"Thanks," Hook said. "I'm sure the powers who matter will appreciate it."

―――――――

Hook waited downline for something headed eastbound. His feet ached, and his elbow burned from having skidded down the right-of-way with that damn kid hanging on to his leg.

When an old steamer came chugging out of the yards with another engine at her back, Hook gave her a wave down. She came in slow and easy, her brakes screeching as she pulled to a stop.

Frenchy leaned out the window. "If it ain't Hook Runyon," he said. "I thought maybe you'd gone back to bumming."

"How about a hitch, Frenchy?" Hook said.

"You ain't got a dead man with you, do you?" he asked.

"Not yet," Hook said.

"Well, climb aboard. I'm headed to salvage with this old battle-ship. She's been sitting 'til the drivers are all rusted up."

Hook climbed up and settled in at the back of the cabin. The bakehead nodded and turned back to his business. Frenchy bled her out and eased up the throttle. The old bullgine took a deep breath and moved off downline. Frenchy checked his pressure and lit his cigar.

"Where the hell your caboose go, Hook?" he asked. "I'd figured on picking you up on my way back from the smelter."

"Bastards towed it off," Hook said.

Frenchy grinned. "Maybe the big boys are trying to tell you something, Hook."

Hook adjusted his sitting place to pick up the breeze from Frenchy's window.

"Eddie put it in the hospital and failed to inform me. I about wore my legs off walking this damn track."

"Walking's got to be a new experience for a yard dog," he said. "Where you headed now?"

"Back to Carmen," Hook said. "Unfinished business."

"You haven't gotten that boy to his people *yet*?"

"It's a possibility I've been looking for the wrong guy all along."

"Well, now," he said. "That might come as a surprise to some what don't know the ins and outs of railroad security, but it damn sure don't to those of us who do."

Within the hour, Hook could see the Avard elevators rising into the blue. Frenchy stuck his head out the window as they pulled into Avard, bringing her down to a crawl.

"You might want to step on it, Hook. Looks like the Frisco's making up a short haul for Carmen this very minute, and I figure it's not in your plans to buy a ticket."

Hook swung out on the ladder and dropped off in a trot. He waved at Frenchy, who answered back with a short blast of his whistle.

Hook settled in on the Frisco short haul and watched the wheat fields slide by at a slow clip. Evening settled in over the plains, and the horizon simmered in an orange glow. Tractor lights blinked on in the surrounding fields, and the night smelled of freshly turned earth.

As darkness fell, Hook pulled up his collar. In the distance, he could see the orphanage, and the wink of lights from its windows. He thought about Celia, her auburn hair and widow's peak. He thought about Eagleman and Buck Steele and little Bet. Most of all, he thought about Bruce Mason and his secret life as Samuel Ash.

32

THE NEXT MORNING, Hook found Skink asleep in the supply room. He fixed coffee and took him in a cup.

"Skink," he said, pushing on his shoulder. "This is Patch. I know what you've been doing, Skink."

Skink groaned and opened an eye. "Oh, damn," he said. "It's you, Hook." He rubbed at his face. "I dreamed Patch was sitting on my chest, and I couldn't breathe. He just kept on grinning and saying out my name."

Hook handed him his coffee. "It's a bad conscience, Skink, from staying up nights doing things you shouldn't be doing."

"What's it to hurt, Hook?"

Hook held up his prosthesis. "Just saying, Skink."

"Ah," he said. "Jeez, Hook, what happened to your clothes?"

Hook looked down at his britches, torn and dirty from his roll down the right-of-way.

"Yard doggin' can be a dangerous business. Now I've a question for you?"

"Okay."

"You ever hear of a guy by the name of Bruce Mason?"

"Sure," he said. "He used to live at the orphanage."

"How well did you know him?"

"Not very. The older kids didn't hang out much with us younger ones."

"What can you tell me about him?"

"They say that he got into trouble with the law and ran off."

"What kind of trouble?"

Skink shrugged. "Robbing someone, I think. I never did know for sure, but Jimmy Weston said he saw it in the paper and everything."

"I see. Maybe I can find something there. Thanks, Skink."

"Oh, and Bruce Mason had a girlfriend," Skink said. "I don't remember her name."

"Is she still at the orphanage?"

"No. They said she ran away, too."

Hook waited outside the newspaper office until it opened at nine. The lady who let him in had on compression socks. She led him to a small room in the back, which served as the morgue for the paper.

"We don't spend much time on organizing, mostly by dates," she said. "No one hardly ever uses these except for wedding pictures and genealogy stuff." Hook looked at the stack of yellowing newspapers. "And we close for lunch, but you can come back about one thirty if you want," she said, shutting the door behind her.

By eleven thirty, Hook knew more about the local football team and the Future Farmers of America than he ever wanted to know. He was about to quit, when he spotted the headline: "Orphanage Couple on the Run." He read on:

> Last night Ron Bolley, of Bolley's Gas Station in Cherokee, reported that a young man held them at gunpoint and ordered them to surrender all their money. Over two hundred dollars in

cash were taken by the gunman, who then apologized to the owner before fleeing on foot.

Shortly thereafter, according to the police, the Spirit of Agape Orphanage in Carmen reported that one Bruce Mason, age 18, and Lucy Barker, age 16, could not be located.

Cherokee Police interviewed Mr. Bain Eagleman, the orphanage superintendent, who said that the boy and the girl were frequently seen together, that neither had living relatives, and that few clues had been left behind as to their whereabouts.

Mr. Buck Steele, orphanage foreman, reported that he saw Bruce Mason and Lucy Barker on the grounds together at about six o'clock that same evening. No one has seen or heard from either of them since their disappearance.

Hook went outside and sat on the steps to think about what he'd just read. Now he understood why Bruce Mason had forged his name on those enlistment papers, but what he didn't know was what had happened to Lucy Barker.

Skink stood at the buffer putting a high shine on a pair of loafers. When he saw Hook come in, he shut down the machine.

"Patch has gone to the bank," he said.

"Listen, Skink, you said that you remembered Bruce Mason's girlfriend. Would her name have been Lucy Barker?"

Skink set the shoes aside and picked up another pair. "Yeah, that's it. Lucy Barker. Pretty, too," he said. "Course, she didn't pay me any mind."

"But she and Bruce Mason were close?"

"Sometimes they held hands on the way to school."

"Did Lucy have girlfriends?"

Skink nodded. "Lots. She was popular, you know."

"I mean special girlfriends?"

Skink scratched his head. "Esther," he said. "They roomed together. They talked all the time and passed notes. Sometimes they giggled a lot, you know, like girls do."

"Is Esther still at the orphanage?"

"Naw," she's gone. "She works in Cherokee, phone company, I heard."

"Do you remember her last name?"

"Rice, I think. Or Reece. That's it. Esther Reece."

"But she hasn't been back since she left?"

"No one comes back to Agape if they don't have to," he said.

Hook dug the phone out from under Patch's latest booby trap and called Celia.

"Agape," she said. "Celia Feola."

"Celia, Hook here. I've some news about Bruce Mason."

"Oh?"

"I need to go to Cherokee and check some things out. Do you think you could take me? I'll fill you in on the way."

"Well," she said, "Mr. Eagleman is back from his conference."

"It could be important."

"I'll try to get away. Where do you want me to meet you?"

"The back of Patch's shoe shop. I'll be waiting."

As they turned on the highway headed for Cherokee, Celia looked over her shoulder at Hook, and her chin dropped.

"Samuel Ash *is* Bruce Mason?"

"I can't be a hundred percent sure at this point, but it looks that way."

"So this girl, Lucy Barker, must have helped him rob the station so they could run off together?" Celia said.

"They disappeared the same night. And Esther Reece, being one of her closest friends at the orphanage, just might be able to tell us something."

Hook rolled the window and let the wind blow through his hair.

"Skink told me you've been out of town," she said.

"They hauled off my caboose," he said. "And Samuel Ash with it."

"Oh my."

"It turned up in the Waynoka roundhouse."

"And Samuel Ash?"

"Safe now in the ice plant," he said.

Celia drove for several miles without saying anything. Finally, she turned to him and said, "Are you telling me that you put Samuel Ash in the ice plant?"

"Or Bruce Mason," he said. "Take your pick."

"Hook," she said, "I consider myself as unflappable as they come, but this is crazy. You can't just haul a body all over the country and then store it on ice while you hunt down a girl you don't even know."

"They were going to bury Samuel Ash in a pauper's grave and forget he ever existed, Celia. If Lucy Barker and Bruce Mason were married or in love, then she should know about his death.

"I set out to bury that boy proper, and that's what I intend to do, though I admit that things have gotten a bit complicated. But it's just a little delay."

Celia shook her head and slowed for the Cherokee city limits. As they came into town, Hook spotted the phone company.

"There it is," he said.

Celia pulled over and shut off the engine.

"Maybe it would be better if you went in, Celia. I might frighten her."

Celia opened her door. "I can't think why," she said, sliding out.

Within minutes they emerged from the office. Celia opened the back door and Esther, a heavy-set girl in her early twenties, got into the back. Hook watched her through the mirror.

"Esther, this is Hook Runyon, railroad security agent," Celia said. "We appreciate you talking to us."

"Hello," Hook said, making eye contact in the mirror. "I hope we aren't interrupting your work."

"We were just closing," she said. "But I don't know what I can tell you."

"You knew Lucy Barker?" Hook asked.

She nodded. "Lucy and I were friends at Agape."

"Do you have any idea of where she might be now?"

Esther shook her head. "The police asked me all that before. Lucy didn't tell me anything."

"Did she ever talk to you about Bruce Mason?"

"She said he was cute, but all the girls said that."

"Did she say she was in love with him?" Celia asked.

Esther opened her hands and studied them. "Yes," she said. "Most of us were, I guess."

Hook asked, "Had she been acting differently? I mean, girl-friends can tell if something is wrong, can't they?"

"I don't know. She hadn't been feeling well, and she'd been kind of sad. But all the kids at the orphanage got sad sometimes. It's not easy being alone."

"No," Hook said. "I'm sure that's true."

Celia turned to Esther. "We're only trying to help her, Esther. Is there something you're not telling us?"

Esther wove her fingers together and looked out the window. "I heard her crying in the night. I asked her what was wrong. She said that everything was going to be fine and that I shouldn't worry."

"But she didn't say what?" Hook asked.

"I woke up later that same night, and Lucy was sitting at the desk writing something. The next morning she was gone. I heard later that she'd helped Bruce rob the filling station in Cherokee, and they'd run away together."

"Did she leave a note for you?" Celia asked.

"No," she said. "And I never saw her again."

Hook adjusted the mirror. "Did you tell this to the police?"

"Yes, but they'd already made up their minds about Lucy and Bruce."

"You have no idea what the note said?"

Esther pursed her lips. "No."

"You've been very helpful," Hook said. "One final question: do you think Lucy Barker and Bruce Mason held up that filling station?"

Hook studied Esther's reaction in the mirror. She lowered her head in thought before answering.

"I don't think Lucy would ever steal anything," she said.

On the way out of town, Celia stopped at the restaurant, and Hook bought them coffee. They rode in silence most of the way home. Celia pulled in at the back of the shop and shut off her lights.

"If Esther is right and Lucy didn't help with the robbery, then Bruce must have done it on his own," she said.

"Or maybe she didn't know about it at all. Maybe he lied about where he got the money."

"Were there no witnesses?" she asked.

"According to the newspaper, Buck Steele saw them together on the orphanage grounds that same night."

"But no one saw her at the robbery?" she said.

"No."

She rocked the steering wheel and looked at him through the darkness.

"So where do you go from here?" she asked.

Hook looked at her.

"First, I have to be certain who's in that casket," he said. "I know of only one way to do that."

33

THE PHONE WENT off at five, and Hook stumbled through the shop, trying to locate it under a stack of insoles.

"Runyon," he said.

"Hook, this is Junior Monroe."

Hook peeked out the window to see the sun just breaking over the horizon.

"Jesus, Junior, do you know what time it is?"

"I've been on that road-rail for hours, Hook. I don't know what year it is. Popeye claimed I owed him two dollars and wouldn't let me take the road-rail unless I paid him."

"And did you?"

"I stole the keys while he was on the phone."

"You're going to make a hell of a yard dog, Junior."

"And the brakes don't work. I have to stand on them with both feet to get the road-rail to stop. By the time I arrived in the Waynoka yards, both my legs had gone dead, and I fell out of the door. Anyway, I'm here. Now what do you want me to do?"

"I want you to go over to the ice plant and pick up Samuel Ash."

"What?"

"He's in the back of the plant somewhere."

"You put Samuel Ash in the ice plant?"

"Load him up and bring him here to the Carmen city park."

Hook could hear Junior breathing on the other end of the line. "Junior, are you there?"

"The city park in Carmen," he said.

"Meet me at the park restroom. You should be here by lunchtime."

"I'm not going to ask why, Hook."

"That's good, Junior. We'll operate on a need-to-know basis. Now, what did you find out about the Pampa bridge and the B&B?"

"I told the foreman we'd be initiating an investigation if the bridge didn't get repaired soon. Apparently, he now thinks the parts might be around somewhere, that someone had probably just misplaced them."

"You did good, Junior. I'll see you later."

Hook had no sooner hung up when Skink arrived. He opened the front door, yawning.

"Morning, Hook," he said.

"Morning, Skink. I'm fixing the coffee."

"Patch said I've been using too much coffee. He threatened to dock my pay."

"I'll pick some up later," Hook said, pouring the water into the pot.

"You might want to put your pants on before you go, Hook."

"Oh, yeah," he said.

By the time Hook got dressed, Skink had fallen asleep at the workbench. Hook poured the coffees and nudged him awake.

"Here," he said.

Skink sucked at his coffee and rested his chin in his hand. "Mr. Eagleman says my time at Agape has expired. He says I better be finding employment soon, but I'm thinking I might not want to be a yard dog just yet."

"Then you wouldn't have to go around shooting up people, Skink."

"Maybe I'll just buy Patch out and run a shoe-repair business right here in Carmen."

"You have the money to buy him out?"

"Not exactly," he said.

"Listen, Skink, you told me one time that you saw Buck Steele going through Eagleman's trash."

Junior sipped on his coffee. "I spotted him spying on me walking the circle out to the cemetery. I figured he'd be telling Mr. Eagleman I shorted my laps, so I followed him back to the orphanage and hid in the stairwell. Sure enough, he went into Mr. Eagleman's office. When he came out, he had Eagleman's trash, and he went through it under the hall light before he took it out to the incinerator."

"Do you know if he found anything?"

Skink nodded his head. "But I couldn't see what, and I didn't want to get caught. Buck would have skinned me out."

Hook went to the shop window and looked out into the morning sky. "You don't remember exactly when this took place, do you?"

Skink twisted his mouth to the side. "I do. It happened the same night Bruce Mason ran away."

Hook turned to him. "Could you meet me at the city park restrooms at noon today, Skink?"

"We going to watch the girls, Hook?"

"No. There's someone I'd like you to meet."

"Okay. Long as I don't have to look at Mildred Bonfield's butt again," he said.

Hook and Skink were sitting in the park swings when Junior Monroe turned into the drive. The road-rail, with Samuel Ash tied onto the back, jumped the curb and lurched to a stop only feet from the swings.

Junior climbed out, rubbed his backside, and pumped the life back into his legs.

"Junior," Hook said. "I'd like for you to meet Skink. Skink, this is Junior Monroe, my associate."

Skink shook Junior's hand. "You're a yard dog, too?" he asked.

Junior straightened his tie. "That's not entirely clear," he said.

"Skink," Hook said, "do you know where the mortuary is in this town?"

"The funeral parlor?"

"That's right."

"Just down the block. It's Juice Dawson's place. He sells furniture out the front and booze out the back. Why?"

"Because I got business there. Now, you boys help me push this road-rail off the curb, and we'll drive on over and see if he's home."

"Maybe I better get on back to the shoe shop," Skink said. "Patch will be docking my pay again."

"Push, Skink, and let me worry about Patch."

As they rambled off down Main, Skink turned and said, "What's in the box?"

"Don't ask," Junior said.

"It's a body," Hook said.

Skink looked at Hook. "What kind of body?"

"A dead body," Hook said.

Skink buried his hands between his knees. "Whose dead body is it, Hook?"

Hook pulled into the funeral home and let the road-rail roll up against the curb.

"That's what we're going to find out. You boys stay here while I see if Mr. Dawson is home."

The man who opened the door had to duck down so as not to bump his head. His arms hung too long for his waist, and his cheeks were sunken.

"Mr. Dawson?" Hook asked.

"Yes," he said. "I'm Juice Dawson."

"My name is Hook Runyon. I'm the railroad bull with the Santa Fe and am the escort for a body that's been shipped from Carlsbad, New Mexico, to Carmen. It's out there in the road-rail."

Juice looked over the top of Hook's head. "That boy they found hung?" he asked.

"Yes," Hook said.

"Been expecting you. I received notice from Carlsbad some days back. Sure took long enough for it to get here."

"You know the railroad," Hook said.

"You brought some help for loading, did you?"

"I admit they don't look like much," Hook said.

"Well, pull around back, and we'll get the paperwork together."

Hook backed around to the double doors. Juice opened them up and rolled out a mortuary truck.

"Alright, boys," Hook said. "Grab hold."

Skink's eyes widened. "You mean we have to unload it?"

Hook nodded. "It's not proper for an officer of the law to be seen doing manual labor. Folks might think he's lost his authority."

"The sheriff paints houses," Skink said.

"I rest my case," Hook said. "Now get hold."

"Being a yard dog's associate is not as easy as you might think," Junior said.

Skink and Junior slid out the container and hoisted it onto the mortuary truck. Juice pushed it into his lab and went to get the paperwork. Skink and Junior stood next to the stainless steel dissection table.

"I'll wait outside," Skink said.

"Hang tight," Hook said. "I've got an assignment for you."

Just then Juice came back in with the papers. "Sign here," he said. "And I'll need to know where you want him interred."

"Here's the thing," Hook said, signing the paper. "We believed this fellow to be Samuel Ash, but now there's some confusion about the identity of the body. I need to have the casket opened so that Skink here can have a look."

Skink backed up, his face pale. "You want *me* to have a look?"

"Well," Juice said, "the body's been prepped for transit. Opening the casket now would be a little unusual. I'd have to break the seal and . . ."

"This is important, or I wouldn't ask," Hook said.

Juice scratched his head. "Well, according to the records here there's no contagious diseases involved, and the body has been cavity embalmed for transit."

Skink leaned against the wall. "I never looked at no dead body before."

Hook said, "There's evidence that leads me to believe that this body may be someone other than who I thought. I've got to know for sure who I'm burying. If it takes a court order, that's what I'll do. But it sure would complicate things for both of us."

"You don't think it's Samuel Ash?" Junior asked.

"I'm no longer sure," Hook said.

"Let me get my tools," Juice said. "But you fellows don't need to be spreading this all over town."

Hook, Junior, and Skink stood back as Juice worked open the transit container. Unlocking the casket lid, he pushed it open.

Hook took hold of Skink's arm and led him up to the casket.

"Do you know who that is, Skink?" he asked.

Skink's knees buckled a little, and Hook steadied him.

"Yes," he said, his voice shaking. "That's Bruce Mason from the Agape orphanage."

"You boys wait outside," Hook said. "I need to speak with Juice."

When they'd gone, Hook said, "Can you postpone interment until I can get this straightened out?"

Juice shut the lid on the casket. "There's no family involved here, is there?" he asked.

"That doesn't appear to be the case," Hook said. "And there's a possibility that this could be a homicide."

"Well," he said, "I don't see what a few days' delay could hurt."

"You said you received word that this body was in transit before we got here, is that correct?" Hook asked.

"Yes. It's customary," he said. "Carlsbad informed me by letter that the body of one Samuel Ash had been prepped and would be sent by train. Details of the embalming procedure were also provided for the health department. The letter stated that the money for burial would be provided by the indigent burial fund if no responsible relatives could be located."

"Nothing out of the usual?" Hook asked.

"Standard operating procedure," he said. "It's important that particulars be provided before a body arrives. There are preparations that need to be made, you understand."

"Did you happen to mention to anyone else that this body had been shipped by train from Carlsbad?"

Juice gathered up his tools as he thought about Hook's question.

"I don't normally talk about my business to anyone," he said. "People can be irrational when it comes to discussing these matters. But, in this case, I may have in fact brought it up."

"Oh?"

"I'm on the Spirit of Agape Orphanage board, and I mentioned at the board meeting that I had a hanging coming in from Carlsbad by the name of Samuel Ash and wondered if anyone had heard of him. No one there had. I hope I haven't caused a problem, Mr. Runyon."

Hook walked to the door. "Who is responsible for the burials at the orphanage cemetery?"

"Financially, the orphanage. As for interments, it's theoretically open to any funeral home, but in practice my establishment takes care of almost all the burials. Being on the board has its advantages."

"Thank you, Juice. I'll get back to you soon as possible." He paused. "What is the procedure for providing markers for a grave?"

"A brass marker is supplied by us until the standard stone marker is donated by the orphanage. More elaborate monuments would have to be provided by the family. Since it's an orphanage, that's a rare occurrence."

"I see, and at what point do you provide the brass marker?"

"As soon as possible, a matter of a few days at most," he said. "You'd be surprised how easily bodies can be misplaced."

34

Hook DROPPED SKINK off at the shoe shop before driving Junior down to the crossing.

He eased the road-rail to a stop. "I need you to follow up on that Pampa deal, Junior. They could still be sitting on their hands. Eddie can get unreasonable about such things."

"Alright," he said. "You want me to drive this thing back to Pampa?"

"Well, not exactly," Hook said, getting out. "I'm going to need it for conducting business."

Junior looked at the line of wheat hoppers that had been emptied and now awaited their trip back to the Avard elevators.

"How am I to get back then, Hook?"

"Same way you got to Kansas City."

"But I thought you were going to get a pass for me."

"It's number one on my priority list," Hook said. "Soon as I get things under control here, I'll see to it. For now, you'll have to hop this short haul back to Avard. There's a westbound at six in the morning and an eastbound at two, seven days a week, regular as clockwork. Got it?"

Junior rubbed at his face. "You'd think the railroad could provide its employees decent transportation."

"Being a good yard dog's all about making do with what you got, Junior. And remember, this is the Frisco, not the Santa Fe. They might not take kindly to you riding free of charge on their short haul."

"What would they do to me?"

"I'd rather not say. Call me if anything comes up on that Pampa deal."

Hook waited until the short haul had pulled out, and he could see Junior scrunched over the wheel truck of the last hopper. Junior gave a weak wave-off as he disappeared down the track.

Hook headed back into town. When he passed the café, he realized he had forgotten to eat.

The waitress, a woman with arm wings and cobalt-frame eyeglasses, took his order. She barked it back to the cook from the table, and within minutes a bowl of boiled cabbage with smoked ham hock and potatoes appeared in front of him. She disappeared and came back with a quarter-loaf of warm homemade sourdough, fresh cow butter, and a glass of cold milk.

When Hook had sopped up the last of his soup, he ordered the rhubarb pie with vanilla ice cream and a cup of black coffee.

The waitress topped off his coffee. "You gonna live, honey?" she asked.

Hook pushed his bowl aside and said, "If it's my time to die, I'm ready."

He watched the waitress bus the tables, and he wondered if Junior Monroe had made it to Avard without falling off or derailing the train. The boy had a knack for trouble, which probably meant he'd either wind up in jail or become governor of the state. He thought about the situation with Bruce Mason and Lucy Barker, and he wondered how she could have just disappeared without a trace.

Maybe Esther hadn't told all she knew. Maybe she'd been hiding something. To date, the only thing he felt certain about was that Lucy Barker, more than anyone else, held the key to the hanging of Samuel Ash.

After leaving a larger tip than he should have, he drove down the street to where the sheriff had just climbed down from his ladder to refill his paint bucket.

"Morning, Sheriff," Hook said.

The sheriff dropped his brush into a can of turpentine.

"You still in town?"

"Using up Patch's rent," Hook said. "Wondering if you remember a fellow around here by the name of Bruce Mason?"

Taking off his hat, the sheriff dabbed at the dent in his head with his handkerchief.

"Boy from out to the orphanage," he said. "He robbed the filling station over in Cherokee, as I recall."

"That's my understanding."

"Not in my jurisdiction, you know, but they called for me to keep a lookout. Nothing ever came up. Seems like I remember a girl being involved, too?"

"Lucy Barker?" Hook said.

"Yeah, that's right. Lucy Barker. They had the hots, guess you'd say, and needed money."

Hook hiked his foot up on the ladder rung. "You never had any trouble out of them before?"

He scrunched up an eye. "The orphanage keeps a pretty tight rein on those kids out there. I've seen them walking that dang circle in the middle of the night."

"Well, thanks, Sheriff. Good luck with the painting."

The sheriff picked up his brush. "You find that Samuel what's his name's people yet?"

"Not yet."

"You know, there *was* that one time," he said.

"What time's that, Sheriff?"

"That girl Lucy came up missing from school one day. About six or so that evening, I get a call from the highway patrol saying they'd picked her up hitchhiking home."

"Oh? From where?"

The sheriff shrugged. "Cherokee, they figured. Guess they got it resolved. Never did hear no more about it. Between painting houses and keeping Momma happy, I don't have much time for nosing around."

Hook sat on the curb with Mixer until school let out. Bet saw him first thing when she came out the door.

"Hello," she said, sitting down next to Mixer.

"Hello," Hook said.

"Hello, Mixer," she said, putting her arm around his neck.

"How did school go?" Hook asked.

She shrugged. "The teacher said orphans get their lunch free."

"Well, that's good," he said.

"Yeah."

"You want Mixer to walk you home?"

"Okay," she said. "Are you going to walk, too?"

"Yeah," he said. "I'll walk, too."

As they walked toward the orphanage, Mixer hung at her side. Bet blew bubbles and skipped down the road. Once, she stopped to tie her shoe.

"You doing okay now, Bet?" Hook asked.

"Yeah," she said. "I get to sleep on the top bunk. I wish Mixer could stay with me, though. But Mr. Eagleman said if he did it for one, he'd have to do it for all."

Hook said, "How's the food now?"

"Fine," she said. "We don't eat shepherd pie no more, and Miss Feola is baking peanut butter cookies for all the kids tonight."

"Your grandma made good food," Hook said.

"Yeah," she said. "I can cook, too."

When they reached the drive, Hook stopped. "Maybe I better go back now."

"Can't Mixer walk me on home? And I bet Miss Feola would give you a cookie."

Hook looked down the driveway. "Sure," he said. "Why not?"

As they walked by the orphanage, Hook could see Bain Eagleman in his shirtsleeves watching them from his upstairs office window. He slipped on his coat, stood back in the shadows, and then disappeared from sight.

Hook and Bet found Celia in the kitchen with a plate of peanut butter cookies, just as Bet had said.

"Hello," she said. "Have one? I baked them myself."

"Believe I will," Hook said, taking one.

"And here's one for Bet," she said. "And one for Mixer, too."

Mixer wolfed his down in one bite and wanted more.

"Well," Hook said, "Mixer begged to walk Bet home until I gave in. I better be on my way. Thanks for the cookie. Bye, Bet."

"Bye. Bye, Mixer," she said, bouncing out of the kitchen.

"Couldn't you stay for coffee?" Celia asked.

"Thanks, but another time. I think I may have worn out my welcome with Mr. Eagleman, and Mixer has a definite attitude about Buck Steele."

Celia smiled. "Another time then."

Hook paused. "I asked Skink to take a look at Samuel Ash today. He identified him as Bruce Mason. There's no doubt about it now."

"I guess you'll be leaving soon, then?"

"There's the matter of Lucy Barker," he said. "And a few too many unanswered questions about the boy's death."

"I see."

Hook looked out at the barn. Buck Steele sat on the corral fence popping his whip over the backs of the milk cows.

"I'm at a dead end here," he said. "I need to find Lucy. If anyone knows how and why that boy died, it would have to be her."

Celia set the tray of cookies on the table. "You're asking me to look in her records, aren't you?"

Hook nodded. "Maybe there's something there that could help."

"Maybe," she said. "I'll call you later tonight." She picked up the tray of cookies again. "You sure you don't want another?"

Hook took one. "Thanks, Celia, and be careful."

Hook sat in the darkness of the shoe-shop office having a Beam and water. He looked at the phone. He didn't like having to place Celia in a situation like this. It could cost her job, maybe worse. He'd gotten a good look at Bain Eagleman's temperament, and he hadn't liked what he saw.

When the phone rang, adrenaline shot through him. Setting his glass aside, he picked up.

"Hook," he said.

"This is Celia," she said. "I'm calling from the kitchen. Everyone has gone to bed. I did what you asked."

"You found her records?"

"Born in Tulsa. Her mother died at birth, and she lived with her father and his sister until the age of six. She turned eighteen about a year ago."

"Go on," he said.

"Her father was an alcoholic, a bad one apparently, because they found him dead in the stockyards. Someone had killed him with a knife and taken his clothes."

"What about the sister?"

"She's the one who brought Lucy to Agape. Said she didn't have the means to take care of her any longer. She didn't leave a forwarding address."

The streetlight blinked on and lit up the rows of shoes in the front of the store. "Anything else?"

"Just the usual. Her medical is up to date, inoculations, physicals, that sort of thing. She fell off the school swing in the sixth grade and broke her front tooth. Other than that, I didn't see anything out of the ordinary."

"No problems at school or at the orphanage? Disciplinary actions?"

"She ditched school one day when she was a senior, but who doesn't? The highway patrol picked her up. Apparently, they found her hitchhiking on the highway."

"Eagleman knew about this?"

"It's in her records."

"No action taken? No walking the circle, anything like that?"

"No, not that I saw."

Hook rubbed the black off his prosthesis. He must have gotten into Patch's shoe polish in the darkness.

"I want to go back and talk to Esther again," he said. "I think she knows more than she's telling."

"Wait a minute," Celia said, whispering. When she came back on, she said, "It's okay, just the cook getting something to eat. I told her you were my mother. Now, you want to talk to Esther again? About what?"

"I don't know. It's a feeling."

"I don't have a car," she said. "Mr. Eagleman and Buck go to the city every few days to buy supplies."

"I have the road-rail," he said. "And Esther might be more comfortable talking with you along."

"Well," she said, "I guess I could."

"Around eight? I'll pick you up."

"Eight's fine," she said, pausing. "What's a road-rail, Hook?"

"It's a surprise," he said. "I'll see you in the morning."

35

CELIA MET HIM at the end of the Agape drive-
way. She wore slacks, white deck shoes, and had her hair up.

"Oh my gosh," she said. "What is this thing?"

Hook got out and opened the door. "Road-rail," he said. "It runs
on road and rail alike, when it runs at all. There are more comfortable rides," he said. "Worse, too, if you've ever hopped a freight
train."

Celia settled in and looked back at the orphanage as they pulled
away.

"Not many freight trains," she said. "I did ride a horse one
time."

"Close to the same thing," Hook said.

Celia found a place for her purse among the tools. "I feel a little
guilty taking off this way," she said. "I've left a lot of work behind."

Hook lit a cigarette, striking the match with his prosthesis. He
looked up to find Celia watching him.

"I forget sometimes that I even have this hook," he said.

Celia covered her mouth. "Oh, I'm sorry. I didn't mean to . . ."

"Don't apologize," he said. "It's a curiosity, I admit. Would you care to know what happened?"

"No," she said. "Not my business."

"It's a part of me, Celia. Without this hook, I'd be someone else and not necessarily for the better. I lost my arm in a car wreck. My girlfriend was at the wheel. After I lost my arm, I hit the skids and wound up bumming the rails. That's how I came about being a yard dog. I'd probably have been in a jail cell or dead by now at the rate I traveled before the accident, so I figure all and all I came out ahead on the deal."

"We're all shaped by something," she said. "My handicap came in the form of religion, large doses of it. At least your disability is out there where you can see it."

"Along with everyone else," he said. "But it's only something I contend with so long as I'm alive." He held the prosthesis up. "I'll be leaving this behind when I die, while you're going right into the hereafter with yours."

Hook turned onto the highway and brought the old road-rail up to speed. She clanked and thumped as he herded her down the highway.

"So, Skink confirmed what you suspected about Samuel Ash?"

Hook nodded. "Not without a certain amount of discomfort on his part, which I regret, but I needed to be certain. The body now resting in the funeral parlor is Bruce Mason and not Samuel Ash."

"And what answers do you expect to find today?"

"All I have are questions, too damn many of them. What we apparently have here is a couple of kids who ran off together after committing a crime. We know where Bruce Mason is and what happened to him, but we don't know what happened to Lucy. Why did he join the army and leave her behind? Where did he leave her? Were they married before he joined? Does she have any idea of who might have killed him? Once we have Lucy, we should have a good many more answers. I'm just hoping that Esther can help narrow this down."

He looked over at her. "And here's yet one more to ponder: if Lucy Barker skipped school, was picked up by the highway patrol, and all that business wound up in her records at the orphanage, why didn't Bain Eagleman discipline her? I mean, here's a guy who's willing to put little girls on the circle for not eating their shepherd pie."

Hook started slowing down a block from the phone office and still ran one tire up on the lawn.

"Maybe you should go in," he said.

"Right," Celia said. "I know the routine."

When they came out, Esther stopped and looked at the road-rail.

"What is it?" she asked.

Celia pointed to the door. "It's alright, Esther. It's a railroad thing and more or less safe."

Esther slid in and nodded at Hook. "I don't have much time," she said. "Someone is covering for me."

"Thanks for coming," Hook said. "Here's the deal: we know that Bruce Mason was hanged off the wigwag signal in Carlsbad, New Mexico. What we don't know is what happened to Lucy Barker."

Esther's face paled. "Bruce was hanged?"

"We've reason to suspect it might have been murder. That being the case, Lucy herself might be in danger."

Esther wove her fingers together and looked out the window. "You think someone might try to kill her, too?"

"It's possible," Hook said. "I need to find Lucy, and I think you can help."

"I don't know where she is," Esther said.

"The highway patrol picked Lucy up for hitchhiking. Are you aware of that?"

Esther glanced at Celia. "Yes," she said.

"Where had she been?" Celia asked.

"Here," she said. "Cherokee."

"Was anyone else with her?" Hook asked.

"No. She came alone."

"Do you know why she came here?" Celia asked.

Esther looked away. "I promised her I wouldn't tell anyone. She made me swear."

"This is more important, Esther. Lucy may be in danger," Hook said.

"To see the doctor," she said.

"The doctor?" Celia asked. "But the orphanage doctor is in Carmen."

"She didn't want to go to him," Esther said.

"Do you know why?" Celia asked.

"She wouldn't talk about it, and she made me swear that I wouldn't tell anyone where she'd been."

"Pregnant?" Celia asked.

Esther shrugged. "She didn't want to talk about it, and I didn't push her."

"Do you know which doctor?" Hook asked.

"The one on Seventh, Dr. Betcher. I better get back now," she said. "Don't tell Lucy I told you. I gave her my word."

"No," Hook said. "We won't. Thank you, Esther."

After Esther had gone back in, Hook said, "We need to know for sure why she went to the doctor, Celia."

"We could go talk to him," she said.

Hook drummed his fingers on the steering wheel. "They won't release her medical information."

Celia took out her lipstick and drew it across her lips. Dropping it back into her purse, she said, "They would to me. The orphanage has legal guardianship of Lucy. As matron, I have access to her medical records."

"You would ask then?"

"Crank this thing up," she said. "And see if you can't get me there alive."

Hook waited in front while Celia went in. After some time, she came out and slid into the road-rail.

"Well?" he said.

"At first he didn't want to release the information. When I explained that I had legal authority, he agreed to discuss the matter with me."

"And?"

"A pregnancy test." She studied her hands. "Positive."

"That could explain why they ran away together," he said.

"It could have."

"But you don't think so?" he said.

"I asked if the bill had been paid. It had, but not by Bruce or by Lucy."

Hook processed what Celia had just said.

"Whoever paid that bill had to have known that she was pregnant."

Celia dropped her hands in her lap. "Exactly."

"But who?"

Celia looked over at him. "The Spirit of Agape Orphanage paid the bill."

36

HOOK PULLED OVER at the orphanage cemetery and shut off the road-rail. He looked out over the row of stones.

"I can feel the sadness here," he said.

"Death *is* sad," she said. "But more so when it's children."

"Children without anyone," he said. "Where's the purpose in that?"

"I thought I knew the purpose of life at one time," she said.

"But not now?"

"Anyone who hasn't questioned the truth of their religion is either lying, or afraid, or both."

He rolled down his window and smelled the freshly turned fields.

"If the orphanage paid that bill, it should have been in Lucy's records. Why wasn't it?"

Celia folded her arms over her chest. "Because they had something to hide?" she said. "Or maybe they were protecting someone else."

"I can't see Eagleman looking out for anyone other than himself," he said. "This is the bastard who puts a little girl out here to walk by herself."

"You're thinking what I'm thinking, that maybe the baby was Eagleman's?"

Hook hung his arm through the steering wheel. "Yes, that would explain it, but it wouldn't explain why Bruce Mason died."

"Maybe Eagleman killed him."

"There's no evidence to support any of this," he said.

"Maybe Bruce Mason hung himself. Maybe he knew the baby wasn't his, and he took his own life. Young boys can be impulsive that way."

"There are too many possibilities here, and they all make sense. We have to rule some of them out."

Celia fell silent for a moment. When she looked up, she said, "Like exactly where *was* Eagleman on the night of the hanging?"

Hook rolled up the window. "Yes."

"Do we know what day Bruce Mason died?"

Hook thought for a moment. "The thirteenth. Friday the thirteenth. I remember the Artesia operator mentioning it."

"Eagleman keeps a calendar on his desk, and he's quite meticulous about entering everything that he does."

"A stickler for appointments, too," Hook said.

"I could take a look."

"Thanks, but too risky. Anyway, I want to think about all this. When in doubt, sleep on it."

"Okay," she said. "You'll let me know?"

"I'll call," Hook said, starting up the road-rail. "Thanks for coming with me today. I wish it could have been a more pleasant outing."

"Next time," she said. "I better get back now."

Hook found Patch gluing up half soles on a pair of work boots.

"Well, you're back in town," he said. "How'd you find Cherokee?"

"I'd ask how you knew I went there, but what's the point?"

"Exactly," he said. "And you better be careful of that goddang digger. He's worn the same pair of dress shoes for fifteen years. A man ain't earning an honest living if he can't wear out a pair of shoes more often than that."

"I went there to deliver Samuel Ash to the funeral parlor," Hook said. "But he turned out to be Bruce Mason instead."

Patch stuck some tacks into the corner of his mouth. "That boy what held up the station in Cherokee?"

"The same. He came back a war hero but wound up on the hanging end of a rope."

"Took that girl with him when he ran away, I hear," he said.

"Guess you wouldn't know where she is now?"

Patch hammered in a tack. "My tracking nose ends at the city limits."

"Mind if I use your phone?" Hook asked.

Patch started another tack and looked at Hook over his glasses. "Don't know why you should start asking permission now," he said.

Hook pushed the door closed and dialed Popeye.

"Clovis," Popeye said.

"Popeye, this is Hook. Has Junior Monroe checked in with you yet?"

"I've been thinking about taking over Eddie Preston's job, given all the time I spend keeping track of Junior Monroe."

"You're too smart and pretty for that job, Popeye."

"Blowing smoke up my skirt works about eighty percent of the time," he said. "Junior Monroe called in this morning."

"What did he find out about that Pampa business?"

"Damned if I know. He's still in Avard."

"What?"

"Said a ballast scorcher came through and when he caught hold the grab iron, it yanked him into the next county. Said he had to walk all the way back to Avard. Had to sleep in the grain elevator, and the Frisco dumped a load of wheat on him in the dark. Said he damn near suffocated, that he had wheat up his nose, and in other places he couldn't mention."

"Damn," Hook said.

"Maybe *he* should take Eddie's job," Popeye said.

"He sure enough qualifies. Do you hear anything about that bridge in Pampa? I'll have Eddie barking up my ass here in about two minutes."

"Oh, it's up and running now that Truman said he'd nationalize the railroad."

"The hell?"

"Said he'd conscript every goddang last striker into the army. There are not many things worse than railroading, but the army's one of them. Looks like the strike business is pretty much over."

"Alright. Thanks, Popeye."

"Listen, Hook, about that money?"

"Don't worry about it, Popeye. It's only a dollar you owe me, and I'm not worried about it."

"I think you owe *me* the dollar, Hook. In fact, I'm pretty damn sure of it."

"I'll be getting it to you payday, then, Popeye. I don't like owing a man money, even if it is just a dollar."

Hook dialed Eddie.

"Security," Eddie said.

"Eddie, Hook here."

"Jesus, Runyon, is payday the only time you show up?"

"Looks like that Pampa thing is under control," Hook said.

"Took the president to do it," Eddie said.

"He has the atomic bomb, Eddie. I have Junior."

"Where is that boy?"

"He's checking wheat cars in Avard. I think those Frisco bastards are picking up Santa Fe hoppers and taking them into Carmen. I been working day and night on it, but I don't figure to be asking overtime."

"I don't want anything happening to that boy," he said.

"Is my caboose about ready? I'm paying rent out of my own paycheck."

"That machinist said there wasn't a damn thing wrong with those bushings, Runyon."

"They wouldn't know from bushings, Eddie. I caught those bastards eating lunch and taking naps on my caboose."

"And another thing," Eddie said. "I get this report about some kind of box being stored in the goddang ice plant in Waynoka. What the hell you up to now?"

"Produce, Eddie. One of the reefer cars crapped out, and the boes were helping themselves to breakfast. I rescued it single-handed, so to speak, and put it on ice to save the company money."

"I hadn't realized you were such a saint," he said.

"No thanks necessary, Eddie. Just one of many sacrifices I've been prepared to make. Working for a boss like you makes a man think, you know."

That night Hook walked to the package store and bought a half-pint of Beam. He missed having his caboose. Living in a shoe shop without his books forced him to pass the evening with a little more libation than he preferred. On top of that, without adequate water, he had to drink the damn stuff neat. He'd just chalk it up as one more good deed for the company.

He'd nearly gone to sleep when he heard the ring of the phone from Patch's supply room. Mixer followed him through the darkness and lay down on Hook's feet.

"Hello," Hook said.

"Hook, this is Celia," she said.

"Celia? Are you okay?"

"Yes. I know what you said about waiting, but I had a chance to get a look at Eagleman's calendar when he went for his evening walk."

"Oh?"

"On Friday the thirteenth, he conducted the Spirit of Agape's regularly scheduled board meeting at two P.M. right here in his office."

Hook listened to the silence on the other end. "Then he couldn't have done it," he said.

"It doesn't look like it," she said. "I better hang up now. I'll talk to you soon."

Hook sat in the darkness and thought about Bain Eagleman. The one guy he thought had both motive and opportunity had suddenly been ruled out.

That left Buck Steele. "One down. One to go," he said to himself.

37

Hook LEFT HIS room early and went out the back door to avoid Skink. He needed time to think, and he needed to be alone to do it. He took a long walk down the tracks as the morning sun broke. Mixer followed at his heels, departing now and again to sniff out the gopher holes that dotted the right-of-way.

Once back to town, he stopped in for breakfast at the café and ordered up a large helping of biscuits and gravy, sausage, hash browns, two eggs over easy, and, for his health, a large glass of orange juice. The morning waitress, a large woman who threw her legs out from the knees when she walked, carried the whole thing out stacked on her arm.

"Anything else, hon?" she asked, sitting the plates down.

"I might need resuscitation at some point," he said.

"Mouth-to-mouth?" she asked, without cracking a smile.

"That ought bring me around," he said.

"Uh huh," she said. "With me sitting on your chest, you might wish you'd gone ahead and died."

* Hook finished his breakfast and checked his watch. The waitress took his money and dropped a handful of change into his hand.

"About that mouth-to-mouth thing," he said.

"Oh, sure, hon," she said, smiling. "But I've another six hours on shift. Think you could wait?"

"For you? However long it takes," he said. "Listen, could you direct me to the pool hall?"

"Down about a block," she said. "Across from the filling station. They don't start that poker game until this evening, though."

"Thanks," Hook said.

He found the door open to the pool hall and went in. A man had just stepped in from the alley with a trash can in tow. He had dark black hair that he swept back on his head and a carefully groomed mustache.

"Be with you in a moment," he said.

Hook pulled up a stool and waited for him to put the lid back on the can.

"No one here yet," he said, coming forward. "Games usually don't get rolling until later on."

"Maybe some coffee?" Hook said.

"Longneck or Coke," he said.

Hook slid up to the bar. "Coke."

The man opened a bottle and set it on a napkin. "Pretzels, chips, pickled eggs?"

"I just had breakfast for five," Hook said. "I may never have to eat again."

"Until supper," he said. "Know how that goes."

Hook took a drink of his Coke. "My name's Hook Runyon. I'm the Santa Fe bull and wondered if I could ask you some questions?"

The owner took a box from under the counter and counted out dollar bills for the register.

"My dad worked for the Santa Fe," he said. "We're Mexican, you know. He came from the old country to work rip track."

"Takes a hell of a man to work rip track," Hook said. "I've seen men beg to be shot rather than go out on another shift."

He nodded. "He never went back to Mexico. Me, I wound up running this place, selling longnecks to rednecks and listening to bullshit until I'm ready to stick a gun in my mouth."

"Thing is," Hook said, "we had a boy from the orphanage killed on railroad property out in Carlsbad, New Mexico, and I'm trying to chase down leads."

"Killed, you say?"

"That's right. Bruce Mason. You may have heard of him."

The owner took a Coke out for himself, wiped off the top with his shirtsleeve, and opened it.

"That boy who held up the station over in Cherokee?"

"That's right."

"Crazy kid," he said. "Putting kids in an orphanage screws up their heads."

"Buck Steele, the orphanage foreman, saw Mason and a girl by the name of Lucy Barker together just before they ran off. I thought you might know something about this Steele guy."

He tipped up his Coke. "Buck Steele? Yeah," he said, "I know him plenty, believe me. He comes in here every night for the poker game. They don't play for real money, if anybody's asking.

"He drinks three or four beers and goes home. Now and then he drinks more. When that happens, he turns mean, and you can just figure on a standoff, usually him against the smallest guy in the pool hall. Keeps him from getting his ass kicked more than three or four times a year that way."

Hook lit a cigarette. "What kind of eyewitness do you think he makes? I mean, you think I can trust what he says?"

He leaned on the bar. "Buck Steele is a great witness, if you're out to defraud the insurance company."

Hook finished his Coke and stood. "Thanks," he said. "I think I get the picture. You say he comes in every night?"

"That's right, 'cept for his vacations. First thing he does is use my john. It's like he don't have one of his own."

Hook said, "Vacations?"

"Yeah," he said. "He takes about a week or so every year. Claims he goes out to one of those Nevada whorehouses and does the whole menu. Can't say I miss the son of a bitch around here, though."

"Did he take a vacation this year?"

"Oh, hell yes. First part of June, I think it was, but then I can't remember my own telephone number half the time."

Hook took a rare afternoon nap and awakened to find Mixer staring into his face.

"Dang it, Mixer," he said, pushing him aside. "Don't you have any manners?"

Mixer went to the door and begged to go out. "Alright," Hook said. "But you stay home."

Hook checked his watch: six o'clock. He put on his shoes and went to the park bathroom to wash up. Once back at the room, he checked the clip in his P.38, put on his coat, and stepped out into the evening. He took a deep breath of fresh air.

Once in the alley across from the pool hall, he hunkered down. Music from the jukebox drifted into the evening, and he could smell hamburgers cooking from the café down the street. Too bad he didn't have time to eat. Maybe later.

He'd been there fifteen, twenty minutes, when he spotted Buck Steele's pickup truck pulling in. Steele got out and cleared his jaw. He wore a western hat and a blue denim shirt. Pulling his shoulders back, he disappeared through the door.

Hook struck out afoot for the orphanage. He'd considered calling Celia but thought better of it. If he screwed this up, she'd have a hell of a lot of explaining to do, and she'd been too helpful for him to let that happen.

By the time he reached the drive, night had fallen, and the orphanage windows lit the darkness. The sounds of cattle rose up from the barn, and the smell of smoke from the incinerator hung in the air. As he approached, he could hear the children inside the orphanage and the clinking of supper dishes.

He made his way around to the barn, double-checking to make certain the gate had been secured and that no lights came from Steele's room. He stepped into the barn, the smells of cattle and hay thick in the stillness, and closed the door behind him. Though nearly black inside the barn, he remembered the direction and worked his way to the back.

When he reached Buck's room, he paused, listened, and stared into the blackness for any signs of life. Some might say he broke in, though entering a barn could hardly be criminal, not seriously criminal at least. In any case, he'd be just as dead in the event someone shot him.

When he opened Steele's door, light bled through a small window in the back of the room. A single bunk had been pushed against the wall, and clothes hung from a shower rod jimmied in between the window frame. A half-empty whiskey bottle sat on a packing crate next to the bed, and Steele's cattle whip leaned against the wall.

Hook searched the room, looking for anything that might give him a clue to Buck Steele. Sometimes what he didn't find gave him the best insight into a man. In this case, there were no books, no magazines, no newspapers, no signs of curiosity or interest in anything beyond a whiskey bottle and a cattle whip.

Hook scanned the room again, his eyes having adjusted to the darkness. What did a man like Steele have in common with Bain Eagleman? What accounted for Eagleman's willingness to hire an expensive lawyer to defend Buck's brawl with the sheriff? Why would Eagleman jeopardize his position in the community for this guy? It didn't click.

He'd decided to leave when his eye caught something white

sticking out of the pocket of one of Buck Steele's jackets. He pulled out a letter and another piece of paper that had been shoved into the pocket. He started to read them when a light swept by the window from the driveway.

Putting the material into his pocket, he worked his way out of the room, eased the door shut, and hid in the shadows of the stanchions.

Within moments the barn door opened. A flashlight panned the area, and Buck Steele stepped in behind it. He opened the door to his room, belched, and clicked on the light. When he'd closed the door, Hook slipped out and headed down the drive. He'd gone only a few yards when something ran up beside him from out of the darkness. Chills raced down Hook's spine as he struggled to see what or who came at him.

"Damn it, Mixer," he said, whispering. "Can't you ever do what you're told?"

Back at his room, Hook turned on his lamp, poured himself a Beam, and took out the items he'd borrowed from Steele's coat pocket, an opened envelope that had been addressed to Lucy Barker, c/o The Spirit of Agape Orphanage, and a receipt for thirteen dollars made out to Bain Eagleman from Dr. Fred Betcher, Cherokee General Hospital.

Hook took the letter from the envelope:

Dear Lucy:

I have been thinking about you ever since I ran away from Agape. You probably have heard by now what happened at the gas station in Cherokee, and I know you must be ashamed of me. I can't explain why I did it, except to say that I had to get away from there before I went crazy. When I asked you to run away with me, and you said no, I figured there had to be someone else. I couldn't take that.

I joined the army under the name of Samuel Ash and saw some really crazy things. They gave me a Bronze Star, but I don't really know why. Most of the time I was just scared and homesick for you.

I've been working on the signal gang for the Santa Fe out of Clovis. The boss has me painting stuff and by myself most of the time because of the strikes.

Payday is only two days away, and I'll have enough money together to come back. Even though I've done some bad things, I've changed a lot since being in the war. Maybe now you'll see me as a grown man instead of just a dumb kid.

My boss is sending me to the potash spur out of Carlsbad to paint the wigwag signal this week. I'll see you soon because there is an important question I want to ask. Love, Bruce

Bain Eagleman had personally paid for her pregnancy test, so he damn sure knew she was pregnant. Hook poured himself another Beam. Steel or someone had somehow intercepted this letter from Bruce Mason, so he knew not only that Bruce intended on coming back but also where to find him. Maybe Bruce Mason's return to Agape was the last thing anyone wanted.

Hook opened the door and let Mixer out. He went back in and studied the letter. Eagleman had been conducting a board meeting the same day Bruce Mason had been hung. He couldn't have been the one who killed Mason, not personally anyway. On the other hand, Buck Steele, who claimed to have been in Nevada, could have been doing Eagleman's handiwork for him, and the fact that Eagleman knew a body had been shipped to Carmen could well account for Hook's string of bad luck as escort.

Mixer scratched at the door, and Hook got up to let him in. He sat down and picked up the letter again. And Steele had the medical receipt. Where did he get it? Perhaps the same place he got the letter.

He finished off his drink. Maybe Skink had it right. Maybe Steele had his reasons for riffling through Eagleman's trash. With this kind of evidence, he definitely had Eagleman by the short hair.

Hook folded the letter and put it in his pocket. At least now he knew what he needed, and he knew that Eagleman and Steele were ass-deep in the middle of it. But he couldn't make an arrest, not yet, because the big question still remained unanswered: where the hell was Lucy Barker?

38

Hook AWAKENED EARLY, his head cranking at full throttle. He made coffee and watched the sun come up. He opened the front door for Skink, who had come in late yet again.

"How the hell you going to run a business if you can't open up on time, Skink?"

Skink rubbed at his eyes. "I didn't get much sleep, Hook."

"You know what I told you about that," Hook said, handing him his coffee.

"Naw, that's not it. Something woke me up, and I had trouble getting back to sleep. Then when I did, I dreamed Mr. Eagleman kicked me out of the orphanage, and I had no place to go. I just walked around looking for something to eat, but nobody would give me anything."

"That's pretty rough, I mean, being abandoned on the streets of Carmen like that," Hook said.

"And then I just starved, see, my body lying out there on the sidewalk. People came by and spit on me for messing up their town."

"I gather being a railroad bull is no longer on your list of occupations?" Hook said.

"I been hoping for something a little more exciting, Hook, no offense. If I wanted to hang around Carmen and sleep in a shoe shop, then I might just as well be what I am."

Hook sipped his coffee. "It's a point, I guess," he said. "Being a yard dog can get downright tedious."

"Maybe I should own my own orphanage. I know a lot about them. If my kids didn't say 'yes sir' and 'no sir' and do their chores on time, I'd make 'em walk the circle. I'd hire Buck Steele to keep watch and pop their earlobes off with his whip every time one of them stopped."

Hook poured himself another cup of coffee and studied Skink.

"You really think Buck Steele watches the kids?"

"All the time," he said.

"You've seen him?"

"Just that once when he watched me," he said.

"Did he turn you in to Eagleman?"

"Well, no, but what else would he be doing out there?"

"I don't know, Skink. I've got a call to make. Talk to you later."

Hook called Popeye and waited for an answer. "Clovis," Popeye said.

"Popeye, Hook. Is that kid there yet?"

"He's eyeing my peanuts right now," Popeye said.

"Put him on, will you?"

Hook waited for him to come on. "Junior Monroe," Junior said.

"Junior, I want you to go to the Waynoka machine shop and check on my caboose. Eddie says it's ready to move. See if you can't line up someone to tow it back to Clovis."

"But, Hook, I just got here."

"You're a yard dog, Junior. Yard dogs are on the move. It's how we solve crimes. You're not supposed to sit around drinking coffee all day like an operator."

"Alright, Hook. How am I supposed to get back there?"

"Just like you got to Clovis. There's a westbound at six in the evening and an eastbound at two in the morning, when they're on time, which isn't that often. First, you jump on the eastbound, and then when you get to Waynoka, jump off. I swear, how hard can it be?"

"That westbound dragged me halfway across the state, Hook, and then I had to sleep in the elevator. I found a wheat seed up my nose this morning. Another day or two and the thing might have sprouted and killed me."

"When you get there, check on my books. Those machinists been hanging around my caboose."

"I wouldn't worry about a machinist stealing your books, Hook."

"Just do it, Junior. If I wanted a lecture, I'd call Eddie Preston."

Hook hung up just as Patch came in the front door. "Morning, Patch," he said.

"I guess you've had your coffee and made your phone calls?" he said.

"That would be correct."

"And I guess Skink here has had his morning nap?"

"I couldn't say," Hook said. "I've been busy conducting business."

"Been at the pool hall, they tell me," Patch said. "How is it a man can draw a salary while shooting pool?"

"Some people get paid for *doing,* some for *thinking,*" Hook said. "I get paid for thinking."

Patch looked at Skink, who had searched out the broom and was busy sweeping the floor. "And some for sleeping," he said.

"I'd like to stay and schmooze, Patch, but there's crime in this world that needs solving. By the way, there's a cricket in my room the size of a small dog, and it cuts into my thinking time."

"Well, I'll ask it to please leave so that it doesn't disturb your thinking. We wouldn't want to set off a crime wave in Carmen, would we?"

Hook went out the back way, leaving the road-rail parked across the street, and struck out for the Spirit of Agape Cemetery. Mixer followed behind, stopping now and again to chew at something lodged between his toes.

The sun bore down hot by the time he reached the cemetery gate. Heat ribbons spiraled up from the rows of stones. Hook waited for Mixer to come in.

The wheat fields surrounding the little cemetery had been plowed, and they stretched off to the horizon like a red blanket. Dust devils, born from the heat, rose up and danced over the fields, disappearing into the blue distance.

Hook whistled Mixer in. "Come on," he said, pulling his ears. "Let's walk the circle."

On the far side of the cemetery, Hook stopped while Mixer marked a fence post to his liking. Hook moved to the shade of an old juniper and sat down. From there he could see the mound of cemetery fill dirt, grass growing on its top.

Mixer circled the mound to sniff out past traffic and then stopped in the weeds just beyond. He circled back to where he'd started and kicked dirt between his back legs.

Hook went over to him and knelt down. The grass had grown tall in the loosened soil, and he could see a sunken place in the earth.

"What is it, boy?" Hook asked.

Mixer dug at the ground, barked, and then dug again.

Hook sat back on his heels. Mixer, as undisciplined an animal that ever lived, could drive a man to distraction with his antics, but this much Hook knew: his nose never lied.

39

HOOK SAT IN the office while the sheriff washed his hands in the back. When he came out, he'd taken off his hat, exposing the sunburn line across his forehead.

He sat down at his desk. "Okay, now what is it you wanted to see me about?"

Hook started with Bruce Mason and how the body had never been Samuel Ash at all and how Lucy Barker had never run away with him like everyone had thought.

The sheriff leaned in on his elbows. "For Christ's sake, Bruce Mason is over at the funeral home now?"

"That's right," Hook said.

"Well, I'm glad you got around to telling me," he said. "Just 'cause I paint houses don't mean I ain't the sheriff, Runyon."

"You're right about that, and I apologize. I just didn't have enough of this put together for it to make sense."

"And you do now?"

Hook took out the letter from Bruce and the payment receipt showing where Bain Eagleman had sprung for the pregnancy test.

The sheriff read them over and laid them on the desk in front of him.

"Are you suggesting that Lucy Barker was carrying Bain Eagleman's baby?"

"That's what I believe to be true," Hook said.

"And what about this letter?" he asked.

"When Eagleman intercepted Bruce's letter, he realized he was about to be exposed, that everyone would know Lucy had never run away at all. He had to do something about it."

The sheriff took out his bandanna and dabbed the perspiration out of the ding in his head.

"And so you think he killed Bruce?"

"Had him killed. That letter has been in the possession of Buck Steele. I believe Buck killed Bruce Mason and then stole this letter and the receipt from Eagleman for insurance.

"Later, Eagleman found out from Juice Dawson at the mortuary about Bruce's body being delivered back here to Carmen. He sent Buck Steele on vacation to try to stop me."

"And how did you wind up with this letter?" He shook his head. "Never mind. I don't think I want to know. Clearly, this suggests that Bain Eagleman might have taken advantage of a girl in his charge, but, if your information is correct, she was of consenting age at the time. It's shit, I admit, but hardly evidence of murder. Without a body, all this is speculation. Without a body, there's just no crime."

"And that's why I'm here," Hook said.

"What do you mean?"

"I think I know where Lucy Barker is buried."

The sheriff reached for his pocketknife and peeled a layer of paint off his thumbnail.

He looked up at Hook. "And just where would that be, if I may ask?"

"In the Spirit of Agape Cemetery."

The sheriff closed up his knife and dropped it into his pocket.

"Now that's convenient, ain't it?" he said. "I take it you've seen her body?"

"Not exactly, but my dog, Mixer, caught the scent of something buried out there."

"I hate to bring this up, but there are a number of folks buried out there."

"Eight feet down, embalmed, and in caskets. Skink says he saw Buck out there the very same night Bruce and Lucy were to have run away. It's possible that Buck killed her and buried her in a shallow grave, figuring it would be the last place someone would look."

The sheriff put his feet up on the desk, exposing the holes in the bottoms of his boots.

"That's one hell of an idea, Hook. Now, I don't mean to be too wary about all this, but Bain Eagleman dragged my ass up and down Main over that foreman of his. I'm not anxious to stir something up I can't prove."

Hook lit a cigarette. "There's only one way to know, Sheriff."

"And what if that dog of yours is just hot for badger holes? What then?"

"I'll shoot him and swear the whole crazy notion came from me alone."

The sheriff dropped his feet and walked to the window, looking out toward the Agape cemetery.

"I'll make a call, see if I can't get a warrant. You go get the digger, and I'll meet the two of you out there."

"Thanks," Hook said.

"You and that dog better be right about this, Runyon."

Hook picked up the road-rail and drove over to the mortuary. Juice Dawson led him into the waiting room. He had on an apron and smelled of formaldehyde and cigarette smoke.

"Thought you might be one of Mable Engle's family," he said. "She fell out of her porch swing and broke her leg. Died this morning."

"They didn't shoot her, did they?" Hook asked.

Juice looked at him. "It's rare we shoot people with a broken leg in Carmen. Now what brings you here? You figure out where you want that boy buried?"

Hook sat down in one of the overstuffed chairs and laid out the story.

"I'll be damned," Juice said. "Bain Eagleman?"

"The sheriff wants us to meet him out at the cemetery."

"Are you certain it's a body?"

"That's what my dog claims. If he's wrong, he's going the way of Mable Engle."

"That body would have been there for a spell, if it's there at all," he said.

"Ever since Bruce Mason robbed that station," Hook said.

"Might not be a whole lot left, you know. Doesn't take long for a body that's not embalmed to just disappear."

"Could you come?"

"If that's what the sheriff wants, but I don't have any legal authority, you understand. You'll have to get the state medical examiner for that."

By the time Hook and Juice rolled up to the Agape cemetery, the sheriff had already backed in to the fill site. Mixer bailed out of the road-rail and made a dash to the area and began circling.

"Juice, thanks for coming out," the sheriff said. "Runyon's got it in his head that there's been a body buried out here. I got a warrant from the judge out of Cherokee to take a look, but it's going to be my ass if Runyon's wrong."

"Well," Juice said, "it looks like there's been some settling over there where that dog is. I guess there's only one way to find out. Did you bring some shovels?"

"In the back of my pickup," he said.

The sun eased below the horizon as Juice and the sheriff dug.

Hook took a turn, but his prosthesis made the digging too slow, so he soon turned it back to the sheriff.

Within the hour, the sheriff stuck his shovel into the ground and knelt down. Hook pulled Mixer back from the edge of the hole.

"I'll be damned," the sheriff said. "Look here, Juice."

"It's a body, alright," Juice said. "There's not much left, though." He took his shovel and pulled away more dirt. "Looks like a woman, too."

"It could be Lucy Barker, then?" the sheriff asked.

"Could," he said. "Could be any woman. The medical examiner will have to do an autopsy before we know for sure."

Hook knelt down. "No identity of any kind?"

"None that I can see," Juice said. "Dental should tell us something. Been there a long time by the looks of it."

"Can you make that arrest, Sheriff?" Hook asked.

"I'll call the medical examiner," he said. "He should be here by morning. Until then, you two keep this to yourselves."

Hook loaded Mixer into the road-rail and drove back to the room. Both Patch and Skink had long since gone home. Having failed to replenish his Beam, he made a quick run to the package store. When he got back, he fixed himself a drink.

Had it been him, he would have arrested both Bain Eagleman and Buck Steele this very night. But then he understood the problems of circumstantial evidence. He understood that these were people the sheriff had lived with his whole life and, in all likelihood, would live with the remainder of his life. He understood how a good lawyer would tear the case to shreds without watertight evidence.

He personally believed that Lucy Barker lay in that shallow grave and that Buck Steele killed her and buried her there. But, like the sheriff, he couldn't be a hundred percent certain, not even after having seen the chipped front tooth in the poor girl's skull.

40

HE'D NO SOONER drifted off when the phone rang. He sat up, his heart pounding. In the darkness, he tracked the muffled ring, finding the phone buried under a stack of wool pelts.

"Hello," he said.

"Hook, this is Celia."

"Is everything okay?"

"I'm not sure. Could you come to the orphanage? Meet me at the back door."

"I'm on my way," he said, hanging up.

Hook dressed and let Mixer out to run. Celia sounded frightened. He checked his P.38 and worked the flashlight into his back pocket.

The road-rail groaned a couple of times before firing off, and Hook rumbled away toward Agape. Soon, he could see the orphanage looming in the moonlit night. No lights were visible from the windows of the orphanage or from the barn. He checked his watch. Eleven. Why would Celia be calling this time of night?

At the driveway entrance, he coasted to a stop and cut his engine. He'd walk in from there. For all he knew, someone could be waiting for him.

As he approached the orphanage, he spotted Buck's pickup parked by the barn. Somewhere in the distance, a lone coyote bayed, and the moon slipped from behind a cloud.

He knocked on the back door and turned to make certain no one came from behind. Celia, still in her house robe, opened the door.

"Hook," she said, "I'm glad you're here."

He could smell baked bread, and the heat of the ovens still lingered in the kitchen.

"What is it?" he asked.

She pushed back her hair, which, now unfettered, fell nearly to her shoulders.

"I went to bed about the usual time," she said. "Something startled me awake. I didn't know what, and I couldn't go back to sleep." She took his arm, and he could feel her trembling. "And then I heard it again. It came from upstairs, from Eagleman's office."

"Go on."

"Then I heard shouting and things being thrown about."

"You didn't go up?"

"No," she said. "Pretty soon it stopped, just like that. Nothing. That's when I called you. Something bad's happened. I just know it."

Hook pulled his weapon. "You did the right thing," he said. "I'll go check it out."

"I'm coming with you," she said.

They climbed the stairs in the darkness. At the landing, Hook could see a slice of moonlight cutting from out of Eagleman's office door. Stepping to the side, he eased the door open. Silence. He handed the flashlight to Celia and pointed to the opening. After taking a quick glance inside, he then stepped in with his weapon leveled.

The filing cabinets were shoved about, and Eagleman's desk lamp lay broken on the floor. The window curtains had been ripped from their moorings, and Eagleman's fedora lay crumpled in the corner of the room.

"Oh my god," Celia said. "What's happened?"

"I don't know," Hook said. "But it can't be good by the looks of it. I want you to call the sheriff. Tell him what we've found in here."

"Where are you going?"

"To have a look around," he said. "After you've made the call, go to where the kids are sleeping. Make sure they stay there until the sheriff comes. Will you do that?"

Celia nodded her head, and he took her hand.

"Good," he said. "Don't worry. It's going to be okay."

Once outside, Hook circled wide, checking for lights in the barn. He figured Buck had been alerted, maybe had seen them at the cemetery, or discovered the missing letter. He could be anywhere, and he could be armed.

Hook put the flashlight into his hip pocket. Handling both a weapon and flashlight at the same time didn't work so well for a one-armed man.

He eased open the barn door and stepped in. He stood, waiting for his eyes to adjust to the darkness. He could see the moonlit corrals out of the front of the barn, and the smell of manure hung heavy in the air. He listened, turning his ear into the blackness at the back of the barn. If Buck Steele suspected that things had turned sour, he could be dangerous.

Hook moved into the interior, inching along, stopping to listen, and then moving forward again. Suddenly, his head bumped into something, and chills shot through him. He struggled to see what it might be, a saddle maybe, strung up by its horn from the rafters.

He holstered his weapon, reached for his flashlight, and turned it on. There, only inches from his face, a pair of wing-tip shoes twisted in the stillness.

Hook panned his light upward into Bain Eagleman's distorted face. His hands had been tied behind his back, and he stared down at Hook with dead eyes. His lips, strutted with blood, stretched over his teeth in a mocking grin. A lariat, tied in a honda knot, had been secured around his neck, and he'd been hoisted up to strangle in the darkness.

Hook traced the rope with his flashlight to where it had been tied off. Working his way over, he double hitched the rope around a barn post and lowered Bain Eagleman onto the barn floor.

He scanned the area with his light. By the looks of it, Buck Steele had fled, a man on the run, a man now unpredictable and dangerous in his escape from justice.

When Hook heard the motor start in the distance, he whirled about. Suddenly, headlights flashed beyond the corrals, turned around, and tore off down the orphanage drive.

"Buck," he said to himself as he headed for the door. If this bastard got out of his sight now, he could be gone forever.

Cranking up the road-rail, Hook goosed her hard. Already Steele's taillights faded in the distance. The road-rail roared but with her heavy undercarriage, she failed to gather up much speed. In the end, the rails were her home. On the road, she floundered along like a landlocked whale.

When he looked again, Steele's headlights had made a sharp left turn as he cut onto the dirt road leading to Avard. The move would cost Steele time, but he probably figured to avoid roadblocks that could spring up quickly on the main highway. Hook pushed the road-rail hard, and she groaned in protest.

Ahead, he could see the crossing signs of the Frisco line. From here it cut a straight run right into Avard. He slammed on his brakes, nearly overshooting the crossing before he got her slowed down.

Pulling onto the crossing, he dropped the pilot wheels onto the rails, and within minutes raced along at a fast clip down the track. At this rate, and a crow's flight route, he just might get there in time to cut Steele off.

Twenty minutes later, he topped the grade coming into Avard. From his vantage, he could see car lights just pulling in near the elevators. Dousing his headlamps, Hook coasted in. Easing to a stop just short of the scale house, he cut his engine. Avard had long since turned in for the night, and darkness prevailed.

Pulling his weapon, he climbed out. He figured Buck to be about somewhere. If he left town on the road, he would have seen his lights. Little traffic, if any, passed through town this time of night.

He eased his way around the scale house with his weapon at the ready. On the far side, he spotted Steele's pickup bumper glinting in the moonlight. He knelt. The door on the pickup had been left open, and the gas-tank cap sat on the fender.

Hook unlocked the safety on his weapon and aimed at the open door.

"Climb out of there, Steele," he said. "And with your hands up."

Not many things in life did Hook know with a hundred percent clarity, but a cold pistol barrel jammed under his shoulder blade happened to be one of them.

"Nice of you to drop by," Buck Steele said. "I could use the ride."

41

"I'LL TAKE THAT sidearm," Steele said.

Hook handed it to him, butt first. "You have to put in gas now and then, Steele."

"Climb back into that contraption you're running, Runyon. I've always wanted to ride one of those things."

"This is the end of the Frisco line," Hook said.

"Throw that switch onto the Santa Fe track, and do it now."

Hook threw the switch and got back in. "This is a high rail, Steele, not some wheat run."

"I figure you got the cops on the way. The odds they'll be looking for me driving down the railroad tracks is pretty damn slim, wouldn't you say?"

"There's heavy traffic on this line, Steele. It isn't safe."

"We'll jump off at the first crossing and be halfway out of the country before they figure out I'm not hiding back there in the elevator. So, if you've no more objections, let's get on with it."

"It's your call, Steele. Eastbound or west?"

Steele looked both directions. "West, toward Mexico," he said.

He leveled his weapon in Hook's direction. "And never doubt whether I can use this thing, Runyon. I can, and I will."

Hook eased off westbound and brought her up to speed. Moonlight lit up the rails, and the rubber wheels sang against the iron.

"Mind if I smoke?" Hook asked.

"Ain't good for your health," Steele said. "But then, why worry about it?"

Hook lit a cigarette and checked his watch in the light: 1:50 A.M.

"You're pretty good with a rope, Steele. First you hang Bruce Mason and then you hang Bain Eagleman."

"One for money. One for fun," he said.

"So, Eagleman paid you to kill Lucy the night Mason robbed that station and bury her in the orphanage cemetery. Then later you took out a little insurance by stealing Mason's letter that Eagleman had intercepted?"

Steele leaned forward and pulled his chew out of his back pocket. He loaded his jaw, all the while watching Hook.

"I couldn't think of a single reason to trust Eagleman. Can you?" he said.

"So, Eagleman laid the whole damn thing at that boy's feet?" Hook said.

"Eagleman was a son of a bitch but not a stupid one. He knew everyone would figure those two robbed the station and then ran off together. No one would have ever known the difference had you not come snooping."

Hook flipped his cigarette ash on the floor and looked over at Steele.

"When Eagleman learned from Juice Dawson that I was escorting a body back by train, he figured out who it had to be and sent you as the welcoming party?"

"You're lucky, Runyon. I usually don't miss."

Hook drew on his cigarette and checked his watch again in the glow: 2:10.

The moon rose overhead like an ivory button, and Steele's

nickel belt buckle glinted in the moonlight. Steele took his hat off and laid it on the seat.

Hook spotted the wigwag signal in the distance, and beyond that, the faint glow of the eastbound's glimmer as she raced to Chicago.

"Tell me, Steele," Hook said. "How did you know we were on to you?"

Steele smiled. "When I came back from the pool hall, that mongrel dog of yours tried to take my leg off. Not hard to figure you were around somewhere. I checked to see if anything had turned up missing. It had."

"You mean your blackmail letters?"

"My protection," he said. "I've been keeping a watch on that cemetery since."

"And so that's when you decided to kill Eagleman and bust out, leaving no witnesses behind?"

"Until you showed up again, Runyon. Say," he said, leaning forward, "ain't that a crossing signal up there?"

"Where?" Hook asked.

The moan of the eastbound's whistle lifted like sorrow in the distance, and her glimmer broke in a pinpoint on the horizon.

"Up there," he said. "Hey, that's a goddamn train!"

Hook said, "I'll run her to the crossing and bail off. There's plenty of time."

Suddenly, the wigwag signal lit up, its light, the color of blood, swinging to and fro, and its bell clanging out the danger of the oncoming train.

"Get the hell from behind that wheel!" Steele yelled, brandishing his weapon. "You're going to get us killed."

Hook released the wheel and moved onto the passenger's side, letting Steele climb over him and into the driver's seat. The eastbound's glimmer lit the track, and her whistle screamed into the night as she bore down toward them.

"You crazy son of a bitch!" Steele yelled, shoving the gas pedal to the floor.

The road-rail hunkered down, gathered up all she had, and roared toward the crossing. Hook waited, gauging his time, his eye on the red lights of the wigwag. At the right moment, he clenched his jaw, opened the door, and jumped.

He tumbled down the right-of-way and veered off into a sagebrush thicket that grew along the fence row. He struggled to his feet just in time to see the road-rail reaching the crossing.

The brake lights lit up like red eyes in the darkness when Steele hit the pedal, but the road-rail shot right on through the crossing. The eastbound's glimmer turned the night into day, and her brakes shrieked as she locked down in a last-ditch effort to slow the massive tonnage at her back.

The eastbound hit the road-rail like a bundle of dynamite, and sparks sprayed into the night. The road-rail skidded down track at the engine's nose, flipping and crumpling into a jagged metal ball.

She passed by Hook and ground to a stop a quarter-mile down track. Hook climbed from the sagebrush and dusted the dirt off his pants.

He checked his watch under the moonlight. "Two twenty," he said. "Late again."

42

Hook, CELIA, SKINK, Bet, and Esther stood at Bruce's and Lucy's graves in the Spirit of Agape Cemetery as the mortician finished lowering the caskets into the ground. Hook took the Bronze Star from his pocket and dropped it into Bruce's grave.

As they walked back to the orphanage, Celia looped her arm through his.

Bet said, "Samuel Ash is home, isn't he?"

"Yes, he's home," Hook said.

"I'll visit him every day," she said.

Hook turned to Celia. "As the new superintendent of the Spirit of Agape Orphanage, maybe you could have proper markers put up."

"They have already been ordered," she said.

Mixer, who had been out in the field chasing blackbirds, came bounding up.

"Miss Feola said I'm getting a dog, too," Bet said. "And he can sleep with me."

Hook looked at Celia. She shrugged. "New policy," she said.

When they came to the orphanage, Hook stopped. The grand

old building lifted up into the prairie sky, and her windows blinked away at the sun.

"And what about you, Skink?" Hook asked.

"Patch is retiring and turning the shop over to me. Said that in another twenty or thirty years I might be as good as him."

"That's a possibility, Skink, providing you get your sleep and keep your mind on the job."

Skink grinned and looked at his feet.

Celia pushed her hair back, displaying her widow's peak.

"And what about you, Hook?" she asked.

"Me? I have a train to catch. Next time I'm through, maybe I'll stop by for a peanut butter cookie."

Celia took his arm, dropped her hand on the back of his neck, and brushed her lips against his cheek.

"We'll be waiting," she said.

Hook turned to Mixer. "Come on, dog, before I change my mind about leaving," he said.

Hook and Mixer picked their way over the tracks to the Waynoka machine shop. Frenchy's old steamer sat on the siding with a half-dozen flat cars at her back, Hook's caboose coupled in on the end. Frenchy came around the front of the engine just as Hook walked up.

"That louse box of yours is on the tail," he said.

"So I see. When are you pulling out, Frenchy?"

"About an hour, if I can find the goddang bakehead."

"You haven't seen my associate, Junior Monroe, have you?"

"I saw a dandy wearing high-water britches and a bow tie. Might that be him?"

"Most likely. Could you throw this mutt into the caboose and pick me up at the depot on your way out?"

"Oh, sure, sure," he said. "We can shut down the whole goddang railroad if you want."

"A slow will do, Frenchy. I'll be riding in the caboose back to Clovis. I need my rest for fighting crime, and I'm not up to listening to you and that bakehead tell lies all the way."

"Well, that suits us just fine," he said. "Some folks have real work to get done, you know."

Hook found Junior sitting on the bench outside the depot. He had a new hat perched on the end of his shoe.

"Junior," Hook said. "See you made it without falling off the train. I'm thinking you're getting the hang of things."

"Hook," he said. "I need to talk to you."

"Well, here I am."

"To tell you the truth, I've had about all the practical experience I can stand. I'm on my way to Kansas City."

Hook lit a cigarette. "That so? What you going to do in Kansas City, Junior?"

Junior took his hat off his foot and screwed it onto his head. "Law school, and I plan to look up Jackie. I can't get her out of my head."

Hook stepped back. "When I told you to catch pickpockets, I didn't exactly have that in mind, Junior."

"It just sort of happened, Hook."

"That's how it is most often," he said. "How do you plan on getting there?"

"I planned to get on a freighter."

"That's against the law, Junior. I'd have to arrest you."

"I've been doing it ever since I came."

"You were working for the railroad then. Doing your duty, so to speak.

"Hang on a minute. I'll be right back."

When Hook came out of the depot, he handed Junior an envelope. "Here," he said. "I don't have time to be running you in to jail."

"What is it, Hook?"

"A ticket on the *Super Chief* to Kansas City. She'll be rolling through here in a few minutes. Try not to fall off, Junior, and remember it's a sin to ride the *Super Chief* and not eat in the dining car."

Junior grinned. "Thank you, Hook."

"And tell that girl I better not catch her picking pockets on my railroad."

The *Super* had no sooner slid out than Frenchy came chugging in from the yards. Hook hopped on his caboose and gave him a wave-off.

Frenchy brought her up, and they were soon clipping over the countryside. The sun lowered on the horizon, and the steam from Frenchy's engine drifted up into the evening sky. The old caboose waddled down the track, her wheels clicking along, and Mixer snored beneath the bunk

Hook fixed himself a Beam and water and lined his books across the table. He studied his new find, the 1902 American first *Hound of the Baskervilles,* the final link in the chain, a task complete after a long and difficult hunt. No one loved that book more than him. No one deserved it more.

He looked out the window at the sunset. Of all the places on Earth, this was where he wanted to be.

Soon, he'd be back to Clovis and with a few things to wind up: a call to Eddie Preston explaining how the road-rail ended up riding on the nose of the eastbound, a debate with Popeye for paying up that dollar he owed, and a trip to the library to return the 1902 American first *Hound of the Baskervilles.*